Blood Diamonds of the Lost Bazaar

by

Rickey Pittman

Blood Diamonds of the Lost Bazaar

COPYRIGHT © 2022 by Rickey Pittman

Cover Art by *Jennifer Greef*

The Wild Rose Press, Inc.
PO Box 708
Adams Basin, NY 14410-0708
Visit us at www.thewildrosepress.com

Publishing History
First Edition, 2022
Trade Paperback ISBN 978-1-5092-4377-8
Digital ISBN 978-1-5092-4378-5

Published in the United States of America

And somehow Hunter felt in his heart that all they had lost, all that had been damaged, all that had been taken from every one of them because of man's greed for wealth and power, all of themselves that they had sold—all would be returned. All of the hands, the dignity, the opportunities that had been lost would blossom in future serendipity and epiphanies. All the lost souls faded with the song, and Hunter walked with Caitlin and Tejan into the Lost Bazaar, a gallery where one can find one's self, one's friends, or the love of one's life. A bazaar, but one where nothing and no one was for sale.

Dedication

To J.W. Dunn, my friend and writing mentor.

Chapter One

When Diamonds are a Legend,
And Diadem—a Tale—
I Brooch and Earrings for myself,
Do sow, and Raise for sale
—Emily Dickinson

Caitlin glanced up as the mineral-gray sedan whipped into a parking space in front of the store. The driver stepped out of the vehicle, tossed his aviator sunglasses into the car, and retrieved a leather briefcase. He wore a charcoal-gray designer suit, and his dark hair was slicked back. He paused and studied the storefront while June heat waves rose from the concrete, bending the air and the man's shape. Caitlin hoped he wasn't a salesman. She sprayed the countertop with glass cleaner and wiped it with a paper towel.

He entered the store and casually strolled toward her with the air and poise of a *GQ* model, and his dark eyes flitted from one display case to another.

"Welcome to Vermeer Diamonds," Caitlin said. "How can I help you?"

His eyes swept down her form. Caitlin felt like she was being inspected and she suddenly felt awkward and overexposed in her blue sundress.

Rapping on the glass countertop, he said, "Which of these bracelets do you like the best?"

This scenario had not been part of her sales training. She quickly scanned the diamond bracelets and her eyes settled on one. "I like this one," she said as she lifted it from the display and set it before him. "A gift?"

"Yes, perhaps."

"She's a lucky girl."

He nodded. "Yes, she is, but I believe the one who steals her heart will be luckier. Why do you like this bracelet?"

Think fast, Caitlin. "Well, the stones have such a luster. I'm not a trained gemologist, but I think it's the most beautiful bracelet in the case. I'm an artist, so I do know beauty when I see it."

"So do I, and I *am* a gemologist." He picked up the bracelet, dangled it in front of the fluorescent lamp on the countertop, and the stones in the bracelet came to life as prisms of light sparkled on the surface and from the heart of the stones. "You chose the most expensive bracelet in the case—worth at least $3,000 dollars. Not a glow-worm or chubby among them. Was that choice by accident?"

"I didn't even think about the price. I chose it because I thought it was the most beautiful." As he had not even looked at the tiny price tag, she wondered how he knew the price. "I'm sorry, but what are glow-worms and chubbies?"

"Inferior diamonds."

"Are you a diamond salesman?"

"Yes," he said. "Put it on."

"Sir?"

"I want to see how it looks on your pretty wrist. The bracelet was made for a woman. You couldn't very well tell its beauty by putting it on mine. No one buys diamonds for men."

Caitlin slipped on the bracelet and held out her wrist. He took her hand and scrutinized the bracelet. One of his fingers rubbed the small dot of red paint on her index finger, paint she had failed to scrub off after painting the night before. The man's nails were carefully manicured, and she made a mental note to have hers done soon and to inspect her hands more carefully after painting.

"Nice. Very nice." He looked at her nametag. "Caitlin. Charming. What a beautifully unique name."

Caitlin blushed. "Thank you." She fidgeted and one of the straps on her blue sundress dropped from her shoulder. She slipped it back into place and smiled. "So, do you think you would like to buy this bracelet?"

The store manager barreled through the door, his arms wrapped around a stack of papers. "This damn heat is oppressive. Monroe is hotter than South Louisiana. At least we had a gulf breeze most days." He noticed the man.

"Hello, Earl," the man in the designer suit said.

"I'm sorry, Von. I wasn't expecting you till later this afternoon. I see you've met Caitlin."

"Yes, and I've truly enjoyed our visit."

"Caitlin," Earl said, "this is Von Vermeer, the CEO and owner of Vermeer Diamonds."

"Oh, now I get it," she said. "That was cruel to test me like that, acting like you were a customer. You came to Monroe just to visit us?"

"Not entirely. I'm a fan of the martial arts, and there's a tournament tomorrow at your civic center and I have business in New Orleans. But New Orleans isn't too far, so you'll probably see me frequently. I intend to drop in on each of my stores at least once a month."

Caitlin mentally reviewed the list of Vermeer Diamond locations. "Are you planning to add more stores soon? If I learn the trade well, maybe I could be a manager."

"Ambitious, are we? Caitlin seems to be an excellent employee, Earl," Von said. "I commend your judgment in hiring her. She seems to possess common sense on how to sell diamonds. Absolutely lovely too. And though the sundress has an appeal, I think she should wear more formal dresses to work. Black dresses would accentuate any diamonds she models for the customers. High heels as well. How long has she worked with us?"

"Three weeks," Earl replied.

"I believe it's time you gave this lady a bonus. Don't you agree?"

"Uh, yes, sir. I'll give her a raise next week."

"No. She's wearing her bonus. Let her keep it. It will be good publicity. Caitlin, I enjoyed our chat, but Earl and I must discuss business. Did Earl tell you that I'm taking both of you to dinner tonight?"

"No, sir. I wish I could go, but I've already made plans."

"Call me Von, please. You can call Earl *sir* if you want, but not me. As for your plans, you need to change them. How many chances will you have to enjoy a wonderful dinner with your manager and your CEO? You do like working here, don't you?"

She glanced at the $3,000 dollar bracelet on her wrist. "Yes, I do. I guess I can adjust my schedule."

"Excellent. While Earl and I talk, make a

reservation at a good restaurant." He glanced at his diamond-laced wristwatch. "At seven. That will give you time to go home and freshen up if you need to. Make sure that the restaurant has a bar so we can meet at six for drinks."

Caitlin flipped through a Monroe phone book, trying to remember restaurants in town that required reservations. She remembered two and called the one she had never been to before.

Just as Earl and Von emerged from their meeting, a young couple entered the store. They held hands and spoke in muted whispers. Von walked to her counter. "I'll take these customers. You watch."

Von said to the couple, "Now, if I'm not looking at a couple in love, then I'm blind. How can I help you?"

The girl blushed. She pulled at the boy's hand. "Tell him, Jimmy."

The boy cleared his throat. "We'd like to look at your rings—I mean engagement rings."

Caitlin tried to imagine her boyfriend Hunter saying this, but the resulting image depressed her.

Von gestured toward Caitlin. "I suspect my beautiful employee is also looking for an engagement ring. We have several rings in the next display case that should interest you."

Von set three rings on the counter. The couple shuffled over and examined the prices, and as Caitlin expected, disappointment etched itself onto their faces.

"These sure are high prices," the boy said. "The cheapest one would cost me two months' salary. To be honest, I need something more affordable. I don't want to buy her no diamond chip and call it an engagement ring, but I can't spend no thousands of dollars neither."

Von smiled and tapped one of the rings. "What if I said I could sell you a ring just like that for five hundred dollars?"

The boy turned the ring box over, looked at the price, and laughed. "The price tag says it cost $2,000."

"I didn't say this ring. I said one just like it. A one carat stone."

"This ring you're talking about ain't hot, is it?" the boy said.

"Would you care?"

"Not particularly."

The girl clung tighter to the boy's arm. "Jimmy, maybe we shouldn't. I can wait on a ring, really. We can just buy bands if you want."

"Nonsense," Von said. "There's nothing wrong with buying bands for the wedding ceremony, but an engagement calls for a ring. After all, one's engagement is a highpoint of one's life." Von removed a ring box from his pocket and set it on the counter. "Take a look."

The girl gingerly opened the black velvet box.

"See?" Von set the ring they had looked at next to it. "The rings are almost identical. This one can easily be adapted into an anniversary ring with three stones— for past, present, and future." He looked the boy directly in the eye. "A ring like this will tell the world how important the love of your life is to you."

"I'm going to ask you again," the boy said. "This ring ain't hot, is it?"

"I was only joking about the ring being stolen. However, it is used. It is a return from a dissatisfied customer. In the trade, we refer to it as a back-alley diamond."

"It ain't damaged, is it?" the boy asked.

Von chuckled. "No, it's in perfect shape. Diamonds are one of the hardest substances on earth and difficult to damage. Does the fact it's used bother you?"

"Some."

Von returned the first ring to its holder beneath the countertop. "Mark Twain said, 'Let us not be too particular. It is better to have old, secondhand diamonds than none at all.' Every diamond has a story and secrets, sometimes many. I personally believe a diamond's rich history charges the stone with energy and power and romance. I think a stone remembers every kiss, every whispered line of poetry that is associated with it." Von addressed the girl. "He is a romantic, isn't he?"

"Oh, yes," she said.

Von continued. "Diamonds are the stones of romance. They are symbols of devotion, fidelity, luxury and wealth. Diamonds outlast people. Some rings have been passed on to heirs and blessed several generations of marriages." He handed the ring to the boy. "Here, slip it on her finger. Let's take a look."

When the boy's trembling hands had placed the ring and he looked into the girl's eyes, Caitlin knew Von had made the sale, and when she glanced down at her new bracelet and then looked up into Von's eyes, she knew his sale's pitch was intended to sell her too.

Yes, he is right. Diamonds are the stone of romance.

****

Caitlin arrived at the Italian restaurant at 6:45 p.m. and joined Von at the bar. At her houseboat, she had changed into a short black skirt and white blouse. On her feet she wore a new pair of leather sandals and a silver toe ring. She loosened the top button of her blouse before she entered the restaurant, smoothed back her hair, and looked down at the diamond bracelet that represented her raise.

Von stood when he saw her. "Caitlin, it's so good to see you, and you look stunning. Knowing Earl, he won't make it till seven, so I'm afraid it will just be you and me for a while. Please, have a seat. What would you like to drink?"

"I don't know… You choose."

After he seated her, Von signaled the bartender and ordered a mojito. "I'm drinking wine, but I think you'll like this drink. I've heard it described as 'a devil disguised as a cocktail.' "

"Von, you're quite a salesman. Where did you learn to read people so well?"

"I suppose you're talking about the couple I sold the ring to. Well, I was raised in New Orleans by my grandparents. My grandfather was a car salesman, and my grandmother worked at a bank. Even in the '60's, New Orleans was not an easy city to grow up in. My grandparents had a strict work ethic, so they insisted I earn my own money. I learned early on that selling was a much easier means of making money than physical labor. My one brother did not learn that lesson. A good salesman must read people well. I learned to do that, and I've been selling ever since."

"I am so impressed," Caitlin said. "Where did you attend college?"

"Like many self-made men, I didn't attend university. I did go to a gemological institute for a while in New York."

"I know this store belongs to you, but how could you afford to sell that ring so cheaply today?"

"I can see we must have a talk about the diamond industry." Von leaned forward. "This is a state secret that you can never divulge: No diamond is worth what people pay for it, Caitlin."

"Explain." Caitlin looked at her new bracelet dangling from her wrist.

"Thanks to the De Beers cartel and some very effective advertising campaigns in the past, we've been able to control and regulate the issues of demand and value. I knew there was no hope of selling the couple one of the store rings—I could tell they were bargain shoppers. So instead, I sold him a ring I had bought at an estate sale for a hundred dollars. I made more of a profit percentage on this sale than I would have on the stones in the case."

"And you made a young couple very happy. There's a lot I don't know about this business, Von, but I want to learn."

Von cleared his throat and adjusted his silk tie and flicked at the sleeve of his charcoal-gray wool suit as if removing dust or lint. "Let's start with this." He reached into his pocket and retrieved a small bag. Unloosening its drawstring, he poured several stones on the counter. "These are diamonds in the rough, but even before they are cut and polished, they still possess a mysterious and captivating beauty." His hand stroked the stones lightly, rolling them with his palm. "Like you, I wanted to learn about the diamond business. I have a passion for diamonds that borders on idolatry. I've seen the Cullinan in the Tower of London, the Hope Diamond in the Smithsonian, the Regent in the

Louvre, the Excelsior—I've actually met Robert Mouawad and seen his entire collection of diamonds."

Caitlin strained her brain to process the stream of facts. "Okay, slow down. Who is this Robert Mouawad?"

"A very wealthy Lebanese diamond dealer who has built an empire. An inspiring story of how a family can rise from a humble state into greatness. He too loved diamonds. Long ago, I memorized one of his quotations. He said, 'It is the human touch that unveils a diamond's beauty. In its rough state it hides its true potential value.' He also said, 'It is difficult to measure the true historical value of a gem, from its formation to its birth on the earth's surface, and the many lives it affects.' "

He picked out one stone and slid it toward her. "Now, take a closer look. Dazzling stone, isn't it? It came from Sierra Leone. You probably have never heard of that country. Sierra Leone is in…"

"West Africa," Caitlin said as she picked up the stone. There was nothing particularly beautiful about it. It reminded her of a quartz pebble. "Our priest talked about Sierra Leone Sunday."

"Hmmm. I've always been fascinated by the church's interest in countries like Sierra Leone, but even more fascinated by your interest in such a place."

"They find pretty diamonds there?" She handed the stone back to Von.

Von smiled. "Ouch. I must have sounded condescending."

"You did, but I forgive you. My uncle is a priest in Sierra Leone, so I've known some things about the country for years. Have you been there?"

"Several times. My business often requires me to go there to broker deals with a mining company. And if it weren't for countries like Sierra Leone, we wouldn't have little beauties like those on your wrist."

"I can't believe that I get to see and touch diamonds every day. There must be a fortune in our store."

"There is, but not in the display counters. A jeweler's best stones are always in the safe, not mounted on rings or necklaces. Educated customers who only want premium stones know that a stone on a ring is usually there because it has flaws. I can tell by your face that you didn't know this. Earl must speed up your training." He took a drink of his wine and daubed his mouth with a napkin. "Or maybe, I'll just train you myself. So, Caitlin, have I completely disillusioned you?"

She twisted her new bracelet around her wrist. "No, at least not entirely. So, the diamond business is really all about making money, isn't it?"

"Of course not. It's also about beauty." Von took Caitlin's hand and dropped a small velvet box into it. "Now, this is an expensive diamond." After she opened the box, he said, "This diamond has been cut and polished. We keep stones of this quality in our safe. Tell Earl I said you could have a look sometime. Fascinating stone, isn't it? Notice its bluish tint, the fire projected by its perfect cut. It is a stone of incomparable beauty. Much like you."

"Thank you. I've never been compared to a diamond before." *You are one handsome devil yourself,* she wanted to say. *Tall, lean, dark eyes and hair—quite handsome.*

"It's difficult for me to believe that your husband or boyfriend hasn't thought of such an obvious comparison. Are you single?"

"Yes. Well, I do have a boyfriend. Sort of... Sometimes." She looked at the bracelet again. "I've been thinking about this bracelet, Von. I can't accept an expensive gift like this. It's not proper, and I wouldn't want you to get the wrong idea about me, and..." She started to unfasten the bracelet but stopped when Von placed his hand on her wrist and shook his head.

Von lit a cigarette and snapped the gold cigarette lighter shut. "Just take the bracelet, Caitlin. It's given without conditions. Remember, I'm wealthy, at least in comparison to most people you know in Monroe, so I can afford it."

Von signaled the bartender to bring them another round of drinks. "About your boyfriend. He should buy you a nice ring. From our store, of course. I'll give him a deep discount. Have you two talked of marriage?"

"One of us has. I don't know that he would find diamonds as beautiful as I do, and I doubt that I could even get him to take the time to come in and take a look. He'd start talking about feeling *pressured*, and how he couldn't afford buying a ring. He can't afford anything that isn't electronic or related to his music or his own personal interests. And heaven forbid that Hunter should feel any pressure to get married."

"Well, as Thomas Carlyle said, 'No pressure, no diamonds.' You Southerners can be so quaint. Hunter. This is an odd name."

Caitlin laughed. "It suits him. He can be very odd."

"You must pardon my questions. My curiosity gets the best of me at times."

"I don't mind. It's good to talk to a man about something other than music."

"I'm sorry, but the music allusion escapes me."

Caitlin fought an urge to take Von's hand. "That's just my boyfriend-frustration talking."

"Ah, your boyfriend is a musician."

"Yeah. He's playing tonight at the Backdoor Lounge. That's where I'm supposed to be. You should meet us there sometime. It's on Cypress near the Well Road exit. I'll get Hunter to put you on his buddy list. I'll buy you a drink."

"I wouldn't think of it."

"What?"

"Of letting you buy me a drink. I'm of the mindset that if a man is interested in a beautiful woman, he should buy the woman—I mean buy the drinks."

"You are such a gentleman. I'm not used to that either."

"And you're an artist, you said?"

"Yes, I have a gallery on Trenton Street in West Monroe. It's called the Lost Bazaar."

"I like the name. Africa is full of bazaars. You can buy literally anything you want there. Life's so simple when things are only about money. You'll have to give me a tour of your gallery. Perhaps one day there'll be a painting of me hanging on its walls."

"I could paint you easily," Caitlin said. "You're a very striking man."

A couple walked by, their arms locked together.

"Ain't love grand?" Caitlin said.

"How curious," Von replied. "I've never heard romance described in such a primitive manner before."

Caitlin blushed. "I sounded dumb, didn't I? It's my

South mouth talking. God, coming to a nice restaurant has made me stupid."

Von smiled. "It's not the restaurant—it's me that rattles you."

Caitlin drained her mojito. "I think you like to do that, I mean, rattle people." Caitlin saw Earl hurrying toward them.

"Perhaps." Von stood. "Earl is here. Shall we go to dinner?"

They left the bar and met Earl at the door. Just as she was about to joke with Earl about being late, Earl said, "I'm on time, Von? You did say for me to be here at seven, right?"

"You're on time. Go find our table. Caitlin and I will be right behind you."

At their table, Von ordered more drinks and a platter of Blue Point and Olympia oysters as appetizers.

Caitlin said, "So, Von, tell me more about your travels."

"I worked two years in London for the Diamond Trading Company, then in Toronto for Diamond Works. In addition to Sierra Leone, I've been to Tel Aviv, Brussels, Antwerp, and several locations in Russia, Japan, India, Thailand, Australia, Liberia, Guinea, Namibia, and South Africa. All travel was connected to the diamond business, of course."

"I bet you have some good stories." Caitlin sampled another oyster. She hadn't realized there were different kinds of oysters, each with a unique taste. She wondered if oysters were aphrodisiacs as she had heard. The way she felt tonight, she suspected they were.

"I do, and I'm willing to tell you all of them."

Earl said, "Von, about our inventory—"

Von waved his hand in dismissal. "Let's talk about work tomorrow, Earl. Let Caitlin enjoy her meal. So, have you traveled much yourself, Caitlin?"

"No, but I've always wanted to."

"You say your uncle is a priest in Sierra Leone. When's the last time you saw him?"

"Oh, years ago."

"How would you like to go to Sierra Leone, do some work for me and see your uncle?"

"You're not serious."

"I am serious."

"I would love that. Our church sponsors a school for the boy soldiers there. Perhaps the school could use me to teach some art lessons. Could I work that in too as well as work for you?"

"I don't see why not, if it doesn't consume too much of your time."

"What would you want me to do there?"

"Some simple bookkeeping, inventory, and shipping. I'll be jammed packed with appointments, so I'll definitely need an assistant. Is your uncle in Freetown?"

"No, I think he's in the north somewhere."

Von frowned. "Not in rebel territory, I hope."

"Yes, he is. But he hasn't had many problems so far. Does the RUF create problems for your business?"

"You are a surprising girl. I bet there aren't ten people in this city who can even tell you what the RUF is. No, my business is prospering. The Revolutionary United Front can be difficult, but if one has the right connections, they can also be helpful. Don't believe everything you hear about them. Much of what you see on the news is journalistic hype and sensationalism. So,

I can count on you to travel with me to Sierra Leone?"

Caitlin looked at Earl and raised her eyebrows.

"Don't worry about Earl," Von said. "He'll give you all the time off you need to get ready—with pay. Isn't that right, Earl?"

"I'll have to hire another employee," Earl said. "I don't want to have another month in the red."

"Then hire another salesman," Von replied. "Monroe seems to be full of people needing work. You'll figure out a way to make up any losses. There'll be a slew of marriages in June, which means if you advertise correctly, you'll sell a good number of rings. You should also begin planning your December campaign. Remember, Earl, ninety percent of all diamonds are sold during the fall holidays."

Caitlin finished her mojito, and the server replaced it immediately.

Von said, "Drink up. I told the server to not let your glass be empty tonight. What do you think of my offer to work for me?"

"I already have a passport—I've never used it, but I have it. What else will I need to go to Sierra Leone?"

"A visa and proper immunizations. I'll take care of the Visa. You'll have it in a week or two. You also need to start anti-malarial medicine. Nasty stuff, the malaria there. You don't want to get it. Your physician will know what you need."

The steaks and seafood Von ordered were served and they settled into their meal. *I'm going to Africa*, Caitlin thought. *I'm really getting to go to Africa.*

After the meal and more drinks, Caitlin wobbled out of the restaurant and drove to the Backdoor Lounge in West Monroe to tell Hunter her news.

Chapter Two

The song is done, the words remain.
—Krio Proverb

Caitlin entered the Backdoor Lounge and staggered into a pool table near the door.

"Damn it," Hunter whispered. He tuned a string on his guitar, then flipped through his notebook, searching for his next song.

Caitlin waved and wobbled toward him. She held a Styrofoam cup, which Hunter guessed would contain whiskey and Coke. Her long curly blonde hair was pulled back into a ponytail.

Hunter mentally outlined the rest of his evening— he would have to drive Caitlin home, put her to bed, then after she recovered late the next morning, drive her back to the Backdoor Lounge for her car. He gritted his teeth. Caitlin had a knack for wasting hunks of his life. She was getting to be more trouble than she was worth.

"Hey, baby," Hunter said when she reached him. He leaned forward and kissed her. "I tried all day to reach you. I didn't know what to think. I was half-afraid that you were avoiding me. Where the hell have you been?"

Caitlin touched his cheek. "I never get tired of looking into your blue eyes—so soft, so sexy, and yet, so lost. Oh, Hunter…"

Oh, brother, he thought when a tear trickled down

her cheek. *Here we go again. I'm cursed with a maudlin girlfriend who plunges into bathos every chance she gets. Drink that cup of suffering down to the dregs, Baby.* Hunter barely contained his laughter. "Are you okay?" he asked.

"Yes, I'm fine, and it was so sweet you called me," she said. "I heard your message, but I wasn't avoiding you. After work, I met my boss and our CEO at a restaurant and had a few drinks. I've got something to tell you, Hunter. I don't think you're going to like it."

This woman lives for her crises. That Mississippi poet girl is looking better all the time. "You went out tonight without telling me?"

"It couldn't be helped. It was work related. Our CEO came in today and insisted on taking us out. But like I said, I have important news."

"What revelation from the big man in the sky do you have this time? The bar's going to close soon, and I've got to get back to work."

"I'm going to Africa—to Sierra Leone!"

Hunter laughed. "Well, at least that's a new one. Caitlin, why the hell would you want to go to Africa?"

Caitlin scowled. Hunter's voice had boomed through his sound system. The bar was now strangely silent. Hunter clicked the off the microphone and gave the crowd an embarrassed wave. "Sorry about that."

"Were you apologizing to them or to me? It's okay. I'm used to being embarrassed around you. Well, if you're through humiliating me, I'll finish what I wanted to say. My company is sending me to Sierra Leone. While I'm there, I can do some church work. Father Robert said volunteers were needed for our missions in Sierra Leone. I've thought about it, and tomorrow I'm going to tell him I'll volunteer to help the mission." She sipped her drink, then said, "His sermon about Sierra Leone last week was so sad, and yet so moving. He begged the congregation's members to do what they can to support our school there financially. People there are suffering so much."

"People are suffering where? In church?" Hunter asked.

"In Africa, smart ass."

"What will you do in Africa? Show them how to pick bananas?"

"That is so like you to say something like that. As far as work goes, I'm going to keep the CEO's books and arrange for the shipment of diamonds to Von's stores. And my uncle is a priest there. I haven't seen him in years."

"Von? Who is Von?"

"The owner of Vermeer's Diamonds. You know, the place where I work that you haven't been to yet. Von took Earl and me out tonight."

"If you're asking my permission, I don't know…"

"It will be a chance for me to help people. At the mission I'll teach art in a mission school. Some really bad things are happening in Africa now. There's a civil war. Criminals are smuggling diamonds and hurting Von's business. The media calls them *Blood Diamonds*. Africa needs me."

"Africa doesn't need you. People have been smuggling for centuries. I think it's ingrained in human nature. So, they smuggle diamonds and don't like their government. So what? As backward as that continent is, Africa must have a crisis like that every year."

"Would you listen to me? It's more than that. I had

never thought about how much misery man's greed could cause. Rebels in the civil war kidnap children and make them slaves or force them to become soldiers and then make them kill people and commit other horrible things. There are so many children there who need help, so the Church has established a special mission school just for the boy soldiers. Many of them are traumatized. That school is where I hope to be working, teaching art. I believe art can help heal them."

"Oh, yeah. Teaching art will definitely fix all of Africa's problems."

"You're one to talk about fixing problems, Hunter. You can't even fix yourself. Why don't you try fixing yourself, Hunter? We'll talk about Africa later. Order me another drink, Hunter. A double."

"No, I won't order you a drink. You're already trashed. I'm surprised you got here without getting a DWI. Unless you want to get sick, you better slow down on the liquor. Your speech is already slurred. You're not a good drunk."

"I feel like celebrating tonight. I'm going to Africa."

"You are definitely too drunk if you're seriously thinking of going to Africa. I mean it. Switch to drinking water. If you stop drinking now, I can follow you home and make sure you get there okay, or you can use the bar's phone and call a friend or a cab if you want." He reached for her cup but she jerked away, sloshing some of the whiskey and Coke on the floor.

"Well, you're not my mama, so mind your own business. I'll drink all night long if I want to." She rattled the ice in her glass at him. "I'll find my way home, thank you. And I can't call a friend because all my friends are out on real dates. They don't have musician boyfriends who always work on weekends. Hunter, I really am going to Africa. I'm going to see things and places and people I've never seen. Then I'm going to come back and paint about Africa. No more moss-on-the-bayou paintings for this girl!"

"You're talking like a drunken crazy woman. Even crazier than usual. Just buy a *National Geographic* and pretend you went to Africa."

She placed her fingers on his lips. "Shhhh. Never you mind. I'll get my own drink. You just be a good boyfriend and play our song." She drained her drink and wobbled unsteadily toward the bar.

Jed, the bar's new manager, stood at the bar. He patted his watch impatiently. Hunter nodded and placed his foot on the tambourine he had set on the floor. After Hunter tapped the tambourine four times, he began "Time of Your Life." Caitlin left the bar with her refill and started dancing alone in the small dance area in front of him. Her eyes were closed.

Three men sat at a table directly in front of Hunter, and they leered at Caitlin. One said, "Man, would you look at those long legs. I just might have to get me some of that." He plopped his black Stetson upside down onto the table and walked to the dance floor.

Caitlin opened her eyes and saw the cowboy dancing with her and smiled. "Well, hello there!" she said.

He moved closer to her. "Hello, sexy thing. You shaking that fine body for me?"

Caitlin laughed. "I'm not shaking nothing for no one."

The man's thumbs were hooked inside his belt

loops, but as they danced his big hands made their way to Caitlin's waist. His friends cheered and clapped every time he made a lewd movement or gesture or when Caitlin's movements revealed more skin.

When Hunter realized that he had sung the lines of the chorus out of order, he cut two verses and ended the song. "Well, that's all of me tonight, folks. I'm Hunter, and I'll see y'all next time."

"That sure was a short song," the dancing cowboy said.

Hunter stood and unfastened his guitar strap. "Song's over, buddy. Sorry. I'm done for the night." He opened his guitar case and laid the Taylor inside it.

Caitlin wobbled over, making a pouting face. "Hunter, you didn't finish our song!"

"I think our song was finished a while back, Caitlin. Where's your car keys?"

She dug the keys out of the small purse slung across her chest, dangled them out, and shook them at him like they were chimes. "Here they are. You thought I'd lost them, didn't you? What did you mean when you said our song was finished?"

Hunter snatched the keys and laid them on a speaker. "I didn't mean nothin'. Just sit down somewhere till I can get packed up. I give up. I'll drive you home. Lord, what would you do without me to take care of you?"

"I'd do just fine, thank you," she snapped. "I don't need nobody to take care of me. You are a condescending, arrogant prick. You talk down to me like you think I need a babysitter." She grabbed her keys and stuffed them back into her purse. "Sometimes I wonder how much you really care for me. Hunter doesn't want to ever have any kids. Hunter doesn't want to get married. But why buy the cow when you can get the milk free, right? All the mighty Hunter wants is to play his damn music and to flirt with his groupies. If you really loved me, you'd think more about what I want, about what I need."

Hunter lit a cigarette and tersely blew out the smoke. "Just sit down and shut up. I don't want you getting sick on me—again."

"Don't you tell me to shut up. You take me for granted. I might just find me a man in Africa who knows how to treat a lady. And he won't be no poor, burned-out musician either."

"Quit talking trash, Caitlin," Hunter said. "I'm really getting tired of that caustic tongue of yours."

"Caustic? That's such an educated word for a redneck like you to use. I wonder where you heard it. Have you been watching *Hee-Haw* again?"

Caitlin walked back to the bar for another drink, and Hunter turned away to pack up his equipment.

Jed left the bar and handed Hunter his money for the night. "Good gig tonight, Hunter, other than quitting early." He nodded toward Caitlin. "Your girl sounds a little worked up."

"Yeah, I guess. How are things with your wife?"

Jed laughed. "Don't you get smart-ass with me. I guess there ain't a woman made whose mind works at a hundred percent. Women are hard to figure, but God, I do love mine."

Caitlin returned a moment later and sat on a table near Hunter, nursing another drink and staring off into space. Hunter figured she'd have to make a dash for the bathroom within the next ten minutes.

The dancing cowboy came and sat next to Caitlin and wrapped his arm around her waist. Caitlin didn't seem to notice. Hunter walked over and lifted the man's arm from her waist like he was moving a dirty napkin. Looking the man in the eye, Hunter shook his head, then set the man's hand on the tabletop.

"She shore is drunk," the cowboy said.

Hunter nodded. "She'll be all right, buddy." He rolled the microphone cord on his arm. The cowboy eyed Caitlin. "Hey, guitar man, how'd you know my name was Buddy? Do I know you?"

"Not hardly," Hunter said. "You still ain't moved. It's hard for me to pack up with you in the way."

"Ah, I ain't in no hurry to go. I think Miss Legs here needs a man for the night." He plopped his cowboy hat on Caitlin's head. "Don't you, baby?"

Caitlin grinned, and her eyes crossed as she tried to focus on the man's face, then crossed again as she looked up. "Oh, what a pretty hat!" she said. "Look, Hunter, I've got a pretty cowboy hat! La-di-da! Would you look at me, Hunter? Why don't you ever wear a hat like this?"

"Yeah, baby, you got you a cowboy hat," the cowboy said. "You can wear it till morning if you want to." He returned his arm to Caitlin's waist, leaned over, and nibbled on her ear. Caitlin squealed like she was tickled and when she turned her face toward him, he kissed her on the lips.

Hunter dropped the microphone cord into the duffel bag and stepped over. "Caitlin, go on and get in my truck. I'll be out in a minute. Look, man. I think you must be hard of hearing. She's my girlfriend."

"What's wrong?" Caitlin asked.

The cowboy placed his arm around Caitlin's shoulder and pulled her closer. "The guitar man's all upset 'cause he saw you give me a smooch. He says he's your boyfriend and that I got to leave you alone. But I ain't gonna leave you unless you tell me to."

"Huh? Tell you what? I don't understand," Caitlin said.

Hunter jerked the man to his feet by his shirt collar. "Look, are you naturally stupid, or do you work at it? She's not going home with you. She's *my* girlfriend, so just keep your hands to yourself. The bar's closing anyway, so why don't you carry your sorry ass out the door." Hunter shoved the man toward the exit and turned to finish packing.

"Hey, guitar man!"

Hunter turned and the sucker punch knocked him to the floor. Hunter's hand found his microphone stand and he speared the man in the gut. Springing to his feet, he pulled the cowboy toward him by his shirt and head-butted his face. Hunter jerked him forward a second time and threw his knee into the plate-size rodeo belt buckle, then he slung the doubled-over man across the dancefloor. The man's nose spurted blood like a water sprinkler as he spun wildly away in a drunken tarantella before he crashed onto a table. Hunter followed. After his fists pounded the man to the floor, he hooked several kicks into his ribs and chest. Squeaking sounds issued from lungs emptied of air, but Hunter continued kicking and cursing.

Caitlin tried to pull Hunter away. "Stop it, Hunter! You're hurting him! You're doing it again! You're doing it again! You promised me! I don't want a savior! I don't want a protector!"

Hunter shoved Caitlin away and kept kicking until the bar's bouncer reached him and locked down his arms.

The ambulance and two deputy sheriffs arrived together. The ambulance took the cowboy and his broken face and ribs to Glenwood Hospital, and the deputies, after some persuasion with their nightsticks, took the agitated Hunter to jail.

****

Von paused at the door of the Backdoor Lounge and watched the deputy stuff a man into the cruiser, then entered. A waitress shouted last call, and he joined the small stream that flowed toward the bar. "What can I get you?" she asked.

"Do you have a wine list?"

"You're kidding me, right?"

"I'll take a double Scotch. No ice." Instead of stuffing money into the tip jar, he held out the twenty-dollar bill. "You can keep the change if you stand here and talk to me a minute. You've had some trouble tonight?"

"Just a fight. I think two guys got into it over a girl—that's usually what it is."

Von studied the bar's clientele. A woman stumbled into the wall beneath the clock that was set fifteen minutes fast. An obese couple in matching overalls stood at the juke box, shuffling the pages of choices.

Then he saw Caitlin sitting alone at a table, dazed and wiping fiercely at her cheeks and eyes. Von tilted his glass toward her. "Would that be the girl?"

The waitress glanced at Caitlin. "Yeah."

Von moved from the bar to Caitlin's table. "Rough night?"

"Oh, Von. Yeah. Hunter trouble."

He sat down next to her. "How are you?"

"Not too good. I'm angry, I'm hurt, and I'm too drunk to drive home."

"I'll drive you."

Caitlin shook her head. "I couldn't ask you to do that."

"You didn't ask, I offered. And if you need me to bring you back in the morning for your car, I'll do that too."

The waitress came to their table. "Need anything else, Caitlin?"

"I don't know."

"Well," the waitress said, "Hunter really showed his ass tonight, didn't he? I don't think it's working out with you two. You had a big fight last time he was here."

"We did?"

"Yeah. You need me to call you a cab?"

"There's no need to call a cab. I'm taking her," Von said. "Home, I mean."

Chapter Three

If you look into the bride's face, you'll know that the bride is crying.
—*Krio Proverb*

Von drove Caitlin to her houseboat on the Ouachita River. The boat was moored close to the Louisville Bridge on the West Monroe side. Von helped her out of his car and with his arm around her, walked her to the boat.

"This is your home?"

"Yes. It belonged to my parents. They died in a car wreck a year ago. I really miss them."

"I'm sorry for your loss," Von said. "Why do you live on a boat? Wouldn't an apartment be more practical?" He looked over his shoulder toward the newly constructed two-story condominiums near them. "Today, I actually thought of making Monroe my American base. I could rent one of those condominiums there. They're only a thousand a month."

"God, you must be made of money. Probably an apartment or house would be more practical for me, but I've never been practical, and besides, I love the river. The boat possesses a good karma, and it also carries very pleasant memories of my parents and childhood. Sometimes I think I can feel them here, and that makes me feel less like an orphan."

She paused at the end of the boarded walkway by the boat. "Thank you so much for the ride, Von." She hugged him.

He kissed her on the cheek. "Can I come inside?"

"No, not tonight. Perhaps another time when I'm not so drunk and I'm thinking clearer."

"Goodnight then, Caitlin."

Caitlin paused on the houseboat's deck and watched Von's shape fade into the darkness. She leaned against the cabin and studied the dark river and the lights and shadows pocketed along its banks. The businesses, restaurants, and clubs along the river, bustling with activity during the day, were now quiet and still and only the gentle sound of water lapping against the side of the boat could be heard. She wished she could etch such river night-scenes permanently into her head and then create the same beauty, the same sensory experience, and the same sense of peace on canvas. Her absent parents had loved the river so much, and Caitlin knew they had also loved her, in spite of the tension Hunter had created between them. They had warned her of the grief that awaited her should she fall in love with him. "He's too wild and unreliable, Caitlin," they had said. "A guitar man like that will only break your heart."

"You were right," she whispered to their ghosts.

Caitlin went inside the boat's cabin, pushed Hunter's clothes of yesterday from the bed to the floor, and faded into a numbed sleep.

****

When Caitlin woke the next morning, she washed down two aspirins with a pint mason jar of ice water and tried to recall and sort out everything that happened the previous night at the restaurant and the Backdoor Lounge, but the memories were muddy.

She made coffee, moved to the boat's deck and gazed through sleepy eyes at the sunrise, and once again wished that Hunter could be here with her. The sun sparkled on the dark river's surface like illuminated diamonds strewn across a dark cloth. She phoned a friend she remembered seeing at the bar last night.

"Jessie, this is Caitlin. I'm sorry I'm calling so early."

"That's okay. These crazy kids of mine got me up early anyway. My God, girl, you were trashed last night. I couldn't help but notice that you and your boyfriend had another falling out. I've never seen Hunter so worked up before. He sure gave that poor Bawcomville boy a beating. Hunter's never hit you, has he?"

"No, Jessie, Hunter's never hurt me physically. It's just—he's just overprotective sometimes. This is the second time he's started a fight over someone flirting with me. Last night's like a nightmare. I've been trying to think what I did wrong."

"You didn't do anything wrong. Hunter is overprotective? Is that your way of saying that he gets crazy jealous? Caitlin, you don't need that kind of man. A jealous, possessive man ain't nothing but trouble. That's the kind of man that will go ape-shit someday and kill you."

"I don't think he could ever hurt me, but after last night… I just don't know what's gotten into him lately. How badly did he hurt the man?"

"The poor fellow couldn't even walk. The ambulance came and they had to wheel in a stretcher to

30

carry his ass out. He's not likely to be such a spry dancer for a while. Hunter wasn't in too good a shape neither after the deputies finished thumping him down."

"I should have left when Hunter told me to go to his truck. What do you think will happen to him?" Caitlin asked. "Where do you think they took him?"

"Well, since it was deputies that came in, I'm sure they toted him to the parish prison. My guess is they'll charge him with assault and resisting arrest. But look, Caitlin, you can't worry about Hunter right now. He brought his trouble on himself. That fellow getting hurt wasn't your fault either. Christ, just because some half-drunk guy flirts with you, that ain't no cause for Hunter to beat the crap out of him."

"I need to find out what happened to Hunter."

"You are such an innocent. Get yourself a Sunday paper and check the police report and see if he's listed, then call me back. If he is, get ready for a flood of sympathy calls. Reading about who got arrested is a favorite pastime of people around here. Do you think Hunter will ask you to arrange for his bail?"

"No," Caitlin replied.

"Well, if he does, tell him to call his daddy. He's probably bailed him out before. Well, I got to go, honey. I think that boy of mine has done climbed into the dryer again. He wants to be a spaceman. I tried to tell him that astronauts don't train inside dryers, but I can't get the notion out of his head."

"I'm going to Africa, Jessie, so I need to meet with you soon. I want to rent out my art gallery. I was hoping your agency could list it."

"No problem. Just let me know when you want me to come out."

"I will. I'm going to have one last show. To try to sell some art and say goodbye to my friends. Promise me that you'll get all gussied up and come to it."

"You know I wouldn't miss it."

Caitlin walked to the convenience store near her boat and purchased the local newspaper. Hunter had been charged with vicious assault and possession of marijuana.

Caitlin dropped the paper into the trash and walked to her gallery on Trenton Street. So that she could push Hunter out of her mind, she spent the rest of the day painting and tidying up the gallery for her show. Tomorrow, she determined to begin preparations to go to Africa.

****

Caitlin drove to St. Michael's. She studied the white stone building with an artist's eye. The white stone church was a landmark of Monroe, one of its oldest buildings. She loved its majesty and form. The Gothic windows, with their opaque stained panes, rose like sentries guarding its ancient, holy rituals. She twisted down the rearview mirror and checked her makeup.

After she powdered her flushed cheeks and applied lipstick, she went inside, feeling the reverent quiet that the building always imposed upon her and knocked on the priest's office door.

"Come," he said.

When she entered, Father Robert looked up from his paperwork and smiled. "Caitlin, I hope you are well."

"I am, Father, thank you. I hope it's okay to drop in like this."

"Oh, yes. I'm glad you're here. I wanted to thank you for inviting me to your art show last month at the university. Wonderful paintings of Bayou DeSiard. Are you making any money from your art?"

"No, Father. In fact, things got so tight that I had to take a job three weeks ago at Vermeer Diamonds. Even though I receive an inheritance of thirty thousand a year from my parents' estate, and I manage to sell a few of my paintings, it's not enough. I still live on the boat, but at least it's paid for. I manage to get by and maybe I'll get out of debt soon."

"Yes, my child. The interest rate on credit cards is pure usury." Father Robert opened his desk drawer and drew out a pack of unfiltered Lucky Strikes. "Do you mind if I smoke?"

"No, of course not."

"Thank you. Thank God social reconstruction policies haven't yet banned smoking in my own office." He lit a cigarette, then fumbled through a stack of papers on his desk. "What's on your mind today?"

"Well, my company wants to send me to Sierra Leone. And my boss was kind enough to say that I could spend some of that time working with the mission you talked about last Sunday, as long as it didn't interfere with my work. Could the school use an art teacher?"

"Caitlin, that is wonderful! Our mission school in Sierra Leone so needs teachers. Your employer is generous. I can't wait to share the news with your uncle. I'll use my ham radio and try to reach him tonight. The Church can provide you with a room if you need it, and we will help pay for some of your expenses. I am confident it will be a life-changing experience." He pointed to a framed painting of St. George's Cathedral. "That Cathedral in Freetown is two-hundred years old. I hope you will visit it. It's a reminder that Freetown was founded on three things: commerce, slavery, and Christianity. Only Christianity remains of the three. And because of volunteers like yourself, Christianity will continue to be a blessing to that dark and troubled land."

"I've never been outside of the U.S., and I've always wanted to travel, but I never thought about going to Africa. The thought of leaving Monroe is a little unnerving. And I don't know what to expect in Sierra Leone."

"The school is in Freetown, so you would have safety and adequate comforts, at least by African standards. You have so much talent, Caitlin. Here's your chance to serve God and develop yourself as well."

"I'll need your help. I'm planning on having one last show before I rent out my gallery. I'm worried about where to store the paintings and sculptures I can't sell."

"Do not worry about that. The church has an empty room you can use to store your art till you return."

"Thank you, Father. That is very generous. I hope you will come to my last art show. Can you announce it to the church? Honestly, I'm a little frightened when I think of making this journey. I don't know how to go about getting ready for the trip."

"I will walk you through every step—all the way to Sierra Leone."

Chapter Four

People say I am ruthless. I am not ruthless. And if I find the man who is calling me ruthless, I shall destroy him.
—Robert Kennedy

At 6:00 p.m., Von sped down Louisville to the Monroe Civic Center for the Open Style Martial Arts Tournament. Ringside, he found Rory Smith, the Northeast Louisiana martial arts instructor who had planned the event. Rory recognized him and stood to greet him.

"Von, how are you? It's been a while. There's a seat here. Why don't you join me?"

"Thank you, I will."

"You're not fighting tonight, Von?" Rory asked.

"No. My work has prevented me from training as I should. I'm only in Monroe for business. I heard about the tournament, so I thought I'd see the competition our New Orleans schools will have to face next year."

A large black man entered the ring. "I especially came to see this man fight," Von said. "His name is Biko."

"You know him? He's the coach for the Sierra Leone team. His boys will give a demonstration later tonight. What do you know about him?"

"I know much about him. He is a Thai kick boxer.

35

He also has a black belt in Tae Kwon Do and is generally just a tough son of a bitch. His team serves with him in a military unit."

After the fighters bowed and the referee began the round, Biko launched a barrage of kicks and punches. One was a low blow. When Biko's Korean style opponent doubled over and wobbled unsteadily on his feet, the man's coach entered the ring. When the referee turned away from the fighters to order the man back to his corner, Biko attacked again, moving in closer this time, delivering hard decisive strikes, his leg whipping repeatedly into the man's kidneys. The last blow was an illegal elbow, slipped in as a curving motion, as if it were a gloved punch, but so quick that few in the audience saw it. Biko's opponent crumpled in a heap. Biko lifted his arms and strutted around the ring. A few in the audience booed when the referee lifted one of Biko's arms in victory. Von heard the fighter shout, "For Biko, and for Sierra Leone!"

Rory said, "Hmm. I can't believe that he beat the Korean so quickly."

"He is not only tough; he is ruthless," Von said. "I like his style."

"You would, Von. After the fight, come meet me for a drink at Monroe's only strip club."

"I can't tonight. I'm meeting Biko at my hotel."

Biko hopped the ropes and joined the Sierra Leone team ringside. He slapped the head of one team member whose eyes wandered while he addressed the team. They filed onto the canvass floor of the ring and as Biko barked out commands they took their positions. Like Biko, the fighters' uniform trousers were short, to the knee, revealing callused shins, the battered nerve endings long dead. Toughened shins would be as effective as a wooden club in combat.

On stage, one of Biko's fighters took the microphone. "Master Biko stresses the importance of the *poomse*. He says our *poomses* reveal that 'Man is born without knowledge and when he has obtained it, he very soon becomes old. When his experience is ripe, death suddenly seizes him.' He has choreographed a new form, one that tells a story as old as Salone. As such patterns of defensive and offensive movements reflect the identity, the principles, and the essence of our fighting system, the form you see tonight reflects the philosophic relevance of the martial arts to soldiers in our country."

The sound system projected ear-splitting music, a mixture of voices and West African drumbeats. The team members formed two lines and rocked on the balls of their feet to the rhythm. The form was a complex series of movements, and the team a model of precision, rhythm, balance, co-ordination, endurance, patience, muscles, discipline, and breath control. Biko's creation, similar to what the Japanese call a *kata* and the Koreans a *poomse*, told a story unfamiliar to the audience. After one line symbolically attacked, the opposite knelt and bowed their heads in surrender. One by one they extended one arm, then another as the leader, wielding a *daab*, a Thai saber-shaped sword, moved down the line, slicing symbolically at the projecting hands, and the hands folded down as if sliced off. The music stopped suddenly and the lights went out briefly on the cue of one final drumbeat. Silence weighed down on the audience, floated down from the ceiling to rest in hearts troubled. When the lights returned, the team formed a single line and bowed in each direction, and then the crowd hesitantly applauded. It was an audacious presentation on Biko's part. Von was certain few in the audience would understand its political and moral symbolism. However, Von understood and he felt a kinship to the ruthlessness, to the power of the form.

After the tournament, Von met Biko at their hotel bar. He sat with two judges from the tournament. Von bowed slightly to the judges, then he and Biko clasped hands.

"Von, how de body?" Biko said.

"Business is good."

Biko rose and bowed slightly to the others. "Excuse us please. My friend and I must talk. Come, Von. We shall go to my hotel room."

As they walked, Von asked, "Did you bring the diamonds?"

"Yes, I have something that may interest you."

At his room, Biko removed a small velour pouch from his suitcase. He shook it. Von's heart raced when he heard the distinctive rattle of stones.

Biko slowly emptied the diamonds onto the coffee table. "These are diamonds from Kono. What do you think?"

Von studied one with his loupe, the special magnifying glass that diamond merchants always carry with them. "A superior grade of diamond. You have a great deal of money here." *A fortune actually,* Von thought. *I've never held so much raw wealth in my life.*

"That is one day's mining from one town in my new district," Biko said. "You like these stones? So, you will pay Biko much dollars?"

"Yes, Biko. I am very pleased. Payment will be deposited into your account promptly."

"It is good. The RUF now controls most of the country. Soon we have Freetown too. Tomorrow, I return to my country. I hope you return to Salone soon. We need your diamond wisdom. We think the Lebanese merchants cheat us. Now, tonight, you can find Biko an American woman?"

"I'll see what I can do."

"You have many fine women in America."

"Yes, we do. However, here in Monroe I haven't seen many for sale."

"All women are for sale. As we say in our country, 'Money in de hand, back on de ground.' Here the women just like to play games first, but the game wearies me, so you must find Biko a woman."

Von left Biko's room and went to the bar. He signaled the waitress, a pleasant and nice-looking girl with long straight hair almost to her waist. She set an open book face down on the counter.

""Hi!" she said. "What can I get for you?"

"I'll take a double shot of Don Julio, chilled, with lime. No salt. And bring me a Corona with lime."

When she returned with his drinks he said, "I see you've been reading in your few slow moments. Is it a good read?"

"Oh, yeah. I can hardly bear to put it down." She held up the cover so Von could read the title, *Under the Witch's Mark*. "This author is just enough on the wild side of the line to excite me."

"Must be a very interesting book. I'm new to Monroe, but happy to find someone here that reads. I don't know why, but as soon as I saw you, I thought you might like things on the wild side. Speaking of wild, and I hope you're not offended by my asking, but do any classy working women come here?"

She nodded toward a well-dressed woman at the end of the bar. "Kind of expensive, I understand."

"Money's not a problem."

"Must be nice to not have to worry about money."

"I've lived without money, and I've lived with it. I'd have to say that life is far better with it. I'm a diamond merchant now, so I can't complain."

"Really? I've never known a diamond merchant before."

He opened his wallet, pulled out, snapped two hundred-dollar bills, then dropped them on the counter. The girl the waitress had pointed out was taking a long slow drink, but it was obvious she had spotted the flashed money and was looking Von over. Von raised his glass toward her. "Take that woman a drink of her choice with my compliments. She appeals to me, but I'd rather have you. Interested?"

"It's tempting, but, no," she said. After the bartender took the girl the drink, she returned, snatched up a towel and again wiped the counter in front of Von. Her eyes were fixed on the two hundred-dollar bills.

Von liked this girl, and her innocence and inexperience attracted him even more, so he laid another hundred on top of the other two. "Easy money."

Her hand froze a second, then resumed wiping. "I need to think about it," she said. "I couldn't tonight. I've got to pick up my little boy."

Like everyone else, she and her virtue are for sale, Von thought. *As Biko said, Money in the hand, back on the ground.* He slid the money toward her. "Keep it then, till a future evening. I'll be back. I'll take you out somewhere nice—if there is somewhere really nice around here." When she hesitated, he said, "Go on, take it. My guess is you can use it. Look at it as a tip for your time and steering me to the pretty lady."

"This is a week's pay. You are a trusting man." She folded the bills and slid them into her back pocket. "It would be so easy for me to just take your money and avoid seeing you again."

Von chuckled. "It's not that easy to get away from me. Do you know what I mean?"

Von picked up his drink, and walked to the hooker, taking the empty stool beside her.

"You must be the gentleman who bought the drink. Thank you," she said.

He laid down a Franklin. "Let's get right down to the point. I'm looking for some company. Are you interested?"

She picked up the bill and slipped it into the purse. "I am. We do need to talk a little more. A private spot would be better to discuss my rates and your particular interests. Do you have a room?"

"I'm open to further negotiations. And, yes, I have an excellent room. Would you care to see it?"

She stood and slung her purse on her shoulder. "Sure. Let's go."

He held out his arm. "My name is Von."

"Oh, a gentleman. I'm Amanda."

When they entered the suite, Biko was playing solitaire. "Biko, this is Amanda, my date for the evening." He winked at Biko.

Biko raised his hand and waved. "Hello, girl."

"Nice to meet you, too." She turned to Von. "Shall

we talk about money?"

"Yes, let's talk about money." Von motioned to the sofa.

Biko said, "The girl would like a drink?"

"Sure," she said.

Biko pointed to the mini refrigerator. "I have rum and coke. Von will prepare us each a drink." Biko returned to his card game.

After Von prepared their drinks, he spread a dark cloth on the coffee table. When he took off his jacket, Amanda's eyes shifted to Von's pistol clipped in its holster to his belt. Von slipped it off and laid it on the table.

Amanda's eyes widened.

"Don't worry," Von said. "I have a license. In my line of work, I need to protect the stones and cash I carry." Then he dumped the sack of diamonds Biko had given him onto the cloth. "These are diamonds, uncut and unpolished." He reached into his pants pocket and pulled out a small silver box about the size of a matchbox. From it he chose a diamond and held it to the light. "Do you know what this is?"

"A diamond," she said. "You said you sold diamonds. It's real pretty."

"Yes, to use the words that came from your pretty little brain, it is a pretty little diamond. But, there is so much you don't see here. This is a three-carat stone, cut and polished. Do you know how much a carat weighs?"

"No, but my grandma raised them. A carrot would weigh a lot more than that."

Von snickered. "Oh, you Southern folks are so witty. I'm not talking about what comes out of the garden, Daisy Lou. You are kidding me, I hope. Hold out your hand."

When she extended her hand, he dropped a paper ßclip on it. "That's how much a carat weighs, one fifth of a gram. Now, hold the diamond." He removed the paper clip and placed the stone in her hand. "Hold it up to the light. Look closely. This stone is brilliant cut with fifty-eight facets. These facets reflect the light from one to another until it's dispersed through the top of the stone. See how it sparkles? See the little flashes of its fire-like rainbow? Clear of color, flawless in clarity, appraised and certified. It's hard to believe that in its raw form it looks like these unimpressive shiny pebbles in the other sack. Do you have any idea how much this one little stone is worth?"

"A bunch."

Von snickered. "A bunch? How about ten thousand dollars?"

"No shit?" she said.

Von continued. "You know, a woman is very much like a diamond. Most people think of diamonds as being perfect, but most are not. The majority of diamonds brought to the surface have at least a few internal flaws, inclusions as we say in the business, and…" He touched her cheek and turned her face as if inspecting her surface for imperfections or blemishes. "Sometimes a 'pretty' stone is not worth much at all. Too many flaws. These flaws are very hard for an untrained eye to spot—feathers and pinpoints, tiny cracks and specks, scratches and chips. Diamonds are much more fragile than people think."

She pushed his hand away. "I feel like I'm in school taking a damn geology class," she said. "And I don't think I like the comparison you've just made.

Maybe you just see too much. I thought we were going to talk about money. Are you interested in me or not?"

"Oh, yes, I'm interested. You must pardon me. My mind fixates on things sometimes, and I get off on tangents. I didn't mean to digress. Actually, I was talking about money. You see, in the dark light of the bar, you had a little sparkle to you—just like a common industrial diamond might have until you inspect it with a loupe—and on that basis I would have offered you a thousand dollars for your services. But now that I have my little gemstone in the light, I think less. Much less."

She lit a cigarette, snapped her lighter shut and blew out the smoke hard. "Bastard." She slapped the Marlboro Lights and the lighter down on the coffee table and leaned back against the couch. "Like I said, if you're not interested, just say so."

"I may be a bastard," Von said. "But I'm not such a bastard that I can't realize that even industrial quality diamonds have some value. I'm not saying I'm not interested." He laid down a hundred. "How's that?"

"Fine," she said. "Fine. That will get you a good hour."

"No," he said. "This and the hundred I've already given you will get *us* a night."

Von slowly and deliberately looked at Biko, then fixed his eyes into hers, and he knew that she knew there would be no discussion. "In Africa, I could buy a woman for life for that amount. So what do you say? And who knows? If you impress us you might get a little more." He deliberately looked away from the girl and down at the coffee table.

The girl followed his gaze to the pistol. "Sure," she said. "A hundred dollars more will be fine."

Biko stood and unbuckled his belt. "Great place, dis America. Come to me, girl."

Chapter Five

I believe there is no sickness of the heart too great that it cannot be cured by a dose of Africa.
—*John Hemingway*

"Hello, Caitlin," the doctor said as he entered the waiting room. He slipped on his reading glasses, sat down on the rollaway stool and studied her chart. "How can I help you today? Are you ill?"

Caitlin tossed the *Delta Style* magazine into the seat of the empty chair next to the exam table she sat on. "No, I'm fine. My company is sending me to Africa, and I need to get shots for yellow fever and cholera." She handed him the visa form. "My priest said that I might need other shots too."

He scanned the form. "Sierra Leone. Excuse me for a minute, and I'll check on those other shots. I'm sorry that I don't know off the top of my head, but I don't have many patients going to Africa."

He returned with a tome that he set in his lap. From the index, he turned to two other pages, his fingers scanning the paragraphs in his hurried research. "Interesting. Yes, if you plan on going to West Africa, I would also recommend immunizations for hepatitis, typhoid, and a tetanus-diphtheria booster. You must also begin taking anti-malarial medicine. I would suggest mefloquine. When do you leave?"

"In two to four weeks if everything goes as planned."

"Just in time. You'll need to start taking 250-mg mefloquine tablets once a week before your departure, once a week while in Africa, and once a week for four weeks after returning home. The medicine is expensive, but it works well. How long will you be gone?"

"I don't know for sure. At least a month," Caitlin said, for the first time feeling some sadness at leaving Louisiana.

The doctor scribbled out several prescriptions. "Well, here's a mefloquine prescription that will get you through a year, and some antibiotics that you might need in case you come down with a bug or something. I'd take as much of your medication with you as you can since there are medical supply problems in West Africa." He ripped the prescriptions from the pad and handed them to her. "Ready for your shots?"

"Do I get the shots in the butt or arm?" Caitlin asked.

"Yes," her doctor said.

****

In a cold misting rain, Larry drifted slowly down Trenton Street in West Monroe, Louisiana, warming his hands in the side pockets of his faded olive-green field jacket. Pausing in front of each store window, he studied the antique furniture and other goods on display. When he came to an art gallery, his eyes were drawn to a wooden sign above him that read: THE LOST BAZAAR. Suspended by chains, the sign rocked whenever a gust of wind nudged it, rasping despondent creaks and groans in the gaps of silence between passing cars. A cardboard placard was taped to the glass of an ancient wooden door. Larry moved his index finger across the page word by word:

HAPPY MARDI-GRAS! THIS WEEK THE GALLERY WILL FEATURE AN EXHIBITION OF THE WORK OF CAITLIN JOHNSON.

The gallery was closed. Larry took off his ball cap and pressed his face to the smudged, tinted glass and peered at several paintings hanging inside on the plaster walls. Adjacent to the window stood a bronze sculpture of a naked man with empty eye sockets holding a guitar with one raised fist. His mouth was opened wide as if he were tortured and howling in rage or dementia. Next to this simulacrum stood another bronze figure of a kneeling nude young woman who held her hands to her face as if she wept for the man's anguish. Larry rubbed his burning eyes.

"Now, we see through a glass darkly…"

For a moment, Larry thought the man-statue had spoken. He shook his head. When he heard a snicker, he turned and saw a man peering over his shoulder. The man clutched a scuffed duffel bag in one hand and with the other he touched his face as a man does when he inspects himself before a mirror when shaving. He wore a pointed stocking cap that was pulled down to his thick black eyebrows. His dark eyes were big and wild, and he grinned, revealing teeth that were stained and crooked.

"What?" Larry said.

The man pointed at the statues. "Dress them up in a few clothes and they might look human."

"I guess."

"I reckon this must be some kind of museum."

"An art gallery actually."

"Well, I'll be. I wonder what else they got on display inside. I used to be a preacher, showing people the way to that great art gallery in the sky. In fact, folks just generally call me Preacher. That's because I quote the Bible so much."

"Glad to meet you, Preacher. My name is Larry."

"You remind me of an uncle of mine. He had a coat like that too. Served in Viet Nam he did. He blew his brains out though. You know what time it is?"

"No. I sold my watch a couple of weeks ago."

"The exact time don't matter much noway. I came in from Mississippi on the train. You?"

"Walked and hitchhiked here. Left New Orleans a while back. I've been out West. Mostly rambling through Texas."

"Ah, you are a true King of the Road, a pilgrim walking till he reaches that better land!"

"Where are you headed?" Larry asked.

"I don't know, my fellow vagabond, but I reckon I'll get there somehow. King Larry, could you spare some change to help a man get a drink?"

"Sure. I got a few bucks and could use a drink myself. I don't have much, but I'm glad to share what I got."

"Like the Bible says, give strong drink unto him that is ready to perish," Preacher said, "and wine unto those that be of heavy hearts. Let him drink, and forget his poverty, and remember his misery no more."

"Are you sure the Bible says that?"

"It does for a fact. Speaks right to the heart, don't it."

"There's a ring of truth to it," Larry said.

Preacher pointed toward the river. "Round the bend

yonder I saw a bar. We could go there."

"Sure. It's bound to be warmer and drier than standing here."

They crossed Trenton Street and walked toward the river. As they walked, Preacher sang, "Little Brown Jug."

Larry looked up at the sky. The gray clouds were thick with moisture. South of town, large plumes of smoke billowed up into the sky from a paper mill's concrete smokestacks. The north wind gnawed its way through his jacket, and the light mist, which earlier floated and drifted to the ground, changed to a light rain mixed with sleet that pelted and stung Larry's face.

"I never can get used to walking in the rain," Larry said. "I hate it."

"The good Lord makes his rain fall on the just and the unjust."

"I still don't like it."

Near the levee they passed through an opening in a concrete block floodwall and sloshed through the parking lot to the Cottonport Lounge. Larry paused outside the door and studied the Ouachita River and the reflections of buildings and lights shimmering on the dark water's surface.

"We're going down the river one by one," Preacher said.

"You must be a hoot at funerals," Larry said. "You probably have a Bible verse ready for every occasion."

"I do indeed. How much money you got, King Larry? The Bible says, 'Money answers all things.'"

"Five dollars." Larry scraped the bottoms of his muddy boots on the edge of the concrete porch. He looked up at the flashing neon sign that said it was

Mardi-Gras Night.

"Tain't much for us to drink on," Preacher said.

"Sorry. It's all I got. Look for unfinished drinks. Shoot them down and no one will be the wiser. Let's go on inside."

They entered and sat down at an empty table near the door. Larry stretched out his cramped legs and felt drafts of heated air push the cold dampness of his jeans against his skin. He leaned his head against the wall and closed his eyes and thought of last week's walk through the West Texas Badlands and how the wind had pushed him relentlessly out of Texas back to Louisiana.

A waitress came to their table. "What would you men like to drink tonight?"

Larry opened his eyes. "Let me have a Budweiser."

She nodded toward Preacher. "What'll he have?"

"A glass of red wine," Preacher said, "for my stomach's sake." He snickered.

The waitress rolled her eyes, took Larry's money, and returned with their drinks.

"You got any free snacks?" Preacher asked. "I'm a mite bit hungry."

"We have some *hors d'oeuvres* and King Cake laid out later for the Mardi-Gras party," she said. She eyed the two men. "You should have come in costume. We're giving a prize for the best one."

Larry looked down at his hard traveled clothes. Not much of a costume. "We're just passing through. Didn't know about the Mardi-Gras party."

Preacher gulped down his wine. "Thank you, cupbearer. I was hungry and you gave me meat."

"Don't drink so fast," Larry said. "The longer your drink lasts, the less they'll hustle you to buy more."

"Ah, wine that maketh glad the heart of man!"
Preacher said. "The Lord shall provide more, King
Larry."

Larry sipped his beer slowly and studied the
motley crowd. The costumes reminded him of a bar
scene in *Star Wars* or folks attending Bourbon Street
festivals. A menagerie of alien humans milled about
him in various stages of drunkenness—mutants,
weirdoes, rednecks, and deviants in mismatched or
bizarre clothes. A bartender in a tuxedo jabbered with a
man in a leisure suit. A plump brunette wearing a
plastic tiara and a short black sequined dress brayed to
her friends with a high-pitched voice. One man sported
a heavily bearded face and a bandoleer of wine coolers
across his chest. He grunted with each step as he
strutted past their table.

"Hey, it's Chewbacca!" Larry whispered.

"Watch this, King Larry," Preacher said. "Hey,
fool!"

Three men at the bar turned and looked at him.

"No, not none of you," Preacher said. He pointed
toward the back of the lounge. "Way back there." He
snickered when they looked that direction.

"I think I'm gonna mingle with the church,"
Preacher said. "You know, check on the indwelling of
the spirits." He left the table and walked through the
bar, talking to various people as if they were lost and
delinquent members of his lost congregation. His arms
flapped wildly as he bellowed out strange Bible verses.
Soon, one man went to the bar and fetched Preacher a
bottle of wine.

"Yes, sir," Preacher predicated. "A man's gotta be
baptized and warsh away his past sins. That old man's

gotta die and be buried in the water before a new one can rise up. Course, baptism don't always take if'n you don't do it right."

A slender blonde woman entered the Cottonport. She wore a gray crewneck sweater and blue jeans. Her pale slender fingers wiped raindrops from her face then nervously tapped her leg. She scanned the bar and when her eyes fell on Larry, she smiled.

"Looking for someone?" Larry asked. For a second, Larry thought he knew her, but then dismissed the idea as wishful thinking.

"My friends, but I don't see them. I guess I need to find a table and save them seats."

"You're welcome to take this one. I'll move to the bar." Larry pushed back his chair to get up.

She sat in Preacher's chair. "I'll take a seat, but you don't have to leave. It's sweet of you to offer me your table though."

"My name's Larry," he said.

"I'm Caitlin. Are you ready for Mardi-Gras?"

"I never seem to be ready for what a day brings.

"Damn. I'm not sure why I came here tonight," she said. "My boyfriend was supposed to be the music for tonight, but he couldn't make it. Most of my life I've waited around this piss-pot town hoping for things to be different. But they never are." She looked at Larry's face. "Your eyes are awfully red. Do they hurt?"

"No more than usual."

Preacher was perched on a pool table, wolfing down sandwiches and guzzling wine. He set down his glass and beckoned Larry to come to him.

"Excuse me a minute," Larry said. "I must consult with my philosopher."

"What?"

"Nothing. Just trying to make a joke."

Larry walked over to Preacher. "What do you want?"

"There is a time to dance," Preacher said, then with his hand dismissed him.

Larry grinned and returned to Caitlin just as the band began a slow song. He slipped off his field jacket and draped it across his chair. "Hey, dance with me, lady."

"Sure."

They danced in small circular movements on the crowded dance floor. Caitlin gently laid her head on his shoulder and sighed. "This is nice. It's been a while. My boyfriend never dances with me since he's always playing his guitar."

Preacher waved a paper horn at them as if it were a wand, as if he were bestowing a blessing upon them.

When the dance ended she said, "Look at that lunatic friend of yours."

"Aw, he's all right. We're probably all crazy in one way or another. It's easy to do, to go crazy."

"Yeah, it is. I've been on the edge a few times myself. What do you do, Larry?"

"I travel."

"Are you in sales or something?"

"No. I'm gainfully unemployed right now."

"Do you just drive your car from place to place?"

"I don't have a car."

"Well, how do you travel if you don't have a car?"

"I either hitchhike or walk mostly. I have hopped a train or two, but I don't like traveling in boxcars. Rough company, and the trains don't run on schedule anymore.

Everything's so damned unpredictable these days—the weather, jobs, trains, people."

"Where will you go next?"

"I don't know. Any suggestions?"

"Are you like homeless or something?" she asked.

"Only by choice, till I get my head together."

"How sad. But you don't look or sound like a homeless person to me. How did you end up like this?"

"I just left one day. Got sick of the way things were, so I just left. Should have done it years ago, but I've always held on to things longer than I should. It's not too bad. I find an odd job now and then, sleep where I can, then I walk somewhere else. I don't know why I'm telling you this crap. Let's talk about something else. What do you do?"

"I'm an artist."

Larry remembered the sign at the Lost Bazaar. "I saw a sign about an art show at a gallery that mentioned Caitlin Johnson. Would that be you?"

She pulled back a little and looked at him. "Yes, that would be me. I've got this last exhibition, and then I'm closing the gallery. Hey, my last showing and reception is tomorrow. Maybe you can come."

He touched her left hand resting on his shoulder. "You have the hands of an artist, Caitlin. I bet you are a good one. Why are you closing the gallery?"

"I'm going to Africa."

"I have… had a brother who spends a lot of time in Sierra Leone."

"You're kidding. That's where I'm going."

"Yeah, my brother Von has made a fortune in diamonds there. We haven't communicated in years. He says I'm a loser and a disgrace. I haven't made up my mind about that."

Caitlin cleared her throat. "Diamonds? Your brother's name is Von? What's your last name, Larry?"

"Vermeer."

Caitlin shivered. "When did you last see Von?"

"Years ago. We did not part on good terms after what he did to me and our parents."

"What happened" Caitlin looked at Larry for a moment, studying his facial features and dark eyes, wondered what had come between the two brothers.

When Larry didn't answer, she gently but firmly pushed Larry away when she saw her friend Jessie enter. "I've got to leave now, Larry. My friend is here. Can I buy you a drink? What would you like?"

"A double whiskey."

When she returned with his drink, Larry watched her leave with her friend waiting for her to turn back and look at him one more time. She didn't.

At 1:00 a.m. the bar manager shouted, "Folks, you don't have to go home, but you can't stay here."

Larry returned to his chair and sipped on the whisky Caitlin had bought him as the crowd filed out—some left alone, others were headed for trysting places or after-hours clubs. "No thanks, folks. I think I'll just stick around here," he said to no one in particular.

On his way out, he stuffed his pockets with leftover peanuts, pretzels and a slice of King Cake that he wrapped in a napkin. Picking up a half-finished drink, he downed it quickly, and the straight whiskey warmed his throat and belly. He set down the glass and looked around for Preacher, but he couldn't find him. Trying not to think of the damp cold he knew would seep into his bones before morning, he walked out of the bar into the darkness of the gravel parking lot.

The rain had ended. Larry sat with his back against the floodwall where he could see the river. He was relieved he hadn't gotten drunk tonight and passed out in the bar. A man ought to choose his resting-place. It's bad when the drink decides. Too many things are lost that way. He fastened the Velcro collar of his jacket and pulled his cap lower. There was no breeze, and the thick moist air was heavy and full of the sour, rotten smell of the paper mill. The stillness oppressed him and pushed his thoughts and being into his own flesh.

Weariness crept up his legs and he closed his eyes and drifted into sleep. His mind was empty at first, but his dreams carried him into the Lost Bazaar where he saw himself and others he did not know hanging on its walls. Barkers and auctioneers in fancy suits stood in front of the gallery hustling indifferent people on the busy street to come in and buy the people on display in honor of the good times past. Larry hung near the door above the statue of the tormented man. One of the auctioneers cursed and flogged him with a whip while Larry raised his fists and howled in pain. Caitlin passed by and he cried out to her for help. Someone gouged his ribs with a stick.

"Hey, you! Wake up."

Larry looked up through his blurred eyes into the face of a policeman. "Oh. Mornin', officer."

"What are you doing here?" He tapped his open hand with his nightstick.

"Sleeping," Larry said.

"Don't you have somewhere to stay? Did you get drunk and pass out here?"

"It's a long story. Do you really want to know?"

57

"Can I see some identification, sir?"

"Don't have any. Don't need it anymore."

"Look, smart ass, before I get real curious about who you are, you better get up and move on or I'll carry your indigent ass to jail. You can't stay here."

"I've heard that before. I'm going."

Larry rose and plodded back to the Lost Bazaar. Preacher sat on the curb.

"I thought you might be coming back this way," Preacher said.

"Where did you sleep?" Larry asked.

"In the back of a truck at the bar, but this morning' a feller woke me up. He seemed pretty riled up. The truck was at some apartments but I managed to find my way here. Where'd you sleep?"

"Down by the river. They're having a reception here this morning. We can get some coffee and breakfast if we hang around a while."

"That's a fine idea, King Larry. Mighty fine."

A huge cloud of blackbirds flew over them, filling the air with the sound of their wings and chirping. Splotches of white splattered the ground around them, and Larry felt a gob of bird shit hit his jacket.

Preacher snickered. "Louisiana's got lots of those blackbirds, don't it? They're like people—you gotta watch out for them when they're in big groups."

They waited on the curb. The gallery had just opened when Caitlin arrived. She stepped out of a white sedan wearing a black formal dress. A priest followed her out of the car.

Preacher slapped Larry on the shoulder. "She's come to see you, Larry! And all dolled up too."

"She didn't come to see me. She's the featured

artist you dumb ass. Be careful what you say."

They followed the crowd into the gallery and Preacher sped directly to a table loaded with refreshments. Larry strolled through the gallery and studied Caitlin's paintings and sculptures, pausing at the bronze man-statue he had seen through the window yesterday. Caitlin noticed Larry and wended her way through the crowd to him.

"Larry!" she said. "You did make it."

"I want to congratulate the featured artist. Your art is exceptional, Caitlin."

"Thanks, Larry."

He pointed to the bronze statue he had noticed yesterday. "If I had the money, I'd buy this to remember you by. The man and the woman both look so sad."

"That's sweet of you to say, Larry." She touched the statue's eyes. "It's my favorite piece. I call it *Tempest in the Mind*."

The priest walked over and took Caitlin by the arm. "I don't mean to interrupt your conversation with this— gentleman, Caitlin, but I think one of my parishioners wants to buy a painting."

Caitlin placed her hand on Larry's arm and squeezed. "Take care of yourself, Larry."

Preacher walked over as Larry was studying the man-statue. Preacher bent over and peered at it closely. "Lord! He ain't got no eyeballs!"

"I'd buy this statue if I had the money, Preacher."

"What do you want a graven image for, King Larry?" he shouted. "You can't afford nothing like this. Besides, he don't seem like he'd be good for anything."

"You're right, Preacher. See you later." Larry

scooped up the statue and ran out of the gallery toward the Cottonport Lounge.

Preacher hollered, "Hey, Larry! Ain't you gonna eat first?" He grabbed a platter of pastries from the table and ran after him. "Hold on, King Larry, I'm right behind you!"

Several in the crowd pursued them. The priest who came into the gallery with Caitlin strode to Caitlin's desk and picked up the phone. "Caitlin, do you want me to call the police?"

Caitlin took the receiver from his hand and hung it up. "No, Father. No police. It's mine to let go. Leave him alone. At least *he* liked it, unlike Hunter who I made it for."

When Larry reached the floodwall, he turned and saw the crowd in pursuit.

Preacher yelled, "You sure do know how to raise Cain. Shall we gather at the river, King Larry?"

Larry willed his rubbery legs toward the river and jumped into the cold water. Preacher stopped at the edge and stuffed a pastry into his mouth. "You done lost your mind, King Larry. This ain't no time to go baptizing yourself. Get out and eat one of these cinnamon rolls."

Larry crooked his arm around the neck of the statue and side-stroked into deep water as if he were a lifeguard rescuing a drowning man. The river carried him downstream past the houseboats, past the plush houses and apartments built along the riverbank. Larry struggled to cut across the Ouachita so he could reach the Monroe side, but the current denied him any progress and sapped his strength. Vice-like invisible hands pulled at him, and a Lethean numbness crept up his legs. Through blurred eyes Larry glanced at the bronze face in the crook of his arm.

"Damn, you're a heavy one, but I ain't gonna let you go. You guitar players don't belong in no Lost Bazaar. We'll go down together. How long you reckon a man can hold his breath?"

Larry Vermeer saw Caitlin the artist looking at him. He raised a fist to the sky and howled at the crowd on the riverbank, then let the river pull them down.

****

The next week when her exhibition ended, Caitlin met Jessie at the art gallery. She could have taken her car, but the Lost Bazaar was on Trenton Street in West Monroe, in easy walking distance from her boat. Caitlin hated the idea of renting the building, but an art gallery is a high-maintenance, time-intensive commitment, and she knew she wouldn't be able to care for it while she was in Africa. Jessie arrived just as she had taken down the wooden sign on which her father had carved the name she had given the gallery—*The Lost Bazaar*.

"Hello, Jessie," Caitlin said. "Thanks for helping me out."

"No problem. Good news. I've already found someone interested in leasing your building, Caitlin. Her name is Melissa, and I think you'll like her. She wants to open an antique shop in downtown West Monroe. After I described the building, she asked if she could live upstairs. I told her the apartment was unfinished and not part of the lease. She offered to fix it up in exchange for lowering the rent. Are you open to that?"

"I guess that would increase the building's value. It would be better to have someone living there, wouldn't it? Hunter's promised a dozen times to do some work on the apartment, but never got around to it. Sure, tell Melissa we'll work something out."

"Good. She sounded so excited about the building. We'll miss the Lost Bazaar though."

"Don't worry. I'll reopen it when I return." Caitlin stepped down from the stepladder and stood the sign on its end.

"They found the body of that homeless man that fled your gallery near the Columbia Lock and Dam. I'm afraid your Hunter statue is on the river bottom somewhere."

"Such a sad man. I kneeled down and wept when I saw him sink. Let's change the subject, Jessie."

"Sure. Tell me once again. Where exactly are you going?"

"Sierra Leone in West Africa. Can you believe it? At last, I'll be somewhere besides Monroe, Louisiana." She folded up the stepladder and slipped her arm through the rungs so that the ladder rested on her shoulder.

"I've never even heard of the place. How's Hunter going to take your decision to go to Africa?" Jessie asked.

"I don't think he gives a rip. The night he got himself arrested, I told him I wanted to go, and he tried to laugh it off. Now, I don't know what he'd say. I've decided I'm not going to see him anymore. Looks like he'll be in jail for a while, and since I'll be overseas, it's probably for the best that I just end it."

"Well, it's sure a rough way to break up. I'm sorry things didn't work out between you two."

"That's okay, Jessie. We probably weren't meant

to be together anyway. God, this has been such a mess. Thanks for being sensitive and not nagging me about it. Just like you said, the story was in the paper's police report, and then the newspaper followed it up with an article, then Channel Eight News mentioned it. My phone's rung constantly. Some of the callers are girls I don't know, and they're asking me about Hunter! God, he must have had groupies everywhere he played. I'm so embarrassed over what happened that I don't even want to go out anymore. I'm tired of explaining it, and I'm damn sure tired of the gossip."

"Caitlin, believe me, everyone will soon forget all about what happened and move on to talking about someone' else's misfortune. That's how some people around here get off—hearing and spreading juicy news about others. Cut off your phone for a while if you don't want people bothering you."

"I guess I should. Hey, Jessie, I need to ask you for another favor. Do you think you and your husband could take care of my houseboat while I'm gone? I'll pay all the expenses, and you're welcome to use it all you want."

"We'd love to. That is so sweet of you to offer. Don't worry about paying us. You can reimburse us for any expenses when you get back. As much as that husband and kids of mine like to fish, I ought to be paying you. We'll take good care of it. Don't give it another thought."

"Thanks, Jessie. I'll drop off the keys and papers you'll need before I leave. God, I've got so much to do yet. Before I can get my visa, I have to buy round-trip air tickets, a business letter of responsibility from the Church, and a letter of invitation from the mission I'll be working with. The damn paperwork is so complicated that it's frustrating. All I want to do is make some money and help some people."

"You should see the paperwork I've got to wade through just to sell a house. I wonder if there's an official reader who reads all these papers the government makes us fill out."

"If there is, he's probably read himself blind like Milton."

"Who is Milton? A relative?"

"No, a poet."

"Don't you go showing off by quoting people I don't know nothing about. Did Hunter call you yet? You know, to bail him out of jail?"

"No. I guess I should try to call and check on him."

"You talk like you're his mother. Do you hear yourself sometimes? Anyway, I don't think that parish prisoners are allowed to receive phone calls. It's not like he's at summer camp. If you're going to dump him, dump him. You don't have to explain anything."

Caitlin tried to call him at the prison anyway. She was told that Hunter could call her collect if he wanted. He didn't. Caitlin thought about visiting the prison and talking to Hunter face to face, but she settled for mailing him a letter the day she left for Africa. She began the letter with *Dear Hunter* and ended it with *Kiss my ass.*

Chapter Six

Kamalu, Sierra Leone 1998

A stranger doesn't know a bad road.
—Krio Proverb

The Xaverian priest clicked off the mission's short-wave radio and slumped back into the wooden chair. "Oh, Lord," he whispered. "I cannot understand your ways, but I must adore them."

The news disturbed him. Kamakwie had fallen to the rebels who had filled its streets with corpses and burned most of the buildings. Kamalu, only a few miles to the south, would likely be the next stop for the advancing rebels, and the bishop had ordered the Kamalu mission to be evacuated. The few units of ill-trained, disorganized government soldiers in Makeni sent to repel the rebels found themselves outnumbered, outgunned, and were now in full flight. Some government soldiers had deserted and joined the rebels who now controlled all territory to the north and east of the Kamalu mission

The priest glanced at the mission staff sitting around him and speculated on the best words to communicate the gravity of their situation. Likely, they had heard the horrific stories of the rebel atrocities. The stories that should make a difference in the way one thinks. Stories like the account of the seven Italian nuns who didn't leave Benduga when they should have and were… He shuddered involuntarily.

"Father Ambrose?" Sister Theresa said. "Did I hear the Bishop correctly? We're being ordered to evacuate?"

He was grateful that her voice had yanked him out of the downward spiral into the darkness inside himself. *You cannot go there, to those dark places inside you. That is a bad road.*

"Yes," he said. "The situation appears to be much worse than even the last time the rebels came through our district. We must reach Port Loko tonight, then move on to Freetown. Freetown is our only sure hope of safety. The RUF could arrive anytime. Likely Makeni itself will soon fall." Makeni was the capital of the Northern Province. Father Ambrose guessed that most of the residents there had already fled to the bush.

"Perhaps we can stay and reason with the rebel leaders," Sister Agnes said. "This mission has been here for so many years. The situation might even reverse itself. Surely Christ will protect us."

Sister Agnes was the workhorse of the mission, the type of woman who could be made a saint after her death. She was a Joan of Arc full of ideals and possessed an energy even the heat and humidity of Sierra Leone couldn't lessen. She seemed immune to any discouragement or even disease. It seemed incredible to him that the malaria and other tropical diseases that typically plagued newcomers had left her alone. He knew of at least four priests who had died of disease here. Perhaps Christ protected her in a special way.

The priest raised his eyes to the crucifix fastened to the wall above the radio and studied the sacred, wounded form of Christ. Handless images of Xaverian priests and Lutheran ministers and the savagely murdered Muslim Imam flashed into his mind like a PowerPoint slide presentation. *Will you protect us from the RUF?* he asked the Christ. *Why should we receive better treatment than others who have fallen into rebel hands? Had Sister Agnes expressed her faith or her naiveté? Had she been in Sierra Leone long enough to know? I must choose my words carefully.*

"No, Sister," he said. "Perhaps, once, some time ago, the RUF leaders were men with ideals and virtue. But now... Papa has done his work well. The good men are gone from his organization. He has conjured up a mindless, vicious beast, and that beast walks this land. A voracious, ungovernable beast, like the devil himself. An army of monsters, a horde of demons incarnate in the bodies of drug-crazed little boys. Soon they *will* come. No, Sister, we must leave."

You sound like an apocalyptic monk, he told himself. *Maybe you're suffering from a fever relapse. Yes, it must be the malaria again that is making you talk this way—like a crazy man.*

Cautiously, Sister Theresa asked, "Could we buy protection from them?"

"That too was once a possibility," Father Ambrose said, "in the days when the rebels were satisfied by our pledge of support and a bribe of a bag of rice or a jug of palm wine. But now their tastes and desires are not so easily pacified. Since they possess enough power to simply take what they want, they are impatient with negotiation. And their demands are greater now. They know they can act with impunity, so they fear and respect no one. They are men governed by a strange logic of violence."

"Perhaps we should cross into Guinea?" Sister Agnes said.

"No. We cannot go to Guinea," he said. "The road is bad now. The refugee camps are too close to the border. The RUF have already attacked the Moola and Tassin camps near Forécariah."

Guinea, only twenty-five miles north of Kamakwie, already hosted an influx of over 250,000 refugees from Sierra Leone and that land's government did not wish the burden of more. In addition, the RUF controlled all border posts, even the bush paths into Guinea. Guinea was not an option.

Father Ambrose could tell the sisters were waiting for him to explain further, but his head had clouded over, and he did not feel the explanation would be worth the effort. "We must go to Freetown, and even that journey will be precarious." Freetown was ninety miles away. By American standards, not too great a distance, but in Africa, ninety miles can be a very long and dangerous journey.

"Will we be safe even in Freetown?" Sister Agnes asked.

Father Ambrose reached for her hand, wrapped his own around it, bowed his head and prayed, *Lord, protect this woman.* He released her hand and looked her in the eyes. "Yes, Sister, we will be safe in Freetown."

Sister Agnes returned his gaze and shook her head.

She senses my inner terror. She is perceptive. I must wear the mask more carefully. But he knew she had silently made a valid point. Conditions had changed for the worse much faster than anyone thought possible. The RUF were weary of their existence in the bush and their juggernaut had been relentless, and so far, unstoppable. Realistically, Freetown might soon fall under RUF control. Once they possessed Freetown, they would have total control of Sierra Leone. *They will not be content until they possess it all. Until they destroy it all.*

His mind drifted to the two American journalists who died last month in an RUF ambush. The pair had stopped to visit with him on their way to the front. He fed them, then warned them of what lay ahead.

In spite of the danger, the reporters refused to return to Freetown, bribing their drivers to take them closer and closer to the front. "If there's no picture, there's no story," one had said. The two reporters possessed the careless fearlessness of men who had often escaped death, having already covered the war in Sierra Leone for months.

As it turned out, their luck ran out, and their dedication and sacrifice was for nothing. Wasted. The American editors who had commissioned them had not published a single story they had written, even after both reporters were killed. America's mind seemed to be focused on other things. The nation's media-guided apathetic conscience was permeated with indifference too deeply seated to be rattled by the deaths of two reporters.

Probably, someday someone would find the reporters' videos, their notes, their photographs, and their story would be told and the world will be shocked for one brief news program, shocked that editors and businessmen would have ignored this heart-rending tale of two men in search of truth. And a book will be published and perhaps a movie made, and many people will increase their wealth as a result, but the citizens of Sierra Leone would continue to be poor and oppressed and the cruel men will continue to roam the land with impunity. And more reporters seeking for the truth would come, and the same story would be replayed, but not told. At least, not truly told.

Father Ambrose had retrieved the reporters' bodies, radioed news of their deaths to the authorities and newspapers, administered last rites, and buried them temporarily in the mission's cemetery until someone could come for their bodies—if anyone would come. He would have to leave their bodies here. Perhaps he should hide or move their grave markings until he could return. In this land, sometimes even the dead cannot abide in peace.

"Father?" Sister Theresa said.

The priest shook his head, again willing the cobweb thoughts of violence, death, witchcraft, and the future to clear his mind, but they clung—web-like, dirty. He felt his thoughts whirl like a dark vortex, sucking his concentration down into those feared dark places inside him.

"We must hurry," he said. "God be with you all." He rose and moved to his study, tossing the mission's records, his journals, and his beloved books into a wooden carton. He stuffed his laptop into its carrying bag and slung it on his shoulder. The sisters and staff remained in their chairs as if in shock. He clapped his hands to wake them from their introspection. "Brothers! Sisters! Hurry!"

After he dropped his personal belongings into the back of the mission's Toyota truck, he loaded the mission's radio. Then he strolled through the mission grounds in order to check on the progress of their exodus. He paused and gathered a handful of flowers from the garden Brother Thomas had worked so hard to create and maintain, and he laid the bouquet at the foot of the wooden cross in the outdoor chapel.

Father Ambrose bowed his head and prayed for the mission's safety. He thought of other villages the RUF had ravaged, and he prayed they would be on the road soon. So little was left in Sierra Leone. "*Concordia res parvae cruscunt,*" he whispered, almost like a prayer. "In harmony small things grow."

Father Ambrose picked up the flowers and lifted them to his nose, inhaling the rich sweet fragrance, then in depression and bathos, clutched the flowers to his breast. The Church had been the people's last hope, the only trusted point of reference among the converts, and now she had failed. Progress had been made for a short while, but now all that work seems to have been for naught.

Frustration gnawed at his gut like a hungry parasite and his head spun. Why had he even come to Sierra Leone? Did he come here of his own will or because of the Church's orders? Had he been driven to this land by the proverbial white man's burden? He could not remember.

Like Ezekiel the prophet, he faced north, staring into the darkening bush like one of Hawthorne's Puritans afraid of the forest. "Neither I nor the Church can save Sierra Leone," he said to nothing and to no one.

He raised his fist and shouted, "I came here to help you find Christ, to find a solution to your poverty, ignorance, suffering. But there is no solution. How lost can a nation become? How far into the darkness can men go?"

A few of the workers looked his way, then resumed their preparations. He did not know what his parishioners thought about his words or what they really thought, felt, or knew about the darkness.

The rebels knew the darkness. They were men with dim consciences whose eyes had grown used to it. Humans without humanity who ventured into the darkness as far as they could go, farther than humans should travel. To such evil men, there are no boundaries, no stopping points, no limits. He remembered how as a child he would say to his brother, "Eat your heart out." Now that flippant childhood idiom stung his conscience because he knew it to be something that a man could do. Something even a child could do. Something RUF boy soldiers had done.

He heard gunfire in the distance, and the sound chilled him. It was not the reports of the archaic, worn-out shotguns and bolt action rifles used by local hunters, but the distinctive rattling sound of AK 47's. Toward Kamalu, an orange halo now ringed the tree line.

"No, God, please not again," he said. He ran in panic to join the others. They had almost finished packing when the first of the rebels strolled onto the mission grounds, herding Kamalu's citizens in front of them.

Chapter Seven

The heart is not made of bone
—Krio Proverb

If it weren't for the AK 47's they carried, the Zebra Small Boys Battalion would have appeared to be an African version of the Boy Scouts out for an afternoon stroll, dressed in a collage of fatigues and American T-shirts and jeans. The young rebel soldiers' clothes wore red spots like medals, and their hands were crusted with the blood of those newly slain or violated. The soldiers surrounded their small herd of captives like malignant spectres. A line of porters, even younger than the soldiers, trailed behind them, and they were loaded down with the looted goods of Kamakwie and Kamalu.

Father Ambrose gathered the nuns and the mission workers together. He said, "Don't run. Do not show fear. If you do, they will shoot you." *Or worse.* The workers huddled together near him, as if to seek protection from his presence.

As the invaders entered the mission compound, Father Ambrose contemplated the scene. Many of the villagers were wounded—all were terrified. The screams, weeping, moans, and prayers blended together into a demented chorus, and the sounds of the choir's grief and terror burned and burrowed into his soul.

After scanning the eyes and faces of the soldiers,

he recognized the signs of drug madness and bloodlust. To Sister Agnes he said, "Calm the villagers. Tell them they must stop the wailing. It will only feed the soldiers' rage and frenzy. Find out what has happened in Kamalu. Minister to the wounded the best you can without attracting attention."

"I will, Father. May God help us," Sister Agnes said. As she tended to the terrified villagers, the priest counted twenty boy soldiers. Two older soldiers hung in the background. One was white, the other mulatto. The aloofness of the two older men suggested they were either mercenaries or senior RUF officers.

One rebel soldier lifted the priest's arm and removed his watch, then searched him and removed everything in his pockets. Others joined in the robbery, and soon every valuable personal item was confiscated from all the mission workers. The soldiers moved on to the packed boxes already on the truck.

One of the boy soldiers sauntered to the truck and barked a command. All the soldiers dropped their prizes and snapped to attention. He spoke again and pointed, and a soldier set Ambrose's wooden chair upon a stack of wooden crates.

A teenager with a Machiavellian smile, he slowly scanned the eyes of villagers and the young soldiers. He clambered up the boxes and sat on the improvised throne, impatiently drumming his fingers on the chair's arm. A soldier rolled a stump to a spot directly in front of the prisoners. The enthroned one spoke dramatically, as if he made an important speech.

Father Ambrose couldn't understand the young boy-leader. He thought the dialect might be Mende. He stepped forward.

"I don't understand you, my son," he said. He addressed the two older soldiers. "Do any of you speak English? Or Temne? Is he your leader? Why does he not speak Krio?"

The white soldier held his hand up, palm toward the boy-leader and caught his attention. The white soldier motioned toward the priest and said in Krio, "The priest-man, he wants to know who you are and what you want. Can I tell him?"

"Tell him," the boy said in English, and then continued speaking in the unknown tongue.

The white man stepped closer to the priest and translated: "The general prefers to address his audience in Mende. He understands some English, and Krio of course, but it makes him feel more important to be translated. God, these black buggers I work with are vain. I'll tell you what he says, priest. He says, 'I am General Share Blood.' He greets you warmly. He says, 'We are soldiers of the Revolutionary United Front. At Papa's orders, we are here to liberate you from the corrupt government in Freetown. You flee from us? Why? Is this a sign that you mean to betray us? You must learn you cannot show such disrespect.' "

General Share Blood pointed to two Kamalu boys.

The white soldier left the priest and yanked two boys away from their parents. Father Ambrose thought that neither boy could be over ten years of age. The white soldier cocked his AK 47 and thrust it into one boy's hands, then pointed to the other who was less than five feet away. "Kill him."

The victim pleaded, "Please, I know you. Do not kill me!"

The mercenary slapped the boy's head. "Do it

now!"

The boy pulled the trigger.

"That's a good soldier. *Gud pikin.*" The white soldier snatched his rifle from the boy's trembling hands and shoved him toward the other soldiers. "Sit down."

Father Ambrose bowed his head and prayed for murdered and murderer. This action had forever separated the young boy from the village of Kamalu. The new recruit could never come home. Ambrose had seen this tactic used before.

General Share Blood pointed to Father Ambrose. "You have diamonds for me?"

"No," Father Ambrose said. "We have no diamonds. All of the diamond mines are far from here."

"You do not speak true. You have diamonds." He clapped his hands three times.

The boy soldiers herded another group of villagers forward and gunned them down. The slaughter was followed by an ecstatic dance around the bodies. As they danced, the drunken and drugged executioners howled and fired their guns wildly into the air.

"Now you have diamonds for me?" General Share Blood asked.

Father Ambrose feared the mission staff might be killed next. He once again attempted to communicate. "I tell you we have no diamonds. This is cattle country." Father Ambrose called out to the white man, "Who are you? Why are you here with these boys? Are you a mercenary? Are you not a high-ranking officer? Do you not see what they have just done? You must order him to stop this senseless killing. These people have done nothing to harm or threaten you. Have you no conscience?"

The white man sat down in front of Ambrose. "No, I don't." He dropped a box of cartridges on the ground in front of him, and slowly reloaded his rifle magazine. The box was covered with Arabic writing.

"Conscience is a luxury a soldier cannot afford," the white man replied. "I'm here as an advisor. About what's happened, I don't try to make sense of these buggers' politics. My guess is the general wants assurance this area will no longer help the government in Freetown."

General Share Blood stood and stretched lazily, then resumed his seat. "It is time for the games," he said in English. He drained a gourd of palm wine, then looked down upon the throng before him as if he were indeed perched on a royal throne. "I am thirsty for my daily drink of blood. Who among you will provide it? Perhaps you?" General Share Blood pointed at Brother Thomas.

One soldier in a Rambo T-shirt grabbed the mission's gardener by the shirt collar and dragged him forward. The gardener's little girl clung to his leg screaming. Brother Thomas tried to pry loose his little girl's hands, but she clung stubbornly. When Brother Thomas and his daughter in tow reached the stump in front of General Share Blood, the Rambo soldier placed the man's arm across the top of the stump and drew his machete.

As he raised the blade, Father Ambrose stepped forward and placed his hand on the young soldier's shoulder. "No, my son. Do not hurt this man. He is good man, good friend."

The soldier holding the gardener squinted at the

priest through cocaine and ganja-glazed eyes. He glanced at the general, then back to the priest. Something human etched itself upon his face. "Father, I do not know what I do."

"Put the cutlass down, my son," Father Ambrose said quietly. "You are a Christian man. I know you are afraid, but God will give you strength."

The trembling blade rose for a moment, then the young soldier stabbed the machete into the earth, and he knelt before the priest with his eyes to the ground.

Some of the soldiers hooted and laughed. General Share Blood shouted for the soldier to continue.

"No," the young Rambo replied. "I will not hurt this man." Then to Father Ambrose he said, "Bless me, Father, for I have sinned."

Father Ambrose knelt and gave the repentant man absolution in an abbreviated form, confident that God would accept the adaptation.

General Share Blood's retort was sharp, and two soldiers dragged the rebellious Rambo forward and held him before the general. After the general clumsily climbed down from his wooden-box throne, he plucked a long, dry leaf from a nearby banana tree, and rolled it up like it was a cigar. He lit it with a cigarette lighter, then as his troops held the man's face, pressed the burning leaf into the soldier's eye.

General Share Blood smiled at the soldier's screams. He swaggered around, looking at his soldiers and his captives, holding a fist in the air triumphantly.

Father Ambrose stood and shouted, "Listen to me, all of you!" He looked at the white mercenary. "Please, do not let him do this. Ask your leader to take what he wants, but please, do not injure anyone else. We will not assist any of your enemies. "

He was cut short when the mercenary barked a command and one of the soldiers pushed him roughly to the ground. The mercenary slung his rifle onto his shoulder and strode toward the priest. On his way he kicked the sobbing young boy-soldier who was clutching his eye and writhing on the ground like a wounded snake.

"That's the problem when you don't take them young enough," the mercenary said. "I thought he was going to make a fine soldier, but I guess I was wrong. Our training was wasted on him. Now, if he lives, he'll only be fit to be a porter."

"You do not talk like a man should, but like an animal," Father Ambrose said. "No wonder the people of Salone fear and hate your soldiers. The RUF once were men of ideals who talked of helping the people of Salone. But now…"

The mercenary knelt on one knee before him. "Priest, I tend to like men in your occupation, but we don't have time for a long philosophical discussion. The situation is actually very simple. The towns of this district and your mission are now under the control of the RUF. The ideals you speak of left Salone with the educated elite émigrés, and the same ideals left the RUF when Papa discovered how much money he could make in the diamond trade. Now, you cooperate and I might get you out of this in one piece. I want you to hook up your radio and call whoever you need to call and have them send money and diamonds. The general wants diamonds, but he and I both will settle for American dollars. Then, maybe he will let you go."

"Diamonds? He wants blood diamonds?" Father

Ambrose felt a rage coursing through his body and he surrendered to it. He shouted, "And you want money? You want us to ask for ransom? You white devil! You want me to cooperate with this sadist and ask for money to buy our freedom? No!"

The mercenary patted Father Ambrose's face, turned to General Share Blood and in Krio said, "The priest, he will not respect the general."

Shouting, the general leaped from the chair to the ground.

Father Ambrose felt boys' hands clutching and dragging him forward. He was thrown to the ground next to the mission's gardener and his daughter, and the three of them knelt together before General Share Blood.

Ambrose looked up into the face of a young girl beside the general. She drew a machete from her web belt and nodded toward Brother Thomas, the gardener. Two soldiers stretched Thomas's arm across the stump, and with a deft stroke, she amputated his right hand. Then she pointed to the little girl. Two strokes this time. The girl swooned and fell to her knees, a Lavinia holding up two bleeding handless limbs.

At the sight, the priest felt his heart crack within himself, and he knew now that all the sadness he had ever felt and all the evil and suffering he had ever seen had reached a culminating point, a climax. As if in the audience of a tragic play, he waited for the drama's catharsis, the purging of his heart through pity and terror.

The machete-wielding girl smiled and pointed to Father Ambrose.

Father Ambrose felt the rough top of the stump

against his skin, felt the wetness of Thomas's blood underneath, saw the whiteness of his own skin in the fading light.

General Share Blood held the mission's gold communion cup in his hands. The general turned dramatically, displaying the chalice to the group. He handed it to one soldier who knelt in front of the stump and held it at the ready. Father Ambrose flexed his fingers, staring at his hand.

What followed seemed to happen in slow motion. A machete flashed in the fading sunlight. He heard a thwack, a thumping sound. The fingers wriggled on his detached right hand, convulsing on top of the stump as if they now had a life of their own apart from his brain. The hand rolled to the ground with the other three hands where it seemed to crawl about. Another boy lifted the priest's arm so the blood dripped into the communion cup. His heart pumped four times and the cup was full. White hands wrapped coarse twine tightly around his arm to stem the bleeding.

The foaming cup was placed reverently into General Share Blood's hands. Father Ambrose stared at the smooth, flat wall of bone and nerves and tissue where his hand used to be. The thought was odd, but he thanked God the machete used was sharp. He had heard tales of how the machetes were often dull and how they mangled the limbs of victims. Ambrose remained on his knees. He knew his body was in shock, but he couldn't think of what he should do or say about it.

He glanced up into the smiling, drugged face of the machete-girl. He studied her blood-splotched face as if it were an icon of a black Madonna. *An amazon*, Father Ambrose thought. *This girl is a true amazon. She would amputate anything, even her own breast if it were in her way.* He heard her chatter to the others in Krio. He felt a strong hand on his shoulder, and he turned. Another icon. This time, it is the tear-stained face of Sister Agnes. "What is she saying?" he asked her. "The machete-girl there."

Sister Agnes drew him to her bosom. Her breast felt soft, warm, comforting. "She calls herself Betty Cut Hands and she is General Share Blood's queen. Here, open your mouth." She pressed two tablets onto his tongue. "Swallow them. They're pain pills. We have no water, so you'll have to swallow them dry. Now, close your eyes. I'm sure you are in shock."

He swallowed the pills but he didn't close his eyes. From within her embrace, he watched as drugs were mixed into the communion cup holding his blood and stirred with the general's finger. The general, still thirsty for his daily blood, drank the priest's blood and thumped his chest with his fist. He pointed to other soldiers who one by one came to the altar of the stump to sup and share in the sacred ritual of his perverted communion. The chalice was returned to the general and after he drained it, he set it on a crate next to him. He licked his lips, and his eyes rolled with delight.

Father Ambrose turned his head and wept. Through the veil of tears, he spotted Tejan. How long had it been since that terrible day when the RUF kidnapped Tejan and five other students? Four years? Tejan possessed the same glazed eyes as the others, and an AK 47 was slung over his shoulder.

Father Ambrose tried to focus his blurred, swirling vision. He raised himself and rubbed at his burning eyes with the stump of his right hand. He attempted to stand

and go to Tejan, but the world spun in a strange mosaic of black and white faces, and he collapsed backward into Sister Agnes's arms.

"Father, here, I will wipe your eyes," Sister Agnes said. "What can I do? What will happen with us?"

He willed himself to answer her, but his tongue was thick and slow. Finally, he uttered, "*Vado mori.*" He buried his face in her bosom. It was time to leave this sad earth. He knew too much now, had seen too much.

"No, Father," she said firmly. "You cannot die and leave us alone."

When he woke, he was still alive in the sister's arms. Everything of value in the mission and village had been piled in front of General Share Blood, who had returned to his throne of boxes. The priest's hand was now buried beneath a pile of black hands, arms, legs, and ears. Several buildings and houses about them were burning. From within one he heard screams and saw black arms reaching out from the flames like anguished souls trapped in a torture chamber of hell.

The general's soldiers had found more palm wine. As they drained gourd after gourd, they fired their guns into the air, and they danced and staggered about a large fire like stiff skeletons in a *danse macabre.* One soldier had donned a nun's habit, another a choir robe. Father Ambrose watched the one-eyed, disobedient soldier embrace a palm tree and struggle to pull himself to his feet. When he finally wrestled himself upright, a machine gun riddled his body and he died with his one good eye open, his arms still clutching the palm.

Father Ambrose thought the RUF soldiers had executed the one-eyed soldier until he saw the mulatto fall. Then General Share Blood and his chair throne tumbled backward. When the general's body hit the ground, the gold communion cup bounced toward the priest. There was no blood in the chalice. Several of the dancing boy soldiers dropped one by one as they too were splattered with bullets. An enemy presence was perceived and the boy soldiers of the Zebra battalion broke and ran.

The white mercenary stood his ground, methodically taking aim and firing his automatic rifle. Bullets peppered his white skin, and he fell to his knees. Then when a bullet struck his forehead, he fell face-first to the dark ground. A group of black shadows swarmed him, and Ambrose heard the sound of the clubs and spears as they struck and tore at his corpse.

Several men sprinted past Father Ambrose in pursuit of the fleeing Zebra battalion. Some of the men were in fatigues, and others wore animal skins. One pushed Ambrose to the ground.

"We have come to help you, Fader," he said. "Please, you are to stay close to de ground."

"Father?" Sister Agnes said quietly as she ducked down next to him. "What's happening?"

"Government soldiers and Kamajors," he said. "And maybe some Nigerian troops from Makeni. Stay down until we're sure it's safe."

"Oh, thank God they have come," she said as she genuflected.

A Kamajor threw a Zebra boy down near them and then machined-gunned him. The young rebel's body bounced like a martinet as the bullets riddled his adolescent body. The Kamajor looked down at Ambrose and smiled. "It be okay soon, Fader," he said.

"Good Christians be here now."

Father Ambrose turned his head from the sight of the boy's body. "Yes, Sister Agnes," he said. "Thank God they have come."

The Kamajors and soldiers returned from their pursuit, herding several of the Zebra boys in front of them, caning them unmercifully every step. The mission captives watched as the Kamajors beat and then executed the rebels one by one with their guns or staves. A few of the younger rebel boys were terrified and began to moan senselessly, as if they were deaf and dumb. But the ruse of being a handicapped child was unconvincing, and the beatings and executions continued. The wails of the boy soldiers filled the night and the sound could have been the audio illustration for the nightmarish paintings of Munch or Goya.

Two more Kamajors returned, dragging a body. Father Ambrose saw that it was Tejan. The priest watched as they kicked him and whipped him with sticks. When one pointed a rifle at his head, Father Ambrose shouted, "No! He is one of ours!"

"Are you sure, Fader?" the Kamajor said. "He look like rebel soldier moment ago. He fight me hard with his empty gun before I conk him on de head."

"I am sure. His name is Tejan," he said. He picked up the gold communion cup and held it out to the Kamajor. "I am sure he is ours. He's probably just frightened."

"You can have him, Fader." The Kamajor stuffed the chalice into his fanny pack and moved on.

"Father!" Sister Agnes exclaimed. "What are you doing? This boy was one of the rebels. He probably did some horrible things to the villagers…"

"Hush, Sister. The sin be on my own soul. I knew this boy and his parents in Guinea, and, demon though he is now, I'm not going to give him up to these murderers. He was kidnapped by the RUF a few years ago. Now, help me with him."

Together, they dragged the unconscious Tejan over to their group. Fortunately, Tejan had not been shot, only clubbed. A cane had stove his head open, and Sister Agnes pressed her hand on the wound.

"Tejan…Tejan…Do you know who I am?" Ambrose asked.

Tejan's eyes opened, and he groaned.

Several villagers shook their heads in disgust at the priest. Ambrose knew they perceived his mercy as another example of the strange behavior and values of the *poo-muis* and that it confirmed their long-held suspicions of the priest-man's naivete.

The mission staff kept vigil that night, caring for their wounded, praying and giving thanks for their deliverance. The next morning, the Kamajors and government troops moved on in their search for more rebels, leaving the mission staff to bury the dead strewn about them. When the mission staff had buried the dead and every body part they could find, they filled the mission's Toyota truck with the weak and wounded, twenty-three in all, and began the drive to Freetown. The villagers who could walk followed on foot, trailing the overloaded truck as it crawled along the pocked, dirt highway.

Chapter Eight

*Enter quickly, leave quickly: If no one sees you,
then ghosts will see you. There is always a witness.*
—*Krio Proverb*

As the priest and his bloodied, numb entourage
neared Lunsar, a jeep plowed forward recklessly,
swerving in and out of ruts, past the rusted carcasses of
cars and trucks burned and stripped by the rebels. The
road was crowded with refugees from the Northern
District, and the driver wove through and around the
people walking, the slow-moving carts, and the
brakeless bush taxis. The jeep bounced on the rock-
hard, crater-filled, dirt road and swerved at the last
minute to avoid a collision with the mission's truck.

Von, the jeep's driver, said to his black passenger,
"Damn these refugees, Biko. They're going to slow us
down."

Biko waved at the priest and smiled at the priest's
icy stare. The priest's bandaged arm rested on the edge
of the truck's passenger window. Biko laughed. "The
boys, they have been busy now in Kamalu. They be in
Freetown soon. The priest-man in the truck, he pray for
us, I know."

As the jeep crossed the bridge over the Seli River,
Biko stretched and shivered in the cool, dry Harmattan
air. A small outboard motorboat chugged slowly up the

river below them. Biko watched a father and son fish. As the man cast his net, Biko closed his eyes and he could feel the net's line slipping through callused fingers, and a trained hand stopping its journey at the exact best moment. As the man pulled in his net, Biko heard the man and son singing. The fishermen were like ghosts pulling at a little string on his heart.

"Ah. Look. The two be fishing. I love to see this. In my land I love I once fish with my father," Biko said. "We would sing the fish songs my father taught me. But it be long time since Biko sing such happy songs."

Von spat onto the dry road. "You're talking mush now, Biko. I heard you and that woman last week singing plenty loud." He laughed and popped a cigarette into his mouth. He dug out his lighter, slowed the jeep slightly, and lit the cigarette while holding the steering wheel with his elbows. "You sound like a sentimental grandfather."

They came upon a bush taxi that had broken down. The driver and a couple of boys were buried underneath the hood of the Toyota truck, arguing about what was wrong with the engine. Twenty or so passengers were scattered along the side of the road. Two RUF soldiers stood next to the truck and eyed the jeep as it approached. Both men wore military fatigues and had AK 47's slung on their shoulders, machetes hanging from their web belts, and both wore small backpacks.

"I know the soldiers," Biko said. "They come from Mile 91. The one on the right is an officer. Stop the jeep." When Von pulled over, Biko laid his Kola nut on the dash, stepped out, and greeted the two soldiers in Krio.

As Biko approached the two soldiers, Von studied

the officer. He was middle-aged with eyes black and hard and empty. He saluted Biko smartly. Von guessed the man was of sufficient rank that he could take a road trip, but then maybe not. Deserting? Smuggling? Von guessed smuggling.

When Biko barked a command, the young soldier snapped to attention. Von admired the iron discipline of the RUF. The boy was young, no more than fourteen, and he wore American jeans, Nike tennis shoes, and a dark, Tupac T-shirt. Biko slapped the boy on the head and pointed toward the jeep. The young soldier sat down on the road a few feet in front of Von. His eyes twitched and crossed, and his arms and forehead were pocked with needle tracks and razor scars.

The young soldier slipped his machete from its canvass sheath and thumbed the edge. He glanced at Von, then at the bush-bus passengers. When he waved the machete in the air, one of the children whimpered. Biko strode over, reprimanded him, and slapped him so hard he bloodied the boy's mouth. The soldier slipped the machete back into its sheath and stared blankly into the bush.

Biko talked with the officer for several minutes, then returned to the jeep.

"Well, Biko?" Von asked.

"It is as I thought. The soldiers carry diamonds from the Kono district and go to the same merchant-man in Forécariah we are to see. The truck is out of petrol, so the driver he makes adjustments to the engine. Soon it will run on *natai*."

"I am truly amazed at how these people can find how so many uses for that stinking brown oil from inside a palm nut. Let's have a talk with them. Will he sell us his diamonds?"

"If Biko say to sell, he sell."

"Bring him over."

Biko signaled for the officer to come over. "Show this mon your diamonds," Biko said. "He want to buy."

Von laid down a cloth and the man emptied a paper sack onto it.

Von inspected a few of the stones with a loupe. "One hundred dollars," Von said.

"For each stone? You are American, yes?"

"No, one hundred dollars for the lot."

"Why you want to steal from me?"

"I'm not stealing from you. On the other hand, you did probably steal them, probably from other RUF officers. Maybe you won them cheating in a dice game."

The man said, "I did not cheat. My sons, they dig them."

Von laughed. "There's probably four-dozen diamonds in this can. That's a day's output of your whole district. I know how you obtained them. The monkey works, the baboon eats. No matter how you obtained the stones, I want to buy them. One hundred dollars."

"You want to cheat me. Two hundred American dollars. *A noh de muv.*"

"Yes, I know," Von said. "You are the immovable waterside stone. But I am the wall where pushing stops."

At times, Von tired of the African negotiation game. Yet, he persisted and finally the officer accepted an offer of a hundred and fifty American dollars, equivalent to over two months' of an officer's wages.

After thanking Von for his generosity, the officer and his cadre moved to the other side of the road to wait for the next bush taxi to the Kono District. Biko and Von resumed their journey, passing through a RUF roadblock on the Guinea border with ease.

****

In Forécariah, Von and Biko parked outside a cinderblock Internet café owned by a Lebanese diamond trader, a middleman for several diamond buyers in Antwerp. A faded wooden sign above the door read: FORECARIAH DIAMOND BAZAAR: BEST PRICES FOR YOUR DIAMONDS.

The café was furnished with card tables and metal folding chairs. Like every Lebanese trader's place Von had ever seen, along the walls were stacks of batteries, of cheap Japanese boom boxes, short-wave radios, and Sony Walkmans. An Anglo, probably a missionary, was the only customer. He glanced at Von and Biko, then his eyes shifted back to his laptop. He blew on his coffee and sipped it. "Wireless reception here is terrible," he said. "Coffee's all right though."

"We didn't come to use the Internet," Von said. "Is the Lebanese here?"

"He's in his office I think."

"I know the way," Von said.

In the office they sat down in chairs in front of the trader's desk. A long fluorescent light hung over them. The trader stubbed out a cigarette in the full ashtray and lit another. An oscillating fan and an ancient air conditioner fed by a generator and held together by duct tape hummed, and Von relished the coolness of the air.

After introductions, the trader's wife brought each of them a cold beer, then the trader spoke. "I am happy,

91

sir, that my cousin in Freetown directed you to me. I am anxious to do business with you, sir, much business."

"Let him see the diamonds, Biko," Von said.

Biko opened the coffee cans and poured the diamonds onto the white velvet pad in the center of the table.

The trader gasped. "Sir, you have many diamonds."

"This is only two days' worth of digging from commander Biko's mines," Von said. "Your Freetown cousin said you would buy them. I can take them somewhere else if you cannot afford them."

"No, no, sir. That is not what I meant. I just was not expecting this quantity. My cousin said you were men of importance, but I am used to only buying a few diamonds at a time."

"Well, there are close to one hundred diamonds in our cans. Make me an offer, a fair one. And don't insult me by offering me less than they are worth."

The trader used a handkerchief to wipe sweat from his forehead. He spread the diamonds with his hand and inspected selected stones with a loupe. After punching in figures on his calculating machine, he tore off the tape and handed his first offer to Von.

After haggling for nearly half an hour, Von accepted a price in American dollars. It was *almost* what he wanted, and more than he expected.

As if on cue, the trader's young wife emerged again from a back room and served them plates of rice and chicken and more beer.

Von contemplated the attractive Lebanese girl, and as she placed his plate in front of him, he said, "Thank you."

"She does not speak English, sir," the trader said, "Nor even much Krio, though she learns quickly. She speaks only the crude Palestinian Arabic of an ignorant country girl."

"So, she is new to West Africa?" Von said.

"My pretty young wife arrived here not long ago from Lebanon. It was not a difficult marriage to arrange. My first wives died from fever you see. I like this one, though I may obtain more wives in the future."

Von heard voices clamoring outside and glanced at the door. "We have articles of value in the jeep. Will they be left alone?"

The trader set down his plate and stood. "Do not worry about your things. My servant is outside. Excuse me one moment, sir. I will direct him to especially attend to your jeep while we enjoy supper."

When the trader had stepped outside, Von gestured to a chair next to him and said to the young girl, "Please, won't you sit and talk with me a moment?"

The girl did not take the chair, but sat down on the floor near Von, modestly folding her legs beneath her. She looked toward the door, then smiled at Von.

Von chuckled and for a moment lost himself in her bold, dark eyes. "Biko, what do you think this man had to pay to get a girl like this as his wife? A mail-order bride. Imagine that. I bet he didn't tell her family a word of truth about himself or Africa. Do you think she feels cheated? I wonder if he would sell her to me."

Biko said, "Mon, put this woman out of your head, unless you want we should kill trader-mon. But if you want her, let us kill him and take her. The Lebanese, we take him to bush and he have accident and bring troubles upon himself."

"Yes, we could kill him, Biko. She's pretty, but the trader's probably worth more to us at the present time. Besides, I have a woman coming from America soon."

"There be too many Lebanese traders already. From cradle to grave, they rob my people. But if you want, we wait and return another time."

"I think that would be best, but God, Biko, look at her. She is indeed exquisite."

Biko laughed. "Biko will buy you pretty Lebanese girl when we reach Freetown. There be many such women for sale now."

"I'll take you up on your offer, Biko. Yet, I'm still fascinated with this one." Von held out his plate. When the girl reached out to take it, he slid his other hand under the plate and placed it so that his fingers covered hers, and when she tried to withdraw her hand, he pressed her hand against the bottom of the plate. As the girl's eyes probed his own, Von whispered, "Just stand there a minute and let me look at you."

The girl smiled again.

The trader entered and saw his new bride smiling flirtatiously. Shouting an Arabic obscenity, he yanked her toward the door. He viciously backhanded her and then shoved her outside.

"You go outside if you cannot behave as a woman should. We will be finished with our business soon."

The trader raised his hands as in supplication to God. "I apologize for my young bride's impoliteness, sir. Women in this age have no shame. I hope she did not offend you. As I said, she is ignorant of many things. I will deal with her later. You must excuse me while I place these wonderful diamonds in my safe." He raked up the diamonds and took the can to a metal safe behind his desk.

Your bride understands more than she lets on, I bet, Von thought. *I know she understood my English better than you, trader-man. There's some fire in her eyes. Some fire in the bed too, I bet. I wouldn't be surprised if she cuts your throat one night. And if she doesn't, I might have Biko pay you a visit and do it for her. Neither you nor your Freetown cousin are indispensable to my plans. I soon won't need either of you.*

The trader returned from the safe and greedily gulped down his beer, then wiped his mouth with a handkerchief. "Mr. Vermeer, I hope you will see me again when you have more diamonds. These today are of excellent quality. They are most excellent, sir."

"Of course." Von and Biko stood to leave. "Until then." Von offered the trader his hand. The trader's hand was plump and soft and limp and sweaty. Von squeezed until he felt the bones in the trader's hand slip in his grip, but the trader's face and eyes did not change.

I could break your hand or insult you. I could do anything, and as long as I sold you diamonds, you'd not say a word, Von thought. He despised this Lebanese trader with the pretty young wife. The Lebanese trader would play out his life on the fringe of the diamond business, then one of his descendants or another just like him would replace him. It grated Von's nerves to think he must waste precious time haggling with this insignificant trader whose ancestors had fled Palestine over a century ago and somehow found their way to West Africa.

Von craved the company and acceptance of the

prestigious diamond merchants in Antwerp and New York. Such men rendered allegiance to no nation, recognizing no boundaries set by God or men. The men who ran the diamond cartels had no political agenda other than the desire to be wealthy, and the chain of greed linked them together. They were powerful, and the world paid them attention and rendered the respect that powerful men deserve.

Von intended to be included in their number.

Von's early months in the diamond business had been in boiler rooms in New York, and since then he had woven many men of influence and power into his web of contacts. Von's present contacts included men from Unita, representatives of Charles Taylor and Savimbi; gun dealers from Bulgaria; and diamond buyers from Zambia, South Africa, England, and Antwerp. He had made deals with Arab envoys of an insane Saudi prince who were raising funds for their campaign of terrorism, mercenaries from the Ukraine, and even a few expatriate Americans like himself, though most of the Americans were only hustlers posing as businessmen. Most were more than willing to help him smuggle diamonds, and would cook their books, break laws, or lie to government or investors—willing to do anything as long as it increased their personal wealth.

Yet, Von felt he had an advantage over other diamond merchants in Africa, an advantage that would quickly propel him into prominence and position. Because of his fortuitous friendship with Biko, Von had won the ear and support of the RUF, who now controlled all of the diamond mining territory in Sierra Leone. As a result, diamond mining was going on at a faster pace than ever, and Von brokered their diamonds. The ruthlessness, connections, and power of the rebel organization insured Von a cheap and endless stream of gem-quality diamonds. Let the rest of the world be afraid of the RUF and their boy-soldier, machete-wielding armies. Von knew the RUF leaders were corrupt and violent, but he also knew that a wealthy man who used his head and money wisely would be in no danger.

Even more than his rapidly increasing wealth, Von enjoyed his newly discovered sense of power. With the help of his growing network of government officials, he had driven several other Freetown diamond merchants out of business. Vermeer Diamonds would soon do the same in America and his stores provided needed legitimacy for transportation of diamonds to the States.

Von's thoughts drifted to the diamond exchange in Antwerp. On his business trips there, he had marveled at the slanted prism-like glass ceiling, and the wealth that the dour men in dark suits generated boggled his mind. Von imagined himself moving in this powerful circle, offering dealers his own gentleman's *cachette* with his monogrammed initials inscribed on the front. He longed for the day he would have his own office in the Diamond Bourse in Antwerp, where he would meet with representatives from De Beers and New York's Diamond District. Of course, someday he would also have the perfect wife to share this world with him, a woman of sparkling intellect and beauty. Someone like Caitlin.

These fantasies pleased Von greatly. He had no intention of living and dying in obscurity like a common Lebanese trader.

Von intended to die a rich man.

****

After Von returned to Freetown, he met with an Eastern District government official with close ties to the RUF and in charge of a weapon storage center. Biko's units needed guns and needed them quickly. After the trip to Forécariah, Von and Biko now had enough funds to obtain the guns directly and immediately, instead of relying on the inefficiently organized and often slow-moving hierarchy of the RUF to supply them.

When Von entered the official's office, he noticed two Europeans who sat with him. Von extended his hand to the Sierra Leone official. "Abadu Bah, thank you so much for meeting with me."

The man shook Von's hand warmly. "Ah, Mr. Vermeer. It is wonderful to see you. May I present Mr. Balev from Bulgaria, and Mr. Van Deusen from Belgium."

"I am pleased to meet you gentlemen," Von said. He could hardly believe his luck. Usually, government officials were reluctant to even mention, much less to involve, their contacts in business arrangements. This was indeed fortuitous.

After coffee, the Sierra Leone official opened the discussion. "What can I do for you, Mr. Vermeer?"

Von eyed the other men. "It is a delicate matter I need to discuss."

"Please, speak. These men are friends of Salone and are supporters of the RUF. All here are friends of Papa."

Von continued. "Commander Biko's unit is in immediate need of rifles and ammunition. I understand that you have recently acquired a cache of government weapons. We want them. We can pay you in American dollars."

"What exactly does Commander Biko need?" Abadu Bah asked.

"Enough AK 47's for a company, a sufficient amount of ammunition, a mortar, grenades, and two machine guns."

Abadu Bah whistled. "In view of present circumstances, this is difficult, but it can be arranged. Tell Commander Biko that tomorrow night, very late, he may pick up the weapons at the disarmament center. He may help himself to whatever weapons are there. However, of course, for security reasons, many of the rifles have been disassembled."

"Biko's boys can easily reassemble them," Von said. "The parts for all AK 47's are interchangeable. Now, might I ask why these gentlemen are here?"

Balev, the Bulgarian, leaned forward. "Mr. Abadu Bah informs me that you are authorized to broker arms and diamonds for Kamara's armies."

"I am."

The Bulgarian took a sip of his coffee. "You are interested in obtaining arms, Bulgaria is interested in diamonds." He handed Von a folder. "Here is a recent inventory of various materials we have available and could ship immediately, about sixty-eight tons of armaments."

"How would the materials be delivered?" Von asked.

"The guns will be delivered by a commercial airline to Liberia, then by boat or truck to any location you designate. We would expect half-payment to be sent in advance to Liberia. When you obtain the weapons, we will expect the remainder. Payment may be made in diamonds, of course."

"I will pass this offer on to Commander Biko and the RUF leadership. I am confident that Papa will approve of your offer." Von turned his attention to the Belgian. "And you, sir? Why are you with us?"

"Mr. Vermeer, I too have a favor to ask of you," he replied. "I have recently been appointed as the CEO of a mining company, Diamonds Salone, Incorporated. Mr. Balev and Mr. Abadu Bah are also on the board. Have you heard of our company?"

Von lit a cigarette. "Yes, of course. It's based in Antwerp, and you made an impressive profit last year. A *reported* income of about five million dollars if I remember correctly."

The Belgian continued. "Mr. Vermeer, the Sierra Leone government for many years has granted concessions to my former mining company in the Kono district. However, currently this district is under the control of the RUF, and our mines have not been operative for months. It appears this scenario is likely to last for some time."

"And what do you want me to do about this?" Von asked.

"Make arrangements with the RUF leadership for a suitable mining concession. We have unsuccessfully attempted to negotiate with them. It is difficult to reach the needed decision makers."

"This will be an expensive proposition," Von said.

"We would expect it to be so. What do you think the leadership would ask of us in return for such concessions?"

"A better question is what I will ask for arranging it. I expect to be adequately compensated for my efforts. I make them a great deal of money, so they will listen to me if I recommend you—or if I don't."

Van Deusen leaned forward in his chair. "So, what will you ask for your services?"

"An adequate salary and a small share of what is mined. An official position with your mining company. An office in Antwerp and one in America."

Abadu Bah laughed, then said in Krio, "The porter says he wants long pants."

Von snuffed out his cigarette and lit another. "Do not take my offer lightly, gentlemen. Yes, I'm ambitious, but so is each of you. The RUF will soon be in total control of Sierra Leone. Without their backing, your mines will remain closed."

"You ask a great deal," Balev said.

"Certainly, but I will also prove to be of great benefit to your company. I know how to conduct business in both Africa and America. I am skilled in all aspects of the diamond trade, a government licensed diamond broker, and I have many other invaluable connections—many in America. You would not have made your request unless you had something to offer me."

"I heard you were resourceful and very determined man. We need such a man to work with us," Van Deusen said as he extended his hand. "We welcome our new partner to Africa's newest diamond corporation."

Von grasped the Belgian's hand. "Thank you, sir. I shall arrange the concessions with the RUF leadership. Regarding my compensation, I will expect written confirmation of your offer by tomorrow."

Chapter Nine

If a person isn't used to dying, once he dies it will be hard to wake him.
—Krio Proverb

As the plane descended at Lungi International Airport, Caitlin viewed the sprawling suburbs and slums of Freetown. The image depressed, and yet fascinated her at the same time. The city seemed to be a jumbled collage of dilapidation and decay, brightened only by the National Football Stadium, a few new government buildings, and a handful of scattered Victorian Age homes. In the bay were tankers, cruise ships, and *pam-pam* ferries. *Bullom* boats of local fishermen lined a portion of the beach. Her eyes traced the coastline until the beaches faded into the thick mangroves of a Harmattan-hazed horizon.

Caitlin whispered, "Hunter, I'm scared to death. What have I got myself into? If only you could have come to Africa with me." She leaned back against the seat and closed her eyes. "Von, you better be there like you promised me."

A flight attendant passed by as Caitlin spoke. "Excuse me?"

"Nothing. Just thinking. I was wishing my boyfriend could be here with me."

"Well," the attendant said. "Welcome to Africa."

Von met Caitlin at customs. He embraced her and kissed her on the cheek. "At last, you are here. I know you probably have jet lag, so let's plan on starting work tomorrow. I'll help get you settled, and then I have business I must attend to. In order to save time, I've already taken care of customs for you."

They claimed her luggage and Von hired a porter to carry it to his Mercedes. They drove onto a ferry that would take them across the bay to Freetown. Von said, "I started to rent a helicopter, but I wanted you to see the bay as the first Europeans saw it—from a boat."

Caitlin gripped the handrail as the ferry bounced on a wave. Across the bay and veiled by a smoky haze, the city of Freetown sprawled along cloud-robed mountains.

"It's a beautiful view, isn't it?" Von said. "You are flushed from the heat. Let's go inside the ferry's sitting area. It's air conditioned."

"I'm fine here, Von. Please don't baby me too much."

"Have you thought of where you will live?"

"Father Robert said I could stay at the mission."

"I wouldn't hear of it. You are more than welcome to stay at my house."

"You have a house here?"

"Oh, yes. And it's quite nice by Freetown standards."

"I might take you up on that later, but for now, I think I should stay at the mission. They said they had an extra apartment I could use. And hopefully my uncle will be here soon. He's a rather strict priest, so I don't think he would like the idea of my living in the same house with a single man."

"Of course. I understand. But the offer will remain open."

"Thank you, Von."

When the ferry docked, Von drove her into Freetown. On a hill overlooking the city, they could see the parliamentary buildings of Sierra Leone. They passed the St. George Cathedral, then the Cotton Tree, where the first settlers had gathered in 1787 to praise God for their newly found freedom. No one knew how old the tree was. It was and is a national landmark, and a symbol of Sierra Leone. A group of men wearing embroidered *lapras* chatted beneath it, oblivious to the flock of huge fruit bats roosting above them. Nearby, Caitlin saw a sign for the National Museum.

"Von, have you been to that museum?"

"Oh, yes. I found their displays honoring the Mandinka Warrior Kings quite fascinating. Before the trouble here started, I even saw the De Ruyter Stone in 1987. Absolutely marvelous. I'll take you there first opportunity."

Near Siaka Stevens National Stadium, a taxi narrowly missed them. "Damn these African taxis," Von said. "I'll never complain about a New York cab again."

"I can't get over how much you've traveled, Von." Caitlin sighed as she turned the car's air conditioning vent so it would cool her face. "Compared to yours, my life seems so dull. Do you think my life is dull? Am I a dull person?"

Von lit a cigarette and rolled down his window enough to draft out the smoke. "How can an artist's life be dull? I mean, yes, you live in a po-dunk town that drives me crazy, and yes, you should travel more.

Perhaps I can help with that. But you, dull? Not a chance. I think you know what's important in life."

"I'm not so sure I do. What do you think is most important in life, Von?"

"Getting what you want." He took her hand. "Don't you agree?"

"Pshaw. What would you want with a country bumpkin like me?" Caitlin said this, but she squeezed Von's hand and wound her fingers into his.

"Von," Caitlin said, "I've told you about my family. Tell me something about your family. Do you have any sisters, brothers? Are you close to your parents?"

"I have no family."

"Do you have a brother named Larry?"

He said fiercely, "Someone's feeding you information about me? I told you I don't have a family and I want you to drop the subject."

"Okay," Caitlin said, "Don't be so touchy." She sensed it would be better to not tell how Larry Vermeer drowned in the Ouachita River.

In the center of Freetown, they stopped at a bazaar. The market was a cacophony to Caitlin's ears. Tourists and vendors argued, at times almost shouting, while boom boxes blasted music so distorted that it was unintelligible. Von took Caitlin's hand and strolled past tables laden with fruits, bags of rice, vegetables, guinea corn, cocoa pods, cassava, jars and cans of palm oil, fish, and kola nuts. Other tables were covered with animal skins, tourist bric-a-brac, bolts of brightly colored cotton cloth, and musical instruments—drums, something resembling a xylophone called *balungi*, flutes, *kurs*, and other stringed instruments of the nomadic Fula herdsmen. Caitlin picked up an oddly shaped three-string instrument and thought about buying it for Hunter. Its resonator was made from a large calabash, with leather stretched across it. The strings were nylon, each string attached to a metal ring on a bow-shaped wooden pole.

"This make good-good music, Missy," the vendor said. "The *bolon* is a harp of warriors and hunters."

Perfect instrument for Hunter. "Can you play it?"

"I can make only a little music." He took the *bolon* and held it with the strings facing him, closed his eyes, and plucked the strings with his thumb. The notes sounded like the strings on the lower register of a harp, the melody that of a forgotten way of life, of a forgotten people.

He paused for a moment with his eyes closed, then opened them and set the instrument on the rickety table. "The *bolon* was played before battle or before a hunt, to praise bravery and urge them on to great deeds of courage and endurance. Trained horses would dance for the warriors when they heard the *bolon*."

Caitlin bought the *bolon*.

After they had lunch at a hotel restaurant along the beach, Von hired a motorbike taxi to take Caitlin's written message to Xaverian school administrators and let them know she had arrived safely in Freetown and would be arriving shortly. Von drove her to see Bunce Island, then drove her on to the mission, which was located on the grounds of an old British Army barracks in the Western District.

At the gate of the mission, an armed guard rose from his wicker chair and raised his hand, signaling for Von to stop the car. He looked inside and waved them on.

"Some security," Von said. "He didn't even speak to us. It makes me feel uneasy about your staying here. Are you sure you don't want to take a room in my lonely house?"

"I'm sure, Von. But thank you. I'll be okay here. The guard was probably told we were coming."

While Caitlin searched for the mission administrators, Von unloaded her luggage. When Caitlin returned, she said, "Okay, I'm set up. I guess I'll see you tomorrow?"

"Yes, I'll pick you up early. We have much to do, you and I. Shall I carry your luggage to your room?"

"No, it will be a while before I get my room. I must fill out papers and such. You go on. I'll see you in the morning."

Von leaned forward and kissed her on the lips.

"Von!" she said. "What are you doing?"

"You know exactly what I'm doing."

Uneasy about Von's earlier harsh reaction when she asked him if he had a brother named Larry, she did a genealogical search on the Internet on Von Vermeer and discovered that he did have a brother whose name was Larry. More unsettling was the *Times Picayune* article she found telling of the murder of Von's parents. The killer was never found.

Why would Von lie to me about Larry, she asked herself, concluding that perhaps the memories were too hard to dredge up. She herself had often refused to talk about the death of her parents. Besides he didn't really lie. He actually did not have a family anymore. She would have to trust Von and give him the benefit of the doubt. He would likely tell her everything when he was ready.

****

Caitlin's roommate was Mandy, an American nurse with UNICEF and who had been assigned to the mission. After Caitlin dropped off her bags, Mandy took her on a walking tour of the grounds and then to supper to meet the two doctors working with the school, one an M.D., the other a child psychiatrist. After a meal of rice, broiled fish, and tea, the M.D. suggested that Mandy immediately give Caitlin a crash course on how to identify various tropical diseases, how to deal with severe trauma, and how to identify and treat the endemic drug addiction. Then he told her a little more about what the school hoped to accomplish.

Before their capture or desertion from the RUF, some of the boys had lived in the bush for four or five years and were in immediate need of medical, psychological, and emotional care. The mission's goal was to rehabilitate as many of the boy soldiers as possible and somehow reintegrate them into society. The intensive education and counseling program was designed to take the boys from their present soldier/savage mentality to their appropriate social, educational, and emotional levels. Caitlin's role in the redemption of these lost boys would be to assist the doctors as and where needed and teach the boys art and English as she had opportunity.

Caitlin had arrived in Freetown during Harmattan, and the suffocating dry heat drained her energy. As she and Mandy walked to a nearby beach to watch the sunset, Caitlin said, "God, this is awful weather. It's a lot drier here than I thought it would be."

"You'll get used to it. We basically have two

seasons: Harmattan, which is dry, dusty, and hot, and the rainy season, which is wet, humid, and hot. The rainy season has its own set of problems, but for now you need to take care of your skin. Use lots of lotion, because if you don't, your skin will dry out and crack."

Caitlin looked up. The sky was enveloped with a yellow haze and thick with dust that clung to her clothes. "Look at this." She brushed at a clump of dust on her shoulder.

"Here, I'll get it." Mandy slapped at her shoulder. "There'll be lots of dust. Our apartment fills up with it some days. I'm told it comes all the way from North Africa and that sometimes thick layers of it are even dumped on ships off the coast."

Caitlin cringed at the thought of days of heat and dust. That first night in their small apartment, Caitlin said, "Mandy, I don't know how much of this I can take. Africa's worse than I could have imagined. And the boys... I didn't know such suffering could exist anywhere in the world."

"Welcome to Sierra Leone, which some say is the most unlivable country in the world," Mandy replied. "I don't think we'll ever get down to the bottom of the barrel of misery here. I've worked here for two years, and just when I think I've seen it all, a worse case arrives. Medically, this group is in fairly good shape compared to some of the other boys I've worked with. I've seen hemorrhagic fevers, tungiasis, typhus, bilharziasis, dysentery, cholera, sleeping sickness, alimentary helminthic infections, hepatitis, Lassa fever, Ebola and Marburg fever. It's very easy to die in West Africa."

"Do you think some places on earth are cursed?"

Caitlin asked.

Mandy shrugged her shoulders. "I think Sierra Leone might be a good argument for the existence of cursed places. People here are certainly having a hard time of it."

Mandy pointed to a small chest-of-drawers. "You can put your things there." She turned on a small oscillating fan and sat down on the bed, leaning back on her arms. "One of the doctors said you had another job?"

Caitlin unpacked her bags and sat down beside her. She found herself longing for the fan to turn toward her. "Yes, my employer had business here and he asked me to come and do his bookkeeping."

"What kind of business is he in?"

"He owns a diamond company."

"Oh."

"What do you mean, *Oh*?"

"Well, there's so much talk about diamonds creating the problems here—you know, smuggling, the whole issue of conflict diamonds."

"Von's a legitimate businessman, and he has a good heart. I'm sure he wouldn't do anything illegal. He's licensed, and he just wants to build up his diamond stores in Louisiana."

"I didn't mean to suggest anything. I'm sure he's a fine man."

"I have an uncle here, a priest. Von knew I wanted to see him, so he arranged the trip for me. I find him incredibly generous."

"Yes, he must be." Mandy stripped down and slipped on her nightshirt. "The mosquito net hanging above your bed—be sure and drape it over you when you sleep. I'm sure you're worn out from your trip. Get some rest. Your first class is tomorrow."

"I feel like I'm the one in school, Mandy."

In spite of bone-weariness from her trip, Caitlin lay awake long into the night. She thought of her past sheltered life, of Monroe, of Hunter, of Von, feeling a pang in her heart when she thought of Von's brother Larry sinking to his death in the Ouachita River. She listened to the fan's oscillations until she finally fell asleep.

Chapter Ten

African art is functional, it serves a purpose. It's not a dormant. It's not a means to collect the largest cheering section. It should be healing, a source a joy. Spreading positive vibrations.
—Mos Def

By the end of the first week, Caitlin ran out of art supplies, so she approached a mission administrator. "I need more materials to do a good job."

He sighed. "Don't we all. Do the best you can with what you have. Make me a wish list. I'll try to get you more, but I can't promise. Be patient, Caitlin. This is West Africa."

"How can I accomplish what you want me to do with these boys without supplies? How can I teach them art with one chalkboard and a couple of buckets of house paint?"

"These boys will be grateful for whatever you can do for them. I'll scrounge paper and chalk, okay? Will that help?"

"Yes, thank you. Maybe I can write some of my friends in the States, too."

"Ask them for money," he said.

Caitlin made do with her supplies. In art class, she instructed the boys to draw pictures of their life, to recreate their memories. The youngsters did so, with seriousness, and the drawings and paintings haunted Caitlin. There were burning villages, stick men holding guns and machetes, and people who shed raindrop-size tears as blood gushed from their amputated limbs. Buried in these story-paintings were other more cryptic images of death and loss. In the artwork, Caitlin saw their fears and dreams, all drawn from a bottomless well of suffering and sadness. Caitlin saw demons on the canvas too—cruel jinn who sought escape from the tightly capped bottles of young boys' hearts.

Yet, the boys' creativity and emotional honesty touched Caitlin, and she regularly shared their drawings with the mission's counselors and psychologists in a weekly exhibition. She even managed to organize a showing of their art at the UN headquarters in Freetown. The UN's staff members were so touched by what they saw that they offered to purchase the entire collection. Caitlin consulted the boys, and they agreed. Once Caitlin received the money, she divided it equally among the young artists. The few dollars each grateful boy received felt like a fortune in his hands.

Caitlin worked late most nights, drawing studies of what she had already seen in Africa, as well as filing some of the boys' drawings. Already a theme was forming in her mind, and she determined to devote a show to Sierra Leone at the Lost Bizarre once she returned to Louisiana.

Caitlin and the other workers labored to get the children to openly discuss the stories in their art and their experiences, and even to act them out. The stories that did surface in the drama and roll-playing sessions horrified Caitlin. Little boys, who should be playing with balls and toys, had been trained by greedy adults to become killers and rapists and arsonists.

Once past the initial *impact* and *recoil* phases of their trauma counseling, the boys were expected to practice *sorry-saying*, that is, to offer apologies to any they had hurt. Boys who required special attention were assigned social workers as mentors.

While many boys made rapid progress, several did not. One fifteen-year-old had been in the RUF army for six years. He lacked concentration and suffered from depression. A counselor diagnosed him as psychotic. He talked constantly, but like many of the others, his speech and thinking were chaotic and incoherent. On a visitation day, his mother and father came to the mission. They left without him.

After the parents left, Caitlin stared in disbelief. "How can they abandon their own son, Mandy? They didn't even look back."

"They're probably afraid of him. Or if the boy hurt or killed anyone in his own village, then they're afraid of what the other villagers will do to him and to them if he comes back. Maybe they feel they cannot afford to take him in, or they're using their poverty as a ruse to try to get money. Perhaps they hate him for choosing to go with the RUF. And after working here, I can understand why they are reluctant to take him back."

"What will happen to him now? He's helpless. There's no way he can survive on his own."

"I suppose the mission will try to place him in an orphanage, if we can find one equipped to care for emotionally disturbed children."

"I tried to help him, Mandy. I did."

"I know, but face it, Caitlin, some of these boys have been so brainwashed that they will never be normal in their thinking again. They will never be anything but soldiers."

"I would like to think we can make more of a difference than that," Caitlin said. "Why are we even here if we can't help them?"

"Because trying to help and failing is better than abandoning them. Oh, by the way, I heard your uncle is here in Freetown. His name is Father Ambrose, right?"

Caitlin squealed. "That's wonderful. I haven't seen him in so long. Where is he?"

Mandy pursed her lips and answered cautiously. "He's in the infirmary at the American embassy."

"What's wrong?"

"The RUF invaded his village, and they hurt him. He lost a hand. But the doctor told me he would be fine. They've put him on an IV and are giving him some antibiotics, just to make sure there's no infection." She hugged Caitlin. "Really, Caitlin. He'll be fine. He arrived alive, and that gives his story a happy ending."

****

The next morning, Mandy had breakfast with Caitlin. A school secretary came to them and said, "Caitlin, guess what! Your uncle has been released from the infirmary and he'll be staying here with us at the mission. He wants you to meet him tonight at Paddy's."

"I can't wait to see him again. He's all the family I have left."

Mandy patted Caitlin's arm. "Family is important, Caitlin. Here so much of the family fabric has been destroyed, and I've resolved to never take for granted or neglect any member of my family. Hey, why don't you help me teach class today."

115

"If you want me to I will. What do you want me to do?"

"After I teach them some English, you have them draw something based on my lesson."

In Mandy's class, Caitlin noticed a new boy who had been badly beaten. During his convalescence, he lay on a mat at the back of the barracks, and he seemed to study her and the other students as they drew and talked about the drawings. Caitlin took him a pencil and piece of paper so he could draw or write something if he wanted, but he set the pencil and paper down by his mat.

"Tejan no write." He turned away so that he faced the wall.

When Caitlin gave the class a short break for tea, she brought Tejan a small glass of the green tea called *ataya* and some starfruit called *carambola*. He tilted his head and looked at her in a funny way, then shook his head.

"Please have some tea and fruit," she said.

He shook his head again.

Mandy joined her. "This one came with Father Ambrose's crew. I understand that some of his workers weren't too happy that he brought him along."

"Why won't he drink the tea?" Caitlin asked.

"He probably thinks it's drugged," Mandy said. "The RUF is telling their soldiers terrible things about us."

Caitlin touched a razor scar on his arm. "What are those?"

"When the RUF leaders ran out of syringes, they cut the boys' skin, put the cocaine inside the wound, and plaster it. A crude, but effective method of injection. This boy will almost certainly have a drug abuse problem."

Caitlin took a drink from the glass. "Mmmm. Good. Now you. I know you are thirsty."

The boy took the glass and drained it, smacking his lips and licking the lip of the glass.

"See? It is good. You are a very thirsty boy. Do you speak English?" Caitlin asked.

"*Englais*? *No*, Tejan speak small-small English. Tejan speak *Francaiz*."

"*Parlez vouz, Francaiz*?" she asked.

"*Oui*." The smile again.

"What is your name? *Comment t'appel tu?*"

"Tejan."

"Tejan. It is a good name, a name of one of the heroes of Salone." She put her hand on her chest. "I am Miss Caitlin."

"Miz Kaytlon."

"Very good, Caitlin," Mandy said. "This one's been really quiet. Father Ambrose rescued him. He knows him and wants us to get his story for the doctors."

"I don't want to know his story, Mandy. Let my uncle get it."

"You're being selfish. You've taken a liking to him, Caitlin. I can tell. Get him to talk. They say that he was a soldier for four years in a group that operated out of Guinea. He's not cooperating with the doctors, and they're starting to get pissed off. The other boys are suspicious of him. Africans are gregarious by nature, and a loner is either considered a witch or an outcast. See what you can do with him in the next few days."

Chapter Eleven

If you are going to the hill to make a sacrifice for the devils there and you meet them on the way, will you still go?
—*Krio Proverb*

Somehow, the rainy season, or as some workers called it, the sick season, changed the rhythm of Caitlin's life. The work slowed, and when not working, she found herself staring into the rain-soaked ground.

The war against the rebels continued to go badly for the government forces, and Freetown swelled with refugees. The United States and England issued stern travel advisories. The Sierra Leone government was considering an evacuation of all Westerners. As a result, the British and American embassies were in lockdown as they struggled with the logistics of arranging emergency travel out of the country by plane and boat. In spite of the growing tension, Caitlin and some other workers took a taxi to Paddy's Bar and Chinese Restaurant, where she was to meet her uncle. Paddy's was a favorite haunt of Westerners and had a reputation for being a place where Africa met the world. The food was good, the drinks affordable, and on most evenings, the bar was crowded to capacity. Mandy had left the mission earlier in the day, saying she would pick up Caitlin's uncle and they would meet her there.

Caitlin shook out her umbrella as she entered, and she slipped past two smiling hookers who had taken their post near the door. She thought them both beautiful. One was a Halle Berry lookalike, and the other an incarnation of a young Whitney Houston. The two prostitutes hissed at men who passed by them, called out to patrons in the restaurant and shouted retorts to other hookers outside who were jealous of their strategic position. Caitlin thought they would make good studies for her paintings. She slipped a dollar out of her pocket, held it up to get their attention, and pointed to her camera. One of the girls took the dollar, put her arm around the other in a pose, and Caitlin snapped their picture. When Caitlin heard gunshots, she lowered her camera and peered over the restaurant's half-wall into the darkness. The rain intensified and the sound of the gunfire faded.

"Don't worry about the gunshots," a male voice said.

She turned and spotted the speaker, who had evidently just entered the bar behind her. He was a tall, striking Anglo with a blonde crew cut, wearing a Panama shirt, cotton shorts, and leather sandals.

"Oh, hello," she said. With her fingers, she brushed her hair back over her ear. *Another African surprise. Nice looking man. Very nice.*

"The shots you heard come from the bay," the man said. "My guess is the Brits are firing on a smuggling boat. Of course, attempting to sneak past the British at night is a sign of a newcomer to the gun and diamond business, one who doesn't know that smugglers can operate with impunity here in the daytime if they just grease some palms. It is truly amazing what a well-placed bribe can accomplish in Africa."

"You seem to know what you're talking about," she said.

"Everyone and anything is for sale here. Africans are much more practical about such things than we idealistic Westerners. I can tell by your speech that you are an American."

"Yes, I am, but your accent suggests that you are British."

"Very good. Though I've been in Africa so long that sometimes I think of myself as African. And you are?"

"I'm Caitlin Johnson. In the states, I worked for Vermeer Diamonds, and I now teach art at the Xaverian child-protection school. What do you call yourself?"

"Rilke. I would have thought you were another Peace Corp volunteer. So they call it a child-protection school now. Most of Sierra Leone's citizens worry about being protected from the children in your school. A teacher, and a beautiful one at that. What a delightful Southern accent. Can I buy you a drink, Caitlin?"

"Why, you flatter me, suh. Since I'm sure y'all don't have mint julips, I'll take one of those Heinekens. I do like that purty green bottle."

He laughed. "Nothing stronger?"

"No, I've got too much to do tomorrow. I don't want to have a hangover."

"I can't believe I haven't seen you about town or at the casinos."

Caitlin blushed. "As for the casinos, I don't go to them. They're tourist traps and I hear that they are very expensive. I couldn't even afford to go to the casinos in

Louisiana or Mississippi. I've been working my little ass off for Von and at the school, and painting in most of my spare time. I can't afford any distractions."

He took her arm and walked her to the bar. They took seats next to a UN soldier who watched a soccer game on the television above the bar. "I am a UNAMSIL military advisor for the army here," Rilke said.

The bartender set the Heineken in front of her and she took a sip. "Impressive," she said. "I'm sure the situation here keeps you quite busy."

Rilke turned and his eyes scanned her from head to foot. "Who did you say you work for?"

She noticed how Rilke's eyes checked her out. *Lech.* "Von Vermeer. Do you know him?"

Rilke turned his face so he could eyeball the hookers at the door. "Everyone here knows Von."

"I'm not surprised. He is a go-getter."

"That's a nice way to describe him. Teaching at the school has to be something, So, are you able to make decent human beings out of any of the little buggers?"

"Yes, actually, some of the boys have made remarkable progress."

"You're a bloody magician or a miracle-working saint if you've changed any of them," Rilke said. "Now, don't take this wrong, but once you've gone and they can't get free food and board, they'll be back in the jungle under the leadership of another psycho. And soon they'll be drugged out of their minds again, playing machete games, and killing each other off."

Caitlin lifted her beer to her lips and said nothing.

"Ah, I've pissed you off now. Don't take my comments personally. I'm sure you're doing a wonderful job with the lads. It's the liquor talking."

Von entered, came up behind Caitlin and placed his hands on her shoulders. "Sorry I'm late, Caitlin. Have I missed much?"

"I haven't been here but just a minute myself. Rilke here bought me a drink and we've been talking. He said he knew you. I told him I worked for you and about my work at the mission."

"Actually, Rilke works for me as well as UNAMSIL. He was formerly an officer with Executive Outcomes," Von said. "I hope he hasn't bored you. Sometimes it is difficult for Rilke to have anything but a soldier's point of view. Even his tastes are questionable. Camouflage is his favorite color, and he knows surprisingly little about anything other than war."

"I apologize for what I said about the boys, Caitlin," Rilke said.

"Well," Caitlin said, "unfortunately, you touched a nerve. I'm really worried about their welfare and future. The mission administrators are convinced that Freetown is likely to be overrun by the RUF."

Von drained his glass and motioned the bartender to bring another. "Do you believe the RUF could be any worse than the banana republic politicians presently in control of the country? Wake up, Caitlin. The RUF *might* be an improvement."

"It looks to me like things are falling apart," Caitlin said.

"Achebe's already used that phrase about Nigeria, the country sending troops to save us." Von said. "Their troops are no different from those in any other African army. One trip to Nigeria would quickly cure one's naivete. However, I'll make sure your trip here is safe and memorable. You might even fall in love with me while we're here."

"Von! You're my employer. Quit talking like that. I'll file a sexual harassment suit."

"No, you won't," Von said.

Caitlin was irritated with Von's arrogance, and yet still attracted to him. *Slow down, Caitlin.* She had heard there were Anglos here whose interior wiring had shaken loose, mostly ones who had lived in the bush. *What was the old English word for someone going native? Fontee. Yes, that's it. Perhaps Von has gone fontee.*

Caitlin turned to Rilke. "So, what do you do for Von?"

"I provide security." He took a swallow of his beer, lit a cigarette, and set it in his ashtray. "And Von informed me that I'm also to watch out for you." He reached in his pocket for a folded piece of paper. "Let's see. Caitlin rises at five, showers, eats breakfast at six. Von arrives at seven. Shall I go on?"

"How much do you know about me?"

"Everything. I'm paid well to know what I'm doing."

"Why do Von and I need a bodyguard? There's so many soldiers here. Who would want to hurt us?" Caitlin wondered how Rilke obtained these details of her life. She also wondered what *everything* included.

"In a tight, the soldiers here, with the possible exception of the British marines, will never be where they can help you. Who would want to hurt you? You can't make as much money as Von does and not have enemies." Rilke snickered and toasted Von with his drink. "Yes, he is a well-known powerful man, and as such, he will have enemies. "

"You haven't lived out in the bush for a long time, have you, Rilke?"

Rilke laughed. "Oh, that's a good one! You're concerned that I might be a little daft. No, I have not lived in the bush for any extended period of time. I much prefer the comfort one can buy in a city." He placed his hand on her leg. "And the beautiful women one can find."

Caitlin was already beginning to feel the buzz of the beer and as she moved his hand from her leg she laughed. "You, sir, are a patronizing flirt. Please keep your hands to yourself."

"Caitlin!"

Caitlin turned just as Mandy and her uncle entered Paddy's. Mandy pointed at a table toward the back.

Caitlin nodded. "Well, thanks for the drink, gentlemen," Caitlin said. "I must join my friend and my uncle."

"Oh, please don't leave me alone," Von said. "We need to talk about work. Bring your friend over. Perhaps she can enjoy Rilke's company."

"As handsome as you are, I doubt you or your friend will ever have to worry about leaving a bar alone. It just won't be with me tonight. And I don't believe that Mandy is Rilke's type. It's been pleasant meeting you, Rilke. Try the Halle Berry at the door."

"He has," Von said. He put his arm around Caitlin's waist and drew her to him so tightly that Caitlin felt the breath squeezed out of her. Then Von kissed her on the lips again. "Caitlin, I think I am in love with you."

Shocked, but slightly dizzy, she gently but firmly pushed him away. "Von, you behave yourself. How much have you had to drink tonight?"

"I'm completely sober. Do you believe in love at first sight, Caitlin?" Von asked.

"No," she replied. *Liar*.

Caitlin saw Mandy carry drinks away from the bar. "Look, I really must see my friend and uncle. Thank you for the drink, Rilke."

Mandy met her and hugged her. "Who are those men at the bar?" Mandy asked as they walked toward her uncle

"My boss, the one who helped me come here. His name is Von Vermeer. The other man is Rilke, his bodyguard. I felt obligated to talk a minute, then before I knew it, Von professed his eternal love and his bodyguard pawed at me. God, are all men here sex-starved lechers?"

"All men everywhere are lechers, as far as I can tell, but they seem to get worse when they drink."

"How do you like my uncle?"

"Oh, Caitlin. He is so funny. I know he'll be glad to see you."

Caitlin's uncle was circled by a group of men. She heard one say, "Why if it's not Father Ambrose. I heard the rebels had you." He extended his hand.

"I'd shake your hand," Ambrose said, "but someone would have to hold my glass, and I already need a refill." He laughed, then extended his handless arm through the sleeve's mouth. "It seems I've joined the amputated ranks of many others here. The Bible says: 'If thy hand offend thee, cut it off.' The experience I had recently gave the verse meaning it didn't have before." His eyes brightened when he saw Caitlin, and he set his glass on a nearby table. "As much as I have enjoyed our conversation, my friends, you must excuse me. My niece is here."

"Caitlin, Caitlin. It's been so long since I've seen you." He stepped back and looked at her. "You look so like your mother." Father Ambrose picked up his glass and saluted her. "May your father and mother rest in peace."

"How are you, Uncle Ambrose? You haven't changed at all." Caitlin glanced at the white bulbous bandage and felt a rough rope of emotion loop and knot itself inside her stomach. "I'm sorry about your hand, Uncle Ambrose, I…"

"No worries, dear. Let me refresh this drink and we can catch up on all the news. I'm drinking far too much tonight for a man of God." He laughed and strode to the bar.

"It's so sad to think that someone would do that to a priest," Mandy said. "I hope none of our boys did it."

Her uncle returned and said, "Well, what do you think of our little African paradise, Caitlin?"

"Working at the mission is not like what I expected. I feel so inadequate. I only know that working here has changed me for the better."

Ambrose glanced down at his handless arm. "Me too, child, me too."

"Father Ambrose worked at a mission in the Northern District until the RUF invaded," Mandy said. "He's known Tejan for several years. Luckily, he saved Tejan from being executed by government troops and brought him to the school."

"You knew Tejan before he came to the school?"

Caitlin said.

"Tejan. Yes, I knew him and his family very well," Ambrose said. "He was a student in our mission school in Kamalu until he was kidnapped by the rebels. I also buried his family."

Her uncle's jaded, matter-of-fact account jolted Caitlin. "Oh, that's terrible!" she said.

The priest continued. "And, as Mandy just indicated, I saved him from being butchered by the Kamajors and our so-called government troops. It speaks well of your heart that you want to take care of the boys at the mission. So many children here will have no one. Ever. You should quit your job and work for the mission fulltime."

The thought had actually flitted through Caitlin's mind. "We'll see. I wouldn't want to leave my boss in a lurch."

"I've heard Tejan is doing much better," Ambrose said. "Mandy says we have you to thank for that."

"Tejan is improving," Caitlin said. "He's growing emotionally, and he has no serious health problems, thank God. And he's so sweet. I'm quite taken with him, Father. He has a sharp mind and speaks French beautifully. He's trying very hard to improve his English."

"I taught Tejan French. He had already learned much from the Guinea traders who did business with his father in Kamalu," the priest said. "He was an excellent student, and if conditions had not changed, I believe he would have become a wealthy trader and leader in the community—just like his father. Sometimes one can sense greatness, and I sensed it in him.

"Tejan was in our mission's school until the RUF swept through our area the first time five years ago. They killed his parents and took him as a slave. I believe he was twelve at the time. The next time I saw him, he was with the RUF when they returned to our village. By then, Tejan possessed the drug-clouded eyes of a boy-soldier, and I don't think he even knew where he was. When I heard Tejan had killed his own grandfather, I was afraid that he was lost forever.

"The rebels did this to me." He held up the stub. "But I'm fortunate. They killed several in Kamalu, and our gardener's daughter lost both hands. And worse, their megalomaniac leader made us listen to his speeches while they did these things. As one of your American travel writers said, 'The rebels here truly have a way with machetes and words.'

"That was when we abandoned the mission and came to Freetown." He drained his drink. "Well, I'm ready for another." He walked to the bar and Caitlin heard him say as his voice faded, "and another, and another…"

"Poor man. He seems so cynical for a priest," Mandy whispered. "Okay, Caitlin, tell me about your boss. Very handsome, don't you think?"

"Yes, he is." Caitlin glanced over her shoulder. Rilke was gone. Von was slouched, leaning on his elbow at the bar and looking at Caitlin. "And though a bit pushy, he has been the perfect gentleman."

Her uncle's voice cut in. "Even Satan transforms himself into an angel of light."

"What do you mean, Uncle Ambrose?" Caitlin asked.

The priest's face flushed, and Caitlin was unsure as

to whether the subject on hand or the drink had caused the redness.

"Von Vermeer is your employer?" Ambrose asked.

"Yes. If it weren't for him, I wouldn't have been able to come to Sierra Leone and to see you."

"Child, you know you could have come here any number of ways. Von Vermeer is an evil man," Father Ambrose said. "I wish he were a demon so I could exorcise him from the land." The priest waved his bandaged nub in the air at Von.

"He's a businessman, a diamond merchant," Caitlin said. For some reason a novel Mrs. Jeanson had made her English class read popped into her mind. She thought the book was called *The Heart of the Matter.*

"Businessman, my arse. Unless one would call gun and diamond smuggling a business. And Vermeer does other things. He lives in a dark circle of greed, ambition, lust, drugs, and diamond smuggling. He has a skill of political manipulation that is frightening. He is known to be on both government and rebel payrolls."

"I think you've confused Von with someone else," Caitlin said.

"No. Vermeer is a gangster who calls himself a diamond merchant. Oh, yes, he peddles diamonds. Blood diamonds. Conflict diamonds for guns. Diamonds for money. Diamonds for soldiers and mercenaries like the Apartheid attack dog who sat next to him tonight."

"Rilke is Von's bodyguard. He was a little rough, but he seems like a nice enough man," Caitlin said.

"Vermeer's friends are as corrupt as he is. Yes, he has an influential circle of friends—politicians, gangsters, businessmen, soldiers of fortune. His interest in you is not a compliment. He is an incubus who will suck you into that black soulless hole where he lives. If he possessed your affections he would show you off at his parties like you were a cheap piece of costume jewelry. On the other hand, it's quite possible that you would like this intoxicating life—the parties, the pretty dresses, moving among prominent people. He could give your art publicity and notoriety you could receive nowhere else."

"Doesn't sound so bad," Caitlin said as she cast Mandy a questioning glance.

Her uncle leaned over and looked into her eyes as if he were inspecting her insides. "No, such a life probably sounds quite appealing. The only problem is that Caitlin would lose her soul in the process. And what then?"

As Father Ambrose spoke, the drink sloshed onto his hand and the ice cubes rattled in the glass. "Men like Vermeer have never brought anything but slavery and death to this country. *Mohnki nohba lehf in blak han!*"

"What did he say, Mandy?" Caitlin asked.

"He said that a monkey can't change his black hands. It's a proverb they use here about thieves."

Father Ambrose's Scotch-wired eyes swept the room. "I predict that everyone in this room will be gone within a month. Conditions have been bad; soon they will be worse. This is a country God has abandoned!"

"Let's change the subject, Father," Mandy said.

"Certainly," he replied. He handed Mandy his drink, took a handkerchief from his pocket, and wiped his forehead. "I am getting agitated. I am so sorry. Ever since I had malaria, my mind lunges into these tangents of thought."

"Did you hear the Liberian ambassador's speech on the radio today?" Mandy asked.

"I did," Father Ambrose said.

"Do you think he meant what he said about Liberia helping us rehabilitate the boy soldiers?" Mandy asked.

"Not a chance in hell," Father Ambrose said. "The Liberian leaders only have power because of their own child armies, so any changes on their part or help from their hands will only be token and cosmetic."

After a few more drinks, Caitlin and Mandy bade her uncle goodnight and returned by taxi to the mission. Once inside their apartment, Mandy collapsed at once under her mosquito netting, but Caitlin turned on her reading lamp wanting to work on the pencil studies which she intended to turn into paintings when she returned to Louisiana. She stripped down to her panties and slipped on a T-shirt. In spite of the draining heat and the drinks earlier that evening, she felt energetic, and an outline of an artist's statement for her next show took shape in her head.

Caitlin listened to Hunter's CD while she drew and wrote down her musings, then listened to the rain, then to the silence when the rain stopped, then to the rain when it started again. In a sudden moment of inspiration, she sketched Von. She felt a strange mixture of fascination and pity for the man. Yes, he was attractive, but her uncle said he was wicked and dangerous. There was also something pathetic about the way he had professed his love for her.

"Oh, Von. Oh, Von. At last I know what true love is!" She laughed out loud held the drawing up to the light, and then titled the drawing: *The Diamond*

Merchant.

After dozing off twice, Caitlin shoved a rubber doorstop under the door for added security and cut off her light. As she patted down her pillow, she saw a man's shadow slip past her window. She slipped off the side of the bed to the floor.

She whispered, "Mandy… Mandy!"

"What is it, Caitlin?"

"There's someone outside our window."

"He'll go away. Besides, there's nothing we can do. It's probably just someone scavenging through the mission's dumpster. You didn't leave anything outside, did you? Is the door locked?"

"No, I brought everything in and the door is locked and propped. Do you think he's a peeping Tom?" Caitlin scooted up to the window on her hands and knees with her flashlight in her hand. She pulled the curtain aside, and in the illumination of a lightning flash saw a white man running across the mission patio. She could have sworn it was Von.

Chapter Twelve

If you close your eyes to facts, you will learn through accidents.
—Krio Proverb

Von watched Caitlin glide gracefully and confidently toward the Xaverian priest. He noticed the priest's bandaged hand and said to Rilke, "I do believe that's the same priest Biko and I passed on the road to Forécariah. I admire the RUF's handiwork. I wonder if the priest can still perform mass."

Rilke unwrapped his arm from the evening's purchased hooker, bent his hand down, and motioned a stiff cross in the air. "Bless me, Fader, for I have sinned." The girl with him laughed. Rilke caught the eye of the bartender and shouted, "Hey! Bring us more beer!"

Von drank down his Scotch. "Rilke, I've figured out how we can move our diamonds directly to America without using human mules."

"How's that?"

"In my art collection—inside the rattles and drums and masks. I should be able to take at least a thousand stones in one trip. All I need is an invitation from an American organization or museum to show the exhibit." His eyes moved to Caitlin. "Or perhaps an art gallery."

"It doesn't matter to me how we get them there. I

just hope you can sell them once we do, and you better hope Papa's men don't figure out that you've been stealing the RUF blind."

"Rilke, I'm making the RUF so much bloody money that the thought of how I could be making my own fortune doesn't even enter their primitive heads. Moving the stones won't be a problem. I've already found buyers. The U.S. Government is so focused on illegal drugs and terrorists that they aren't looking for uncut diamonds."

"Have you heard from Biko yet?" Rilke said. He slammed his empty beer bottle on the counter. "Hey! I said to bring me another beer!"

"Yes. Biko is in New York as we speak, meeting with Black Muslim groups who support Papa. He has successfully raised a great deal of funds and even recruited some experienced soldiers who should be excellent officer material for his units. After New York, he has appointments in New Orleans. That's where he wants to meet us. From there he will fly to Libya."

"Blood lucky you met Biko. I suppose he thinks the same about you since he's now got a bank account that rivals Taylor's. He better watch his back. I'm told Taylor doesn't trust anyone who is successful."

"Yes, Biko enjoys the money, but I think Taylor better watch his back when Biko's around." Von's eyes returned to Caitlin. "Rilke, Caitlin is the finest girl I've ever met. I wonder how Monroe, Louisiana could produce such a beauty. You know, I've held many fine gems in my life, but I've never seen a jewel like her. I think I just might have to marry her."

"You're joking me, right? You want to marry that flaky Yank who was just with us?"

"I am dead serious. I intend to marry her."

Rilke snorted. "I think all your bloody money and the damned heat has made you daft, Von. You couldn't be that desperate. There's a boatload of drop-dead gorgeous women available here for little or nothing. Why don't you buy one or two of them and get your mind off this girl."

Von leaned against the bar, placing his head on his hand, his eyes glued on Caitlin. "Unlike you, Rilke, I can't be satisfied with bush girls or the serpents we passed at the door. I've been searching all my life for a woman like Caitlin. More than that, she's an artist with her own gallery."

Rilke laughed. "I see. Is it her art gallery you're thinking of sending the diamonds to then? Come on, girl. Let's leave this lovesick fool. I'll see you at the house, Von. Do you want a girl tonight?"

Von slapped Rilke's girl on the ass when she stood. She smiled and chattered Krio vulgarities. "Sure," Von said. "Make sure she's pretty, but don't pay her up front. Tell her I may be delayed, so if she wants money, she needs to stay awake. Take a cab to my house and leave me your jeep. I'm going to need it for a while tonight."

Rilke pitched him a set of keys. "Be careful where you go. Stay on the main roads. Biko's not with you. In spite of what you think, not everyone here knows you. I'll call my boys on curfew duty and let them know you'll be in my jeep."

When Von turned and saw Caitlin and Mandy walk toward the door, he moved to the other side of the bar where they would have to pass by him. Caitlin stopped and opened her umbrella.

"I'm so sorry we didn't get to talk more tonight, Von," Caitlin said, "but I hadn't seen my uncle in so long. What time do you want me tomorrow?"

"I'll pick you up first thing in the morning. We'll go to breakfast, then to work. I think someday soon, I'll ask you to marry me."

"I think you must be very drunk, Von, to say something silly like that. But it's nice to hear, so thank you for the compliment." With that, she stepped out into the dark and the rain.

Mandy followed a few steps behind her. Von pinched her ass as she walked by. Mandy turned and slapped his hand. "Psycho," she muttered. "Get a life."

Von turned his attention back to the few left in the bar. Their eyes were on the priest, who now was preaching to all about him, his voice more agitated and louder than before. He waved his arm sans hand in the air, crossing himself and slinging the bandaged stump forward as though he flicked holy water on unseen supplicants.

The bartender wiped the table in front of Von and pointed at Father Ambrose. "The priest, he's drunk and needs to be taken back to the mission. It's nearly curfew. If he doesn't get out, he'll have to spend the night on the floor."

"I'll see him out and home, Edward," Von said. "Don't cause a scene."

"You're sure you want to fool with him?" Edward said. "He looks like a crackpot to me, priest or no."

"I'm sure." Von slipped a ten-dollar bill into Edward's hand. "Let me take care of the priest. Can you help me get him into Rilke's jeep?"

"Sure, Von."

****

Von drove the very drunk Father Ambrose back to the Xaverian mission. The same guard who had stopped his car earlier in the day roused himself from his nap and stood at the gate.

"*How de body*?" Von asked.

"*I tell God tank ya*," the guard said.

"As you can see, I need to get the priest to his quarters."

"Father Ambrose, he have party tonight? I go for the sister. The sister, she show you where his room be."

The guard returned a few minutes later with a nun. The rain had slowed, and she guided her way with a flashlight.

The nun directed the beam of her flashlight to the priest's face and gasped. "Is that Father Ambrose you have there? Is he hurt?"

Von laughed quietly. "No, Sister. He's fine. The good Father just overindulged tonight a bit. Would you be kind enough to direct me to his quarters?"

After Von pulled the limp and unsteady frame of the priest from the car and to his feet, he supported him with an arm around his waist and, following the nun, walked him into the mission compound.

The nun ushered them to a tiny, sparsely furnished room at one end of the barracks. After she lit a kerosene lamp she said, "The power's out again. I'll have the generator on in a moment and you can turn on his fan." She pointed to a small oscillating fan by his bed.

The nun helped Von carry Father Ambrose to the small bed and they stretched him out.

She picked up the priest's hand, kissed it, and whispered, "Sleep with the saints, tonight, Father."

"I know one of your volunteer workers well, Caitlin Johnson. Are her quarters in the compound?" Von asked.

"She and her roommate Mandy live in the first small barracks you passed as you came through the gate. You say you know them?"

"I know Caitlin. I am not acquainted with her roommate yet."

"Ah, all the boys love Miss Caitlin. She is indeed an angel. She has done so much for the boys since she came."

"She's smart and beautiful and talented," Von said, "and a wonderful artist."

The priest began to snore.

"You talk as if you know Miss Caitlin well," the sister said.

"She is my employee. And besides, how else should one talk of his fiancée?"

The nun clasped her hands together. "Miss Caitlin's engaged? Why she hasn't breathed a word of it!"

"Nor should you," Von said. "We wanted to keep it rather quiet." Von marveled at the gullibility of the typical person. They will believe anything you tell them. However, he rather liked the sound of what he had said. Yes, *fiancée.* The nun's face beamed with the joy that only a not-of-this-world person can possess. He said, "So, please, can I trust in your discretion?"

"Not a word will come from my lips." She glanced reverently upwards. "Thank you, Lord, that you have the power to work upon the human heart by bringing us love!"

"Sister, if you'll leave, I'll prepare the father for

bed. It's too hot for him to sleep in those clothes."

"Of course. And again, thank you. Such a Christian man you are. You are welcome to spend the night here. We could find you a bed if you wish."

"No, thank you, Sister. I borrowed a car and must return to my own lodging."

After the nun left, Von raised Father Ambrose, removed his clothes, and laid him back down. He studied the priest's body, touching it, wondering at its softness and the stories of its scars. Finally, he touched the bandaged stump at the end of the handless arm and speculated as to whose handiwork it was. When Von poked the bandage a little harder, the father opened his eyes.

"Get some sleep, Father," Von said. "You're safely back in your own room."

"Thank you for helping me," Father Ambrose said. "But I've forgotten your name. I'm having trouble focusing, and I can't make out your face. I feel I should know you."

"Von," he said as he clicked on the fan. "My name is Von. Goodnight, Father. We haven't met, but I think you know me. Don't thank me. I'm just doing my Christian duty." Von heard the generator start, so he turned down the lamp, turned on the fan, and left.

****

When his strange helper had left, Father Ambrose rolled from the cot to the floor and knelt in the African darkness at the side of his bed, intending to pray. Out of habit, he clasped his hands together, but his left hand passed through phantom fingers and wrapped on the cloth bandage gloving his wound, and he held his hands up to God in a Chinese martial salute.

"God, my father," he began, but he could not dredge from his mind the rest of the words of the memorized prayers of a lifetime. "God, I am really drunk tonight, and I can't remember what to say. We'll deal with it tomorrow, okay? Brother Jon will receive my confession tomorrow and I will offer proper penance."

He shook his head, again intending to remember his Vespers, but he could not. "I must see to the boys, tomorrow, Father. Please help me to help them."

And he resolved that tomorrow he would minister to these lost boys, he would look into their empty eyes and try again to absolve them of incomprehensible sins, to convince them they could be forgiven. And he would help them, though he himself be drunken tonight, though he himself be empty inside and abandoned by God, though he himself wished to cry out "'My God, why has thou forsaken me?'"

"I will not lose faith!" he shouted. "My God, I will not!"

Hoping that the dreams tonight would not be too harsh, hoping that someone somewhere had heard his cry and that he would have a peaceful night, he fell asleep on his knees. But the dreams were harsh, centered on the boy the mission had lost last year. He had met the boy when he had taken a two-week holiday and come to Freetown. He listened to his own voice as it narrated the sad story.

****

Benjamin, yes, that was the boy's name. He had deserted the RUF and came to the mission on his own accord. He truly had a penitent heart. I walked with him to his parents' home. The father came to the door, but the welcome was icy, and a stony silence was all the returning prodigal received. Benjamin knelt and begged his father to forgive him for having fought with the rebels.

"No," Benjamin's father said. "The priest be welcome, but you must stay outside."

"Father, I am Benjamin, your son."

"You be no son of mine. Papa Sankoh, he be your father now."

"Father, I did wrong thing. Please forgive me."

"Forgive you? No. I will not forgive."

"Father, I am sorry. Sorry, please. Why do you reject me? One does not cast even a bad child into the bush!"

"You ask me why? Angie, you come here girl!"

A little girl shuffled to her father. When she saw Benjamin, she screamed and clawed at her father, hiding behind his back. Benjamin's father reached behind himself, took one of the little girl's arms, then another, and forced into view two little handless arms.

"This be your work, Benjamin," he said. "With your own cutlass you cut off the hands of your sister. And you do things to others that night. You will find no forgiveness here. There be no one here who wants you."

Benjamin nodded, pulled a small sack from his pants pocket and tossed it at the father's feet. "There be diamonds and gold in that sack, Papa. Enough to help you live well." Then Benjamin turned and walked away.

I followed and tried to console Benjamin, but there was no balm in Gilead, no exorcist for this young man's demons. Instead of returning to the mission, Benjamin marched toward the West Side Boys' territory. I

141

begged, threatened, and attempted to reason, but Benjamin walked on, and left me far behind. From a distance, I saw him talk with a group of boys who wore women's wigs and bizarre clothes. After I finally caught my breath, I reached Benjamin only to see him place a revolver against his head and pull the trigger.

I ran to his body, then ran back to Benjamin's house. The father returned to the door.

"Your son, he is dead," I said.

"My son, he be dead a long time. I wish to have kill him myself. Angie, come here child."

From another room trod the barefoot handless girl, and the handless arms wrapped around a sonless father's neck. "It be good now, Angie," Benjamin's father said. "Your brother, he no come back again."

The sound of their weeping tore my heart out. I went back to Benjamin's body and kicked away two pye dogs sniffing his body. I scanned the ground for the pistol, but someone had already taken it. I tried to lift Benjamin's body, but my strength failed me, so I left Benjamin's body on the street and walked back to the mission to minister to the other boy soldiers who had surrendered. I sent someone for Benjamin's body later.

****

As Von left, he closed the priest's door and scanned the mission grounds. The rain had died, and he heard music coming from a lit window of the small apartment the nun said was Caitlin's. He slipped quietly toward it, and up to the curtained pane. The darkness about him felt like a warm cloak as he peered inside.

Caitlin sat cross-legged on her bed. She wore a white T-shirt and white panties, and she held a sketchpad in her lap. He studied her as she drew and chewed thoughtfully on her pencil. He saw the sweat glisten on her body and the dark outlined circles of her nipples through the T-shirt. Von stayed and filled his eyes with her beauty, even after it had started raining again. When she held the sketchpad up to the light, he saw the outline of a man who looked very much like himself.

"She loves me already," he whispered. His breathing quickened with his lust. Her lips moved and he was sure he heard her say, "Oh, Von, at last…"

****

Every day Caitlin probed Tejan to talk about his experiences—always unsuccessfully. However, he did begin participating in the classes. He appeared interested in learning anything he could from Caitlin, especially English. Tejan listened to her intently, slapping his head whenever he failed to remember or when he mispronounced English words.

Caitlin's uncle took Tejan on walks occasionally. They would walk the compound together, talking in French, and when Father Ambrose left to return to his work, Tejan wept and clung to the priest desperately.

No matter what Caitlin or any of the other staff members tried, Tejan refused to talk about his experiences as a boy-soldier. He remained a loner, aloof from the other boy soldiers. Whenever the other boys would be outside during recess, playing soccer with local Freetown boys, or playing on drums and dancing, Tejan would sit by himself, staring into space or endlessly recopying his lessons.

One day he had an altercation with another boy who tried to take his sleeping mat.

After the workers broke up the fight, one of the

doctors cornered Caitlin.

"I appreciate what you and Father Ambrose are trying to do with this boy, but if he does not make progress, he will be put out of the shelter," the doctor said.

"You can't do that," Caitlin said. "He doesn't seem to have been affected as deeply as the others. Maybe he just needs some space."

"Oh, so you've worked here long enough to become the expert? For one thing, personal space is nothing that a socially adjusted African wants or expects. And I can put him out of the mission, especially in view of his recent violent episode. He's only used his fists so far, but who knows how long it will be before he uses a weapon. The head of the mission agrees with my assessment of Tejan. Resources here are limited. All of the boys here are traumatized. We don't have the luxury of being generous and giving unlimited chances. Tejan's cover-up and denial is a coping, a survival tactic. I've seen such behavior before. If we ignore it, he'll only turn on us and return to the rebels. If he wants to get well, he'll cooperate and allow us to give him what he needs."

"What does he *really* need?" Caitlin asked.

"The chance to be a child again, to regain his humanity and the years the RUF took from him, but we can't do that if he doesn't let us help him."

"I can help him," she said.

The doctor shrugged his shoulders. "Perhaps. I'm sorry. I don't mean to sound harsh. But I do want to say this: Your optimism is admirable, but it is also naive. You must admit the possibility that Tejan and several of the other boys are damaged goods beyond rehabilitation. Some of these boys have committed enough murder, rape, and cannibalism to make Jeffrey Dahmer look like a sissy. They have no concept of what affection is. They refuse to trust adults. It's a hard, long road they have to travel before they be a part of normal society. And the odds are against them."

"He's only a child!" Caitlin said. "You're so cynical."

"No, Tejan never had the chance to be a child. And the odds are that he will never get that chance. Not here," the doctor said. "Not in Sierra Leone."

Caitlin looked at Tejan sitting across the room. He seemed to be lost in a daydream again. Yet, Caitlin felt certain that she could somehow reach him. "You're right. I can't do it here."

"What are you talking about?" the doctor asked.

"I'm not sure yet."

That night she made a drawing of Tejan. She sketched him standing on the deck of her houseboat, with the Ouachita River and the Monroe skyline as a background.

The next day she found Tejan sitting outside under a jacaranda tree. She handed him the portrait she had made. "Look, Tejan, Miss Caitlin made a drawing of you. I want you to have it."

Tejan took the drawing. First, his eyes widened, then he smiled. "Thank you, Miss Caitlin. This is good picture. Only important men have pictures made of them."

"That's true, Tejan. And you are very important to Miss Caitlin."

He held the picture up, looking out of the corner of his eye to see if the other boys were watching. "Where is Tejan in this picture? I do not know the place."

"It is on my home on the Ouachita River in Louisiana. That's where I imagined you in my mind."

"Your boat is very big, like *pam-pam*?"

"No, it is not a ferry. It is what we call a houseboat. Tejan, you are doing very well. Would you like for Miss Caitlin to give you some extra help learning English?"

He fixed his eyes on hers. "Why? What does Miss Caitlin want from Tejan? Does she want diamonds like other *poo-muis*?"

"I don't want anything but you to get well."

"Tejan is still sick? What is wrong with Tejan? He will die soon like the others?"

Caitlin felt a stab of pain in her heart. Some of the boys had died. One had passed away in his sleep just last night. Tejan had watched the workers wrap the boy in a sheet and carry him out to the new cemetery outside the compound. Another in the cemetery named Benjamin had killed himself after he had tried unsuccessfully to reconcile with his family. She patted Tejan on the chest. "No, Tejan you will not die. But you are sick. Sick on the inside. There are things you have lost that you must get back. It may take a long time."

"Miss Caitlin, will the British soldiers send Tejan to Pademba Road Prison? Tejan thinks now he has done many bad things. If it take long time, they send me away?"

"No, they won't send you to prison. And Tejan, nothing that has happened is your fault. Not your fault, do you hear me? And I promise to help you get well. Do you have any family we can find who will help us?"

Tejan plucked a stem of grass and chewed on it.

"Miz Caitlin does not need to look for Tejan's family. He has no one but Father Ambrose now. My mamá and papá, they die when Papa Mohamed took Tejan."

Caitlin struggled to control her emotions, but she heard her voice breaking up as she spoke. "So, Tejan is an orphan like me."

"How did Miz Caitlin's parents die?"

"Not in a war like yours. In a wreck—a car accident. I really miss them, just like you miss your parents."

"Tejan is sorry, Miz Caitlin. He did not mean to make you sad. Tejan's head thinks too much." He looked at her. "Tejan wish you be his mamá and to help him with *Anglais*. It make Tejan very happy."

At that moment, Caitlin knew she wouldn't be able to leave Sierra Leone without Tejan. Here in Sierra Leone, this orphan faced a bleak and uncertain future outside the mission. He would have to eke out a pathetic living in civilian life, and he had no trades or skills to rely on even if stability returned to the nation. Worse, he might be drawn into gangs and live on the streets or be forced to join another army. If she left him here, he would die.

She rubbed the top of his head. "Yes, Tejan, I will be your mamá. But you must promise me you will get well. And Tejan, you must start talking to Father Ambrose, and to Miss Caitlin and the doctors about everything that has happened to you, everything they did to you, everything you have done. They will not let me be your mamá unless you do."

"Miz Caitlin will not like Tejan if he tells these things. Tejan hear what others say about boy soldiers."

She wanted to pull him to her and squeeze him, but

she followed the voice of caution in her head. "I will love you, Tejan, no matter what. I want to take you with me to Louisiana, but you must get well. You can't live like you used to. Never again can you be a soldier. You know that, don't you?"

"Yes, Tejan know this. My grandfather said when Tejan was little boy, 'A dance that makes a person poor, you *nah* forget the song.' Tejan will not forget."

At lunch, Caitlin sat next to Mandy. They watched the boys play the tunnel game. In this game, the boys stood in two lines facing each other. They joined hands with the boy across from them, creating a tunnel through which the first two boys would run. When the first two reached the end, they would face one another and lock their hands in the air, becoming part of the tunnel through which the next pair at the front of the line ran. In some ways, it reminded Caitlin of the Virginia Reel.

For the first time, Tejan played too. Caitlin immediately saw the psychological dimensions and implications of the game, a game designed to repair the war-torn fabric of trust. So much can be said in the simple act of holding hands with someone.

"Mandy, how hard is it to adopt a child here?" Caitlin asked.

"It depends on the child's situation. If you're talking about adopting one of the boy soldiers, I'd have to say that you were crazy and that it was probably time you thought about returning to the States. Adopting one of these lads, even Tejan, whom I presume you're talking about, would be risky. You would really want an ex-killer as a son? Besides, I've heard most adopted kids taken to another country miss Africa and become so homesick they don't do well."

"Do you know anyone who can help me adopt Tejan? I mean, he has no parents, no living relatives. He has no village to return to, no money, no future here. If he's left alone in a war zone, and the RUF gain control, they will kill him for quitting them."

"Your uncle has helped arrange adoptions for some girls from his mission in the Northern District. I hear he has friends who are government officials. I bet he'll tell you what you need to do. But you live in Louisiana. I thought you had race problems there. How would people feel about a young white woman adopting a black teenager?"

"He would have far fewer problems than he'd have here. The worst we'd experience there is some social ostracism. Believe me, compared to the violence and hate in this land, Louisiana is a Utopia. I think Uncle Ambrose will help me, don't you?"

"Probably. He's quite fond of Tejan."

"You are a sweetheart," Caitlin said. "I'm going to start giving Tejan some extra attention."

The next afternoon, there came a hard rain. When Tejan heard the thunderclaps and the raindrops hitting the tin roof, he dropped his sketchpad and pencil and ran outside. Caitlin followed. Tejan stood, his arms extended horizontally as if he were hanging on an invisible cross, his eyes closed and his face turned up to the sky, and she heard the raindrops slapping at his skin.

"Wash Tejan away, rain!" he sobbed. "Wash Tejan away!" He turned and saw Caitlin in the doorway. "Miss Caitlin, Tejan will tell you his story. But there is much I do not remember. Tejan is sorry. Please, Miss

149

Caitlin, be Tejan's mamá."

She rushed out in the rain and embraced him. "Tell me what you do remember. The rest will come back to you. I will always love you and be your mamá, Tejan. No matter what you have done."

In her trauma training, the doctors instructed Caitlin to look for such signs of intrusion—for those emotional outbursts, when thoughts and direct or symbolic responses occur spontaneously, when the human mind acknowledges past trauma and tries to break through the denial barriers the mind erects as a survival tactic. Though often painful, without this breakthrough, the mind becomes a denial prison.

Caitlin and Tejan stood together in the rain. Somehow the sound of Tejan's words and sadness reminded her of a song Hunter played often. Hunter said he had written the song when he was sixteen. Hunter would have been Tejan's age.

Chapter Thirteen

The memories we make with our family is everything.—Candace Cameron Bure

The next day, Caitlin was given permission to spend the whole day with Tejan and to record his story. After breakfast, they sat in chairs on the mission grounds, or walked about dodging rain showers. Caitlin had already written down much of Tejan's life's story from talking to her uncle. Father Ambrose told her that his earliest memories of Tejan and his family's life was in Kono, the hometown of his mother.

"Do you know what a farmer's life is like in Sierra Leonne, Caitlin?"

"No, I do not."

"It is not an easy life. Every January his father brushed new swampland. With a stone-sharpened machete, Tejan and his father cleared as much of the grass and brush as they could and marked the boundaries of the plots with split poles. A leaf stuck on the top of the stick indicated that the ground had been spoken for. A sorcerer, whom they call a *looking gron man*, instructed his father to offer a *yaasi,* a sacrifice of rice flour and yams, and to hang a bell on a strip of white satin to placate a bush devil the sorcerer felt was fond of the location.

"In the spring they felled trees. After the first rain,

the termites appeared. His father said this was a good omen, a sign that the crops would not be late. After the land had been thoroughly brushed, they burned it. In May, the family sowed the rice seed, along with corn, okra, small beans, cotton, benne, and cucumber seeds. While his mother weeded, his father wove twigs and saplings into a fence around the fields to keep the muskrat-size cane rats from devouring the young rice shoots. He showed Tejan how to make a noose-snare and place it in a hole or two in the fence deliberately left open. This way, some of the rats would indeed be with the rice as they wished, but as part of the meal. As the rice grew, Tejan was assigned the task of driving any marauding birds away from the crops. At harvest, the rice was stored in their rice barn.

"He spent the first ten years of his life in this yearly cycle at Kono, until his father, fearing for their safety, moved the family to Kamalu, an isolated town in the Northern District.

"At Kamalu his father gave up farming and became a skillful trader, and he prospered almost immediately. After trading for several months with our Catholic mission, Tejan's family converted to Catholicism. I warned the father that I sensed changes coming in Africa, so to better equip Tejan for the future, he should enroll Tejan in the mission school to receive an education that would help him become a trader like himself. Tejan did well, especially in French and when school was not in session, his father took Tejan on trips deep into Guinea, the land of his birth, and even into Liberia where he learned to negotiate with city officials and the crafty Lebanese traders.

"I could tell that Tejan loved the mission school,

but the happiness he felt was not meant to last. It was in those days that Papa's armies came into their district, killed his parents, and took him as their slave."

Caitlin read her notes to Tejan, and when she looked at the boy, choked and only with difficulty kept herself from weeping. "Do you remember these things, Tejan?"

"Some of these things. Some memories come to me in my dreams. It is good that Father Ambrose can remember these things."

She set down her notebook and turned on the cassette recorder. "Tejan, I want you to tell me what it was like in the rebel army." She turned on her cassette recorder.

He held up his fist. "The first lesson I learned as a soldier was that the RUF commanders ruled with this."

When Tejan finished talking, they sat in a sad silence, listening to the rhythm of the rain that had started again. It was now time for supper. She led him by the hand to the barracks, and after the meal, ordered Tejan and the other boys to bed, and then shut herself in her room and raged and cried and cursed the men who had done these things to the young boys in her care. She cursed them as devils though she knew neither names nor face the devils wore.

Between the recording of Tejan's stories and those of her uncle, she was able to write out Tejan's story as a boy soldier.

The RUF did indeed rule with an iron fist. Every act and thought was under their leaders' control and every order carried out immediately and without thought. If a soldier disobeyed or even hesitated, he was punished brutally. The boys were told that there was no escape, no quitting the glorious ranks of the RUF. Deserters would be found—no matter where they fled. And when found, they would be killed, or worse.

One of Tejan's friends was beaten to death by a RUF commander as an example of what would happen to any soldier who did not obey orders. Two others were killed in a skirmish with Kamajors. One deserted. The commander sent two older soldiers to search for him. They found him just before he crossed the border into Guinea and they left his body in the bush.

Those boys had been Tejan's friends. They had played together in the mission, and at school studied and dreamed together—dreamed of attending the university in Freetown, of owning farms, houses, and wives, of starting businesses. Yet, the RUF's training and brainwashing had been so effective that Tejan shed no tears at their deaths. He said he wept for no one. His tear ducts were as dry and as withered as his heart. He knew his parents had been killed, but he never thought about them. He no longer thought of anything but the drops of blood on a machete and the daily fire of cocaine the officers injected into his blood.

At first, he was just a mule for the RUF in the mountains—the Sula Kangari, the Loma, and the Tingi Hills. He with other boys were sent to work the diamond mines, work that required them to stand in water, filling basket after basket of gravel in search of the precious little stones. The guards searched the boys every day to make sure they did not steal.

When the leaders were sure Tejan could be trusted, he was made a guard for the groups sent to Liberia. They took in diamonds; they returned with weapons. Eventually, Tejan was made a soldier and trained to kill. He hid from government troops in the dense mangroves of the coast, tormented by mosquitoes and snakes. He marched across the dry savannas of the north, his skin stung by the tsetse fly, and helped destroy village after village. He fought the Kamajors in the bush, the leopard men who clothed themselves in animal skins and hunted the rebels. He often slept in trees at night for fear of lions and leopards.

He marched, stole, burned, and killed. And this life had lasted four years. When he first came to the mission, he said he did not know what the future would bring, and some nights, he said he did not care.

Chapter Fourteen

Adoption is a journey of faith, from beginning to end. — Johnny Carr

Later that week, Caitlin went to her uncle. He looked up from the paperwork and folders piled on his desk. "Good morning, Caitlin. How are you? I hope you don't have a hangover like I do. I must slow down on the drinking. I can tell by your face that something's on your mind. Do you need confession?"

"No. I need your advice and help."

"What is it, child?"

"I want to adopt Tejan and take him back with me to Louisiana."

"You don't want to wait to have children of your own?"

"Perhaps later, but now I want to adopt him."

Ambrose nodded. "I see. And what makes you think you are ready to raise a child? And why Tejan? Why not one of the other boys? Why not a girl?"

"I just know. I feel my heart is going to burst every time I'm around Tejan. If I can't adopt him, I don't want to adopt any."

"You are not married. Do you intend to raise this boy without a father?"

"If I have to."

"I hate to state the obvious, but the child is black.

Do you think any prospective husband in Louisiana will be able to accept him?"

"If he can't, then he's not much of a man. Tejan and I will be a package deal. I'm not desperate to get married, Uncle Ambrose."

"Good." Ambrose stubbed out his cigarette and lit another. He blew smoke toward the open window. "I too love Tejan. I want to talk to him myself, then have a psychiatrist evaluate him. If those talks go well, I will help you adopt him if I can. There are some strings I can pull. We may not have much time. There are rumors of a coming evacuation of all foreigners. So, we must quickly find out which hoops the government will require us to jump through and whom we can bribe to speed things up. As the American embassy in Freetown only has a skeleton force, we will have to work through the ambassador in Dakar, Senegal. I'll get right on it. Tomorrow, I will give you the I-600 form from the U.S. Naturalization Service. You will need to fill it out immediately."

"Thank you so much, Uncle Ambrose," Caitlin said. "This means the world to me. I've always wanted a son."

Chapter Fifteen

I've seen the future and it is murder.
—Leonard Cohen

As Caitlin and Mandy sat together at breakfast the next morning, a large truck lumbered into the mission. A slogan was scrawled on its side: GOD SAVE THE TRAVELERS. Soon, one of the mission workers came to her, arms filled with flowers.

"Caitlin, these are for you," she said. "Aren't they beautiful? They are from Mr. Von Vermeer. And here's a note for you too."

Mandy chuckled. "You must have made quite an impression on your *boss*."

"Must have." Caitlin opened the envelope and read the note.

"What's the lorry unloading?" Mandy asked.

"That's the best news," the worker replied. "Mr. Vermeer sent the mission a truckload of food and supplies—rice, palm oil, soap, pencils, paper, and even some battery powered games for the boys. The priests and nuns are ecstatic."

"You said there's pencils and paper too?" Caitlin asked.

"Yes, several boxes of colored pencils and four big cartons of paper. The pencils and paper were designated especially for your art program."

"Okay, Caitlin," Mandy said. "Enough suspense. Read the letter."

Caitlin clutched the note to her chest. "No!"

Laughing, Mandy snatched the letter and read it out loud, holding Caitlin at bay with one arm:

Dearest Caitlin:

I hope you enjoy the flowers, and I trust the supplies will be useful for your mission and for the very important work you are doing. I know your time in Africa is limited, so take as much time off as you need from Vermeer Diamonds. Please allow me to take you to dinner this evening. I will pick you up at seven. During dinner we can talk about my art collection and possibly your using it for a show in Louisiana. I never thought I'd say this to any woman, but I love you, Caitlin. I've loved you since I first saw you.

Affectionately yours,

Von

Mandy scrunched her face. "I wuuvvv you, Caitlin? Christ, this note sounds like he's a schoolboy who has his first crush!" She made kissing sounds. "I hope you aren't seriously thinking about getting serious with this bobo. He's got *loser* written all over his face. Did you know he pinched my ass at Paddy's?"

Caitlin laughed at Mandy's smooching sounds. "Mandy! You probably liked his pinching your butt. I admit, Von is a little frisky, but I don't think he meant anything by it. Calling this date a sign of a serious relationship is stretching it. He's just my boss taking me to dinner." Caitlin turned and looked at the pile of boxes the workers had taken from the truck. She wished Von had left out the *love* words and she wished she hadn't let Mandy read the letter at all. "It really was a generous thing for him to do for the mission. You know how badly we needed those supplies. He might think I'm ungrateful if I 'don't go. Besides, I won't be here much longer. I've worked hard, and I want to see something else of Freetown besides the mission. I'm entitled to have one night out with a handsome, rich man, even if he is my boss."

That evening, Caitlin slipped on some jeans and a red button-down blouse and waited for Von by the compound gate. He arrived in a chauffeured Mercedes, and he wore a suit and tie.

"Hello, Caitlin," Von said. "You look lovely. Allow me."

When he opened the back door of the Mercedes, she said, "I'm a little embarrassed at my clothes, Von. I wasn't expecting a formal evening. I feel very underdressed. I thought we might be going to Paddy's. You'll have to excuse me while I go in and change."

"So, I've succeeded in impressing you?"

Caitlin couldn't recall Hunter ever wearing a suit. "You've impressed me, Von, but I'm still going to go inside and change. I would feel out of place."

"No need for that. Besides, we don't have time." Von extended his arm toward the car, and they slid into the backseat. He had hired a private driver for the Mercedes, and though it was not a limousine, it was air-conditioned, and Caitlin found the drive through Freetown very pleasant.

Von took Caitlin to the Bintumani Hotel and Casino. When they arrived, Von led her by the hand to the casino's shop. "Let's pick you out a dress. They have a decent selection." He flipped through a rack of dresses and picked out a black, silk evening dress.

"Here," he said. "Let's see, you are about five-foot-five? This should fit you nicely."

She stepped into a changing room and slipped it on. The dress fit her perfectly. She felt as though Von knew the exact size of her clothes. Caitlin never remembered any man ever buying her a dress. It certainly was not something that Hunter would have done.

Caitlin smoothed the dress down and admired herself in the mirror, then stepped out.

"Stunning," Von said. Von charged the dress to his room and sent a boy to deliver Caitlin's clothes to his car. "We'll send for your clothes when you're ready to call it a night."

Caitlin could hardly believe her eyes as she studied the cut of the dress. The dress *felt* expensive. She again ran her hand over the fabric in disbelief.

"Von, I can't accept this dress."

"Nonsense. We've had this talk before. It's already paid for. If you don't accept it, I swear I'll throw it away."

"How much does the dress cost, Von?"

"Don't ask such things about a gift. It doesn't matter. I'm embarrassed that I didn't have time to find you a better one. Let's move along to the restaurant. I hope you have a good appetite tonight."

"I'm starving," she replied. "Thank you, Von. It's a lovely dress."

Throughout the evening, Von showed himself to be extravagant and ostentatious, spending by Caitlin's calculations nearly a thousand dollars on the meal and a few games of roulette and blackjack. Her conscience was piqued by the contrast between the wealthy who crowded the tables around them and the poor she knew to be the majority of the nation's population. She wondered what the mission could have done for the boys with the money she helped Von squander.

Yet, Caitlin felt pampered and special, and her attraction for Von intensified. Handsome and a brilliant conversationalist, he didn't seem to be the soulless beast Father Ambrose ranted about or the loser Mandy perceived him to be.

"What are you thinking, Caitlin?" Von asked as he scooted his chair a little closer.

"I just realized how nice a man you are for giving me such a wonderful evening. I've never had an experience like this before. These people here have so much money! I mean, I've lived a rather sheltered-on-the-poor-side type of life. I was sixteen when I learned that chester-drawers were really what people called chest-of-drawers. I was twenty-one before I found out that prime rib was a kind of steak. I feel a little bit like a Cinderella tonight."

"I think you underestimate yourself," Von said. "I already see you as a princess, and I want you as a part of my kingdom."

After the dress, the meal, a great deal of drink, and the lavish attention Von showered on her, when he suggested they go to his room, she agreed. She had not been with a man since she had broken up with Hunter, and that seemed so long ago.

****

During her last week in Sierra Leone, Von came to the mission every day to see Caitlin. He seemed to enjoy watching her teach and work with the boys. At the end of the day, after she helped put the boys down for the evening, Von would take her to Paddy's or one of the other Freetown restaurants for supper and drinks. One night, he offered to take her back to the casino, but Caitlin refused. Instead, Von drove her to his Freetown house so she could view his collection of art and artifacts.

Caitlin gasped when she entered the room. On one wall hung several handcrafted masks from the various secret societies of Sierra Leone, and Von spoke eloquently of each mask and its implied symbolism. There were various musical instruments, including a score of leather-wrapped rattles and a *kele* drum made of a hollow log with slits in its side. There were gourd castanets, various stringed instruments from the Fullas, and marimbas from the Kabala district. On another wall were paintings and tapestries created by Sierra Leone artists, as well as primitive and certainly ancient wooden sculptures that stood on small tables in each corner.

There was a judgment mask of the Poro secret society, made of wood and decorated with iron pins and cowry shells. Caitlin touched it. "Von, this collection is breathtaking. I had no idea that you possessed such an aesthetic eye." Caitlin tried to imagine Hunter having and appreciating such a collection, but the thought was too difficult to hold on to.

"I only obtained it recently. I know you've been wondering what I've been doing while you've been the good Samaritan at the Mission. It seems I've been named a partner for a mining company. I had planned to sell the collection immediately upon my arrival in New Orleans, but I've told the interested parties that I wish to hold on to it a bit longer. I would like to loan this to your gallery for display, to go along with the African art show you have planned."

"I'm speechless. This collection must be priceless."

"Oh, you have no idea of its value." Von's blue eyes scanned the room. He lifted a rattle from its holder, shook it, and placed it in her hands. "For example, Caitlin, I have a buyer who is willing to pay me one hundred thousand dollars for this one rattle."

"Just for one rattle?" In spite of herself, she shook the rattle, listening to the stones inside make their delicate music against the hard skin of the gourd.

"So, you'll use the collection in your show?"

"Von, I couldn't... I couldn't take a collection this valuable. What if something were to happen to it?"

"It's insured. You can take it. Please? For me?" He returned the rattle to its holder and slipped his arms around her waist and drew her close. "I'll pay for the shipping. All you have to do is keep it on display until I can make arrangements to pick it up."

Caitlin contemplated the magnificent pieces of Von's little museum, picturing the items in her gallery. This collection would be an excellent illustrative backdrop for her show on her African experience and would certainly help draw a huge crowd. "Thank you, Von. You do know how to find a lady's weak spot."

Caitlin called and left a message for Mandy that she was safe but wouldn't return to the mission that evening. She spent that night with Von in his Freetown house.

****

The night before Caitlin was scheduled to leave, Von came to the mission.

"Well," he said. "Shall we go to dinner?"

"No, Von. I told you yesterday that I've got to pack tonight. I'm glad you came to see me though."

"I'm going to miss you, Caitlin," he said as he took her hand. "Let's at least go for a walk."

"Sure."

After they had made their way to the beach, Von said, "I want something more than casual employee contact, Caitlin. Much more. The next time I see you, I want to talk about our future."

"Von, I am so flattered, but as far as our future together, let's just take it slow, okay? I can't promise that we'll ever have more of a relationship than we have now. I don't think I'm ready for that kind of commitment. I just don't want to promise too much, and anyway, you probably will forget about me a week after I'm gone. As handsome and rich as you are, the moment you return to New Orleans, you'll have women climbing all over you."

"Caitlin, you're the only one I want climbing over me." Von pulled her close. "A kiss before I leave?"

Caitlin discreetly glanced around them to make sure no one was watching and kissed him. "Now, you've got to leave and quit distracting me. I must pack."

"I'll drive you to the airport tomorrow."

"No, Von. I promised Mandy the whole morning. She'll take me there, but you can meet us and see me off." She shooed him away. "Go on now." When he reached the gate, he turned to look at her and she blew him a kiss.

****

Von drove his Landrover to the Lungi airport and walked directly to customs. There, a man sat on a stool

165

reading a copy of *The Pool*, a Sierra Leone newspaper.

"How are you, Bashir?" Von extended his hand.

Bashir took his hand. "I am doing well, sir, very well."

Von thrust a small envelope and a wrapped package into his plump hand. "An American lady will come through here to take the weekly flight to London." He took a picture of Caitlin from his pocket and handed it to him. "This lady is *very* special to me. Her name is Caitlin Johnson. Please give her the package. It's a rattle from a tribe in the interior in case you're wondering. I trust she and her baggage can get through customs speedily with no problems. And this envelope is for you and your family. Be sure and give my wife your best."

"Thank you, sir." Bashir smiled as he slipped the money into a small briefcase at his side. "My wife will be very happy that you came to see me. This Miss Johnson will one day be your own missus?"

"Without a doubt."

"I will take care of my friend and his future bride." He held up the envelope and the package. "I will deliver this to her myself, as she boards the plane. And thank you."

"There's one more thing, Bashir."

"Yes, sir?"

"I am shipping my art collection with my fiancée to America. Please send your men to my truck when it arrives and have them load it carefully on her flight."

"I will see to it immediately, sir. The plane is filled to capacity now, but if necessary, I can remove some luggage to make room for your collection. Those suitcases can follow on the next plane."

"Excellent." Von returned to the airport later, in time to watch Caitlin and Tejan board the plane.

****

Caitlin was about to board when she heard a voice calling, "Madame! Missy!" She turned and saw the Lebanese man who had checked her through customs running her way. "This is for you." He handed her a wrapped package.

"Thank you," Caitlin said. "What is it?"

Bashir wiped his forehead with a handkerchief. "It is a gift. You should be honored. The gentleman who sent you this is a very important and powerful man. I must go now. Have a good flight to America."

Caitlin glanced at the package. *For Caitlin* and *Rattled* was neatly written on the front. "Who is this from?"

"A Mister Von Vermeer, Missy," Bashir said. "You must excuse me now. I must return to my work."

After Bashir left, she opened the package

Inside was an African leather rattle. The handle was made of a dark hardwood and the gourd bell was leather covered. The leather was etched, painted, and beaded. Caitlin was sure that it was the rattle Von said was worth over a hundred thousand dollars. "My, oh my," she said. "Would you look at this?"

"What's going on?" Mandy asked. "Who is it from? No, let me guess. It's from your boss and lover boy, Von."

"Yes, it must be a goodbye present. Get this. He says that I rattled him. See?" She shook the rattle at Mandy. "Look Tejan!" She handed the rattle to Tejan.

"I have often seen such rattles. It is very beautiful, Mamá." Tejan shook it in a rhythm, then frowned.

"This does not make music as it should, Mamá." He shook it again. "Something is wrong on the inside."

"Let me see it, Tejan," Mandy said. She shook the rattle a few times, then handed it back to Caitlin. "Yes, a very nice rattle."

"You are such a stick-in-the-mud, Mandy. Von said it's our destiny to be together. Do you think he'll really propose to me? He asked me if I believed in love at first sight."

"I don't believe in love at first sight, Caitlin, especially when at least one of the parties involved is *blind!* Von's assuming a lot, isn't he? I mean it's not like you slept with him or anything."

Caitlin's face took on a squeamish, embarrassed expression.

"No!" Mandy said. "You didn't! Caitlin, I've got a bad feeling about this man, and it's not just from what Father Ambrose says either. Von is too clingy. He's too eager to latch on to you. You're not in love with him, are you?"

Caitlin laughed. "No... At least I don't think so, but oh, the time with him as been so wonderful! It's been so long since I'd been with anyone. And he was so sexy and charming, and I just felt weak and vulnerable. At first, it was just a one-night-fling-thing, Mandy—I think, then it turned into something else. I'm not sure I can call it love, but I am extremely attracted to him. And he's shipping me his whole art collection to display at my next show."

Mandy slapped her forehead in disbelief. "What is it about Africa that makes white people so crazy? You are absolutely nuts for leading this idiot on."

"I'm not leading him on. I told him that if he came

to see me in Louisiana, we'd talk about a relationship. Imagine. Somebody as rich and handsome as Von proposing to a Southern country girl like me."

"Well, get married if you want, but I'm going to stay single as long as I can. Give me a hug, Caitlin. The room will be lonely without you and your stack of stinky paintings. Say a prayer that the rest of us can get out soon. I'm getting nervous as hell about this place."

For some reason Caitlin thought again about the man-shadow near her window during the rainstorm. "You be safe, Mandy. Get another roommate. I don't want you living alone. And call me as soon as you arrive in London."

"No, I don't think I'll look for a roommate. With my luck I'd get another artist who paints all night long. Being alone for a while actually seems appealing. But I will call or write you when I get the chance. Don't be stupid and marry Von when he comes to Louisiana."

"Mandy, I'm flattered by his attention, but to be honest, I don't know what I'll say if he proposes seriously." She gave Mandy a hug and kiss. "Goodbye, Mandy!"

****

That night, Von went to Paddy's. Mandy was there also, sharing a table with two female Peace Corps workers. They were very drunk, laughing and talking loudly. He walked up to their table.

"May I buy you ladies a drink?"

The two with her tittered but said nothing. Mandy curtly replied, "No."

Von felt his face redden as Mandy ignored him and resumed her conversation with the women sitting with her.

He tried again. "There's fewer Westerners in Freetown every day."

Mandy's eyes bored into his and she said in a loud voice, "I think you are confusing me with someone who wants to have a conversation with you."

Mandy's friends laughed.

"I just want to talk to you about Caitlin," Von said. "You must believe that I'm very sincere when I say I care for her. She needs me."

"Oh, I know. I read the letter you gave her. I wuvvv you, Caitlin. Jesus, man. Just in case you're more out of touch from the real world than I think you are, let me say this: Grown men don't come on to women with premature declarations of love and marriage. She was attracted to you and all that, but she has a new son to take care of and a life to rebuild in Louisiana. Let her do that. She's bright, talented and independent, and she doesn't need you or your money at all."

"Who are you to say?" Von said.

"I was her best friend here. And I know more about her than you'll ever know. Just so you'll understand my true feelings about you, I told her you were a loser and that she shouldn't have anything to do with you. I've already talked to Father Ambrose about you, and I've heard some other things just today that just might make her *totally* lose interest. Now, get lost."

"Caitlin won't believe anything you say about me."

"I'm calling her as soon as she arrives in Louisiana and gets a phone. Would you care to wager a bet on which of us she will listen to?" Mandy held up a wad of bills. "But if I were you, I'd keep your money in your pocket."

Von walked back to the bar, anger burning in his gut.

"You bitch," he hissed. "You stupid bitch."

****

Inside her apartment that night, Mandy dressed for bed, then wrote Caitlin a letter telling her the latest news about the mission and about her most recent confrontation with Von. She missed Caitlin already. She put on one of Hunter's CD's that Caitlin had given her and contemplated Hunter's photograph on the CD jacket. She quietly said, "Caitlin, what were you thinking when you let this one go? And God, his voice, so much feeling in it."

After she finished the letter, she addressed the envelope and laid it on the table. She lay down, buried her face in the pillow, and lost herself in Hunter's music. She imagined herself the girlfriend of such a creative man, wondered if the poetry in his music could be seen in his eyes and heard in his voice when he talked, wondered what such a man would say when they made love. She turned out the light, fell back on the bed, and allowed Hunter's Southern voice to be the lullaby to pull her into sleep. Her last conscious thought was about how bad it would be to die alone, without ever knowing the kind of love she felt a man like Hunter could give.

****

The man-shadow outside Mandy's window watched as she fell asleep, and he hated this woman with a hatred as great as the love he felt for Caitlin. He tried the door first, although he knew it would be locked and braced. Then he examined each of the windows. One was open. He cut the screen and crawled inside. Mandy had left music on, and he wondered how one could sleep listening to such horrible music. He moved closer and listened to her tired breathing, then opened the mosquito net and sat on the bed next to her. He placed one hand on her mouth. Her eyes opened, and he growled, "Not a word. Nod your head. Do you understand?"

He felt her head nod. She whimpered, and he leaned closer. "Shhhh. Oh, Mandy, Mandy, you and that insulting mouth of yours. You really should have let me buy you a drink. We could have had a wonderful evening together. There was so much I wanted to ask you about Caitlin." He pressed the pillow over her face until she stopped struggling. When he left, her brown eyes were still open.

****

Mandy's death jolted the psyche of the mission staff and reminded them how quickly the situation in Sierra Leone was deteriorating. Rumors spread that one of the newer boys had strangled her in her room that night. Others were sure that the RUF leaders had sent assassins into Freetown and that for some reason the rebels had targeted the rehabilitation school and its workers. One nurse suggested that since she was smothered, it had been done by a secret society.

Father Ambrose arranged for a small unit of UN soldiers to be stationed at the mission for added protection and dutifully wired Mandy's family the sad news of her murder. That evening, as he mulled over a bottle of Scotch, he wondered if he should try to contact Caitlin, who seemed to be Mandy's closest friend here. After several drinks, he realized that he didn't have the heart at that moment to face any more hurt or to talk about anyone's death. Besides, the evacuation order had been issued. The mission workers would all be gone and the school closed within a week anyway, so he put off this delivery of bad news till a more convenient time.

Chapter Sixteen

A bad husband is better than an empty bed.
—Krio Proverb

The wake of a passing barge rocked the houseboat. The movement woke Caitlin from her daydreams and mental flight into her past with Hunter, and she laid down the newspaper. She watched as the tug and its two barges chugged slowly past. Two men sat idly on the tow. One was smoking and staring idly at the water. The other noticed Caitlin sunning in her shorts and bikini top on the houseboat and whistled and gyrated his lower body.

"Dream on, deckhand," she called out. As the barge chugged by, she hummed Johnny O'Neal's song, "Snaggin' on the Ouachita." She knew it to be one of Hunter's favorite songs, and in her mind, she could hear him singing it again. When the barge had faded into the distance, she picked up her cell phone and dialed Melissa's number.

"Hey," Caitlin said. "It's Caitlin. I've been getting some sun and reading the paper. You'll never guess who's playing at the Back Door Lounge tonight."

"Who?" Melissa asked.

"Hunter. I'm going to hear him and give him the African instrument I bought. Want to go with me?"

"Oh, your old boyfriend. I thought you had sworn

off the Hunter addiction."

"I know, I know. And I treated him so badly that he probably won't even speak to me, but it still would be good to see him again, even if I have to admire him from a distance."

"Oh, don't worry, you love-sick fool. I bet money he'll speak to you. You're probably the only reason he came back to Monroe. And it's more than just you wanting to see him—I think you still care for him, in spite of all your talk about this Von guy. Did you know that after I signed the lease, all you talked about was your breakup with Hunter? And then when you came back from Africa, you asked if I had seen him? I don't think there is a cure for what you've got. What will you tell Von when he comes? Weren't you like thinking of getting serious with him?"

"I was, but now, I don't know. He's my boss and I probably shouldn't be dating him anyway. Isn't there a law against that? I'll probably have to handle the Von situation by ear. He's so damn good-looking that I may change my mind once I see him. I really think I'm over Hunter, Melissa. Maybe I need some sense of closure."

"Bullshit. Would you stop with the love clichés already? You're not over him, and I'd bet money that he's not over you. Some part of you will always love him. And I'm not cutting you down for feeling anything. I know what it's like to be love-sick with no known cure available."

"Well, do you want to go?" Caitlin asked.

"Sure, we'll go, if I can snap out of my dreamworld we writers like to slip into. I'd like to meet him because I do like his music. Remember his CD you gave me? I play it all the time. I just hope that the rednecks at the bar will leave us alone." Melissa sighed. "Sometimes I don't understand how we can love living in the South like we do. There is so much pathology here. If we had any brains we'd move to a civilized part of the country and get away from this mess. Do you realize how many psychotics there are in Monroe? Maybe I should move to Dallas."

"What and leave your best friend alone in Monroe?" Caitlin asked. "Like Dallas isn't a Southern city with its own share of psychos. Listen, no one will bother you at the Back Door. I know Jed, the owner, and I'll tell him to have his bouncers kick their ass if they do. I'll pick you up around eight."

"Sounds good."

"Thanks, Melissa. I just need you with me tonight. This may be hard."

"I understand."

Caitlin laid down the phone, crossed her legs into a lotus position, placed her hands palms up on her knees, and allowed the warm afternoon sun to drench her skin. She closed her eyes and breathed like her Yoga teacher in Bastrop had taught her to do, savoring the moment, searching for the green light on the inside of her heart, trying to block the alternating images of Hunter's and Von's faces that appeared in her mind.

When she failed to find the green light, she opened her eyes and glanced over her shoulder at Tejan who was fishing at the other end of the houseboat. Tejan's health had greatly improved and she thought him handsome, sure to be a heartbreaker someday. He was bare to the waist, and as usual when she sunned like this, his back was turned modestly to her.

One of Tejan's hands held a rod and reel, and the

other hand shook Von's leather rattle while he softly sang a French song. The words caught her attention. The song was one of the few good memories he had retained from his turbulent childhood. Singing always seemed to lift his spirits and calm him, in the same way her yoga mantra helped her. She closed the fingers of her open hands, as if to clutch the beauty and sensations of the moment. As if to close a part of their life she and Tejan both wished they could forget, so that she and he could only hold on to the wonderful present.

She had just heard on the National Public Radio that most of Freetown itself had fallen into the hands of the RUF. Nigerian and British troops had dug in and were trying to hold on to the little bit that was left. She was so grateful that she had left Sierra Leone when she did. Grateful too that she had managed to get Tejan out. She hoped Mandy and her uncle were safe.

Caitlin glanced at the stack of books outside the cabin. She knew she should be helping Tejan with his schoolwork. Yet, for now, this was what they needed to be doing, this was where they needed to be—here, on her houseboat on the Ouachita River, fishing and sunning and enjoying a warm summer afternoon together.

Tejan glanced her way. "Mama, the sun has not yet tilted out of the center of the sky, and your skin is red. Tejan is hungry. We will eat soon?"

She lay down and stretched. "I know. I'll fix supper in a bit. But I need to sit here a few minutes more."

"Okay, Mama. And I want to fish. The priest, Father Ambrose, said my grandfather was a fisherman. To fish feels good for Tejan. Do you go somewhere tonight, Mama?"

"Yes. I'm going to see a friend I haven't seen in a long time. Will you be okay alone on the boat?"

"As long as Mama loves Tejan and doesn't leave him, I am never alone. Tejan is home here on the river. The Ouachita River, in America."

"You will never lose me, Tejan. I will always be your mama." Caitlin smiled as she fought down her nervousness about her plans for the evening. *Damn you, Hunter.*

"Why does my mama look sad?" Tejan asked.

"I was just thinking of someone I knew a long time ago."

"It makes Tejan sad to see his mama this way. Mama told Tejan she would be happy in Monroe."

"Really, I am happy here. It's just hard to forget some people sometimes."

Tejan stared down into the water. "Tejan knows. Sometimes it is hard to forget many things."

Caitlin winced, hoping she hadn't stirred any bad memories of Sierra Leone.

"Who makes you sad, Mamá?" Tejan asked.

"His name is Hunter." Caitlin wondered how much she should tell Tejan about Hunter. Even in Africa, so far and so different from Louisiana, Hunter had proven to be impossible to forget. Mandy had commented about Hunter's music she listened to constantly, and the sketches she had made of Hunter playing his guitar, sketches that Caitlin refused to talk with her about. Maybe she had loved Hunter more than she had realized. And now, after over a year, she would be able to see him again.

Then, there was also the Von factor.

Von had written and called her several times. He would arrive in New York any day, then go on to New Orleans to handle some business for Vermeer Diamonds. He promised to come to Monroe in time for Caitlin's show. She would have to find a way to fix the clinging-Von problem soon.

She wondered if Hunter had changed since she saw him—if his hair was still long and wavy, if he was still lean in body and restless in those blue eyes. She wondered how the months in the parish prison had affected him. Months, at least in his mind, he had spent because of her. She wondered if he would see the changes that had taken place in her since Africa, inside and outside. Wondered if Louisiana had changed for him, if he could see or sense the Von episodes when they met, or if she should even tell him. She shook her head. There was just too much to think about.

She glanced at the billowing clouds of smoke to the south rising from the paper mill, eternally permeating the air with its sour, sulfuric smell. Visitors to her art gallery often asked what the smell was, and she, like other residents would reply, "That's the smell of money." The paper mill was probably the largest employer in the area. Maybe Hunter would get his fill of the music world and take a steady job there.

She spread out a towel and lay down on her stomach near the edge of her boat. She stared down into the river's calm surface, a green-brown veil deceptively covering its opaque heart, masking the strength of its currents and undertow, concealing its mysteries. This river healed her and drowned her sorrow with the same certainty with which it drowned drunk and reckless swimmers every year at Lazarre Point.

Tejan stood and dived into the river. He was a strong swimmer, swimming nearly every afternoon in good weather. After a few minutes, he climbed back onboard, grinning. She rose and pitched him a towel. As he dried himself, she said, "Tomorrow, we've got to scrub the mildew off the walls and change the engine's oil, Tejan. God, sometimes I hate fooling with things like that. Living on the river is getting to be a lot of trouble."

Tejan sat on the gunwale, scooped his hand into the river and watched the water drip from his fingers as if it were the holy water of a god. "These are small things, Mama. It is the soul of the Lady River who is important. She loves Tejan like you do, Mama. I can feel her heart. It is true—sometimes she is very angry. Sometimes she sinks with sadness when she carries sad stories past us."

"Yes, you're right, Tejan. Mama shouldn't complain. This river is our home now."

Tejan smiled. He picked up his rod, cast out his bait, and sat down on the deck. When the tip of his pole bent, he set the hook and reeled in a large blue catfish. "See Mama, I think the Lady River heard us speak of her and is pleased. She gave us a big catfish." Stepping into the cabin, he returned with a zip-lock bag and a kitchen knife. He plopped the fish on his cleaning board at the edge of the boat and deftly gutted it, tossing the entrails into the river. Making two quick slices, he dropped two white filleted white slabs into the baggie.

"Mama would like Tejan to cook fish now?"

"No. I don't have time. I've got to clean up a little before I go out. Just wrap it and put in the refrigerator. Let's just eat sandwiches tonight and save the fish for tomorrow. Why don't you cook that red-gravy fish dish for our reception party? Everyone will love it."

"How many will be at this reception?"

"The boat will be full." *I hope*.

"Then Tejan must catch more fish for Mama's party." And he turned his eyes to the river and sang to her. A song she had never heard him sing. The lyrics were in French and about a woman whose lover returns after many years.

Chapter Seventeen

If you're not dead yet, you haven't heard all the news.
—Krio Proverb

Hunter felt that the months spent at the parish pea farm had been hard, yet he felt lucky he hadn't landed in Angola. Hunter knew a man who had done ten years there. He claimed that Johnny O'Neal had even written a song about him. Blacky talked a great deal about anything—anything that is, except what Angola was like. The only thing he said about Angola was that it was a place no man should be sent to, that it would be more merciful to just kill him.

Before his time in the parish prison, Hunter noticed, but didn't understand Blacky's intense criticism of his incarceration. Now he felt he understood Blacky a little more. Prison changes a man. It empties him, wounds him. He understood to a minor degree the misery and lostness that two of his friends experienced when they were arrested crossing the border and ended up in a Mexican prison—because of a single bullet the police found in the floorboard of their truck. They were still in prison there, and the two white boys would probably have to fight every day of their short life. Now he understood the sadness in the ballads of the old musicians who had sung about their own prison experience, the rage of poets and prophets and political prisoners. They all had stories that needed to be told. Hunter hadn't been in prison long before he knew his music would change dramatically once he returned from his Ouachita Parish grave.

Hunter did his time, taking every work detail he could to pass the time and get out of his cell. He wrote Caitlin at least one letter every week, but he never mailed them. The one letter she had sent him when she left for Africa, made him think there would be no more letters from her. And there 'weren't. Not one letter from a girl he had loved like no other.

During those months in prison, he also had no guitar, and his hands, so used to their world of movement along the six strings of his Taylor, felt awkward and lost. He still sang, silently in his head while around other prisoners, and softly to himself while he worked. Shortly before his arrest, Johnny O'Neal had given Hunter his new CD. At lights out, Hunter turned one of those songs into a nightly ritual and used it to pull him into troubled sleep. *It's true, Caitlin,* he whispered every night. *It's true.* His heart cracked a little more each time he sang the song and every time he thought of how he had lost her.

During the day, he kept to himself, managed to stay out of trouble, and in his little bit of spare time filled three steno pads with song lyrics and ideas. Most of the songs were about Caitlin. From the small prison library, he managed to obtain a map of Africa that he taped to his cell wall. Once in a while he placed the tip of his finger on Sierra Leone. The only thing he knew about West Africa was that Caitlin was there, and he wondered if she could feel the breaking of his heart.

After his release, his father gave him an old pickup. Hunter put a small camper on the truck, loaded his equipment, and went to Mississippi. He traveled, drinking himself senseless most nights, living in cheap motels while he played the clubs and casinos.

After disappointing gigs and a failed romance with the poet girl in Hattiesburg, Hunter went to Texas. He crossed Louisiana without stopping. He had some good times in Austin, even opening one night at Antoine's for Jimmy Vaughan, Lou Ann Barton, and James Cotton. The club owners liked his music and guitar playing, so they hooked him with up with some producers who asked him to play guitar and sing some harmonies with them the next night at Austin City Limits. He accepted their offer and opened for the featured acts. After he was finished, he played backup rhythm guitar, perched on a stool next to a black percussionist who played a tambourine with a drumstick.

After the show, he went out with some of the band members and got trashed at a club while they listened to Miss Molly and the Whips. Hunter figured he must have had a good time because afterwards he couldn't remember the musicians' names or even the bar they had gone to.

When the gigs in Austin ran out, he moved on to Dallas where he found plenty of work. He was running high in creativity, yet Dallas felt empty. The money was good, the music came out okay, but his new songs never arrived, never connected to any heart as far as he could tell. The audience was distant, disinterested, and aloof, not at all like the crowds in Louisiana. The audience changed nightly, and Hunter noticed that a new audience never knew his music, and really never knew how to take his ballads and love songs into their hearts. One night he decided he had suffered long enough in Texas and phoned his parents and told them he was coming back to Louisiana.

"I didn't think you'd be able to stay away from Louisiana too long," his father said. "You reckon you'll be here a while? Or will that Viking blood your mama's family put in you get to stirring again and push you somewhere else?"

"I think I got most of that out of my system. After Dallas, I realized what a white-trash Southern peckerwood I am."

"I don't know what that's saying about your mama and me, but I am glad you're coming back this way. When will we see you?"

"I've lined up a gig in Ruston this Thursday, and one in West Monroe on Friday. I ought to make it home sometime after that."

"Well, your mama's been worried about you, Hunter. Time to settle down some, don't you think?"

"Yeah. But I still have to find my way in some things."

"Hunter, how are things with you and that Mississippi girl?"

"I don't think things are going to work out with her."

"I'm sorry, son. She sounded like a nice girl. You call us as soon as you get in."

"I'll do that, Daddy."

Chapter Eighteen

Songwriting is too mysterious and uncontrolled a process for me to direct it towards any one thing.
—*James Taylor*

That night, Hunter collected the money owed him and left Dallas the next morning. At Marshall, Texas, he stopped at a mom-and-pop restaurant for lunch. He ordered coffee and the daily lunch special. While he waited for his meal, he opened his notebook and tried to write a song that he could feel bubbling on the edge of his consciousness, but no clear words or lines came to him. The image and emotions were there, but the right words were choked out somewhere between his heart and his gut.

An eighteen-wheeler parked along the service road. Hunter watched the trucker lock his rig and make his way to the restaurant.

"There's Louis," one of the waitresses said to the cook. "He's such a hoot. I bet he was a wildcat when he was younger. Best get his steak going."

As the trucker entered, he stuffed his John Deere cap into his overalls' pocket and sat down next to Hunter. He called out to the waitress, "Hey, Sally. I'll take the usual."

"Louis, when are you going to order something different?" Sally asked.

"When you quit cooking me good steaks." The trucker looked over at Hunter. "How you doing, young fellar?"

"All right, I guess."

"Where you headed?"

"West Monroe. My name's Hunter." He held out his hand.

Louis' callused hand pumped Hunter's. "Louis. I live in Winn Parish. Was a logger most of my life. When I retired, I went to driving a truck. My route usually don't take me beyond Shreveport, but when it does, I always like to stop here. The food here is top-notch, and Sally there provides some nice scenery. Why, if I were younger, I'd…"

"You behave yourself, Louis," Sally said as she set Hunter's plate down and refilled his coffee.

"What's taking you to Monroe?" Louis asked.

"I'm from there, but I'm a musician. I've been working in Dallas, but things slowed down a bit. I know logging and truck driving are hard ways to make a living."

"It is for a fact, but you guitar pickers ain't got it as easy as folks think. I couldn't do it. Too much temptation. I had a buddy that was a guitar picker. Wore himself out in the honkytonks, drinking himself senseless and chasing women. But that boy could sing. Sounded just like Jimmie Rogers. You know who that is?"

"Yeah. He was a good songwriter. There hasn't been many equal to him, my daddy always said."

"Your daddy is right about that." Louis closed his eyes and sang out a verse of "'Women Make a Fool of Me.'"

Ain't that the truth, Hunter thought.

"I like that song. Makes me think of what an idgit I could be at times. I was lucky though and found myself a good woman," Louis said. "She's been gone from this earth a couple of years, but I still got her in my heart. I knew right away that she was the one God had chosen for me. She gave me a devil of a time getting her though. I'd get pissy and we'd break up, but then she always took me back. Finally, I married her. But I wouldn't trade one moment of my life with her for nothing. You married, young fellar?"

"I had a girlfriend, but she and I didn't work out, so now I'm just married to my music."

"Folks need music and good musicians like yourself, but music ain't no substitute for a good woman." He signaled Sally. "Sally, I'm going to pay for this young fellar's meal, okay?"

"Sure thing, Louis," Sally said.

"That's nice of you, but I got money," Hunter said.

"Don't you get uppity just because someone tries to do something nice for you. You can return the favor on someone else. There ain't no shortage of people who need a helping hand in this world. So, what happened between you and your lady?"

"Hard to say. I think I mostly didn't pay her enough attention. Things got stormy between us. More problems and complications than before. She ended things last time."

"Every woman comes with her own set of difficulties. So does a man. You reckon you contributed to this storm you're talking about?"

"I'm sure I did. I can really get the dumbass sometimes."

"She still on your heart, is she?"

"Yeah. All the time."

A woman close to Hunter's age entered the restaurant. A young boy and girl trailed in behind her. Louis's tan, wrinkled face beamed. It seemed to Hunter as if his face were one big smile.

"Here's another reason I like to stop here," Louis said. "That's my daughter and grandkids. They live up in Jefferson."

The two children ran up to Louis shouting, "Grandpa! Grandpa!" He rubbed their heads as they hugged on him, and then he kissed his daughter on the cheek.

"Rose, I want you to meet a new friend, Hunter. He's a guitar picker, a durn good one too, I bet you. On his way to Louisiana."

"Pleased to meet you, Hunter," she said. "I hope my daddy didn't talk your ears off. He never meets a stranger."

"Let's move over to a booth," Louis said. "Hunter, you're welcome to join us."

"Thanks, but I'll let you folks enjoy your visit. I'm almost done eating anyway."

Louis pounded Hunter on the shoulder. "If Hunter here looks a little addled, Rose, it's because he's in love with some woman he's trying to run from."

"You just say whatever you think, don't you," Hunter said.

"Yes, he does," Rose said. "He's not often wrong either. That's what made living with him so bad."

"I ain't wrong this time neither. If I was you, son, I'd go back to Monroe and patch up things. She's just waiting for you to do that, bet you money."

Rickey Pittman

Hunter left the restaurant and drove on to Ruston. He arrived at the Sundance Tavern an hour early. After he found the manager, he opened the topper camper on the back of his truck and unloaded his equipment. He set up his P.A., lights, music stand, and amplifier in the outside patio, then kicked back on one of the iron chairs to enjoy a cold beer. The stucco-walled patio courtyard was furnished with metal-mesh tables and chairs under umbrellas. Flowerpots of impatiens, petunias, and daisies were set in corners. On one wall hung a dozen ancient, small chairs, handmade and once the thrones of small children in rural homes. Moonflowers were planted in large pots and their vines wound and scaled posts of the tin-roofed covered stage area. A pair of long, swirling purple and white mobiles hung on either side of him and one had already mesmerized a lone drunk in a corner muttering to himself or an invisible friend.

Hunter studied the crowd trickling into the Sundance. For a moment, he was afraid the evening would be a repeat of Dallas. Most weren't there to hear him but had spent the day at Ruston's Peach Festival and simply were ending the day by grabbing a quick sandwich or drink. Even though he had played two nights a week in Ruston for over two years before his stint in the parish pen, he doubted that anyone tonight would recognize his name. A musician learns early in his career that even people who like him can forget him.

A year ago, his evening gigs at the Sundance Tavern and the other clubs were crowded with college students, most of them there only because they chose to trash themselves with pitcher beer rather than hole up in

190

stuffy, sterile dorms in a conservative town studying for exams. Yet at every gig there were usually a few groupies and loyal regulars and some old farts who followed him everywhere he played.

Finally, a few folks he knew entered the tavern. Then, a few more, and he slipped deeper into his music. He was surprised when some mouthed every line to every song. Several made song requests, and Hunter recalled many of their names by the song they requested. Hunter thought that certain songs must seat themselves in peoples' memories—change them, wound them, touch them in an existential experience that helps them define and understand past moments.

He played on without a break, remembering and loving this feeling of performing outside on balmy Louisiana nights. A few dropped bills in his tip jar and requested songs. *Memento mori*. He had not played some of the songs in over a year. Though he kept his notebook open before him, he was able to recall the words and the feelings of the songs without relying on it.

As he played and sang, he watched the sun set, and watched the stars as they slowly pierced the dusk and become faint dots in the overhead darkness. The moonflowers and other night flowers on the patio opened and glowed—luminous, iridescent, in the light of the neon beer signs and black lights, and the Scotch and pot kicked in and to Hunter's mind the patio changed into a faery garden. And Hunter and a few in the crowd lost themselves in the songs and the feelings and memories, and he and the crowd drank, sinking and singing together into another Southern night.

As he packed up his equipment, a young man

walked up to Hunter and held out his hand. "Man, Hunter, I've sure missed your music. True Americana. No one does it like you, Hunter."

Hunter snatched his hand and shook it. "Good seeing you, Robert. You still in school?"

"Yeah. As my dad says, my senior year will be the best three years of my life. I'm president of our fraternity too. Why don't you play for our frat party this fall? It'll be good money."

"Sure, if I'm in the area, but to be honest, I don't know I'll be here then."

"Well, I hadn't seen you in a long time. I heard you got busted."

"Yeah. Did a few months at the Ouachita Parish prison farm. Technically, I assaulted a man, but I also happened to be carrying a matchbox of pot. The guy I fought didn't want to press charges, but the D.A. wouldn't let the pot charges go."

"You know this is really a coincidence. I saw your girlfriend last week in Monroe. Let's see, what was her name?"

"Caitlin."

"Yeah. Caitlin. Hadn't seen her for a while either. Did you guys split up?"

"Yeah. Last I heard she had gone to Africa and was working for some humanitarian organization. I guess she's back by now."

"If you don't mind me asking, why'd you two split up?" Robert asked.

"It's a long sad story. If you were my psychiatrist, I'd tell you all about it—there's bound to be some meaning in that amount of suffering. Where did you see Caitlin?"

"At her art gallery in West Monroe. It was closed for a while, but it looks like she's back in business. Caitlin's got some kind of big show planned soon; I think it's got an African theme. I asked Caitlin about you, but she didn't have much to say."

"Figures. I'm playing in West Monroe tomorrow night at the Backdoor Lounge. You come out too if you're that away."

"Might do that. Do you have a girlfriend now? My girlfriend has a friend who always liked you a lot. I could fix you up."

Hunter laughed. "Fixing me in any way would really take some doing."

Chapter Nineteen

Sometimes life gives you a second chance...It's what you do with those second chances that counts.
—*Dave Wilson.*

After settling Tejan in for the night, Caitlin, showered, threw on jeans and a blue silk blouse and drove to West Monroe. She parked on Trenton Street outside her gallery. She paused a moment to study the Lost Bazaar's sign and thought about how good it was to be home and to be back in the art business. The street was crowded with Saturday afternoon shoppers and tourists and yuppie couples with children in tow. Directly across the street from the gallery two transients sat on the curb in front of the coffee shop, a pair of the many homeless nomads who often traveled Highway 80 and wandered onto Trenton Street looking for handouts or a place to spend the night. One of the men fixed his eyes on Caitlin. The face was blank—no anger, no desperation, just the nothingness the homeless must have to live with. She thought the man's eyes hollow and hungry. He reminded her of Von's brother Larry. She had seen the same eyes in Sierra Leone. Glancing up into the loft window, she saw Melissa as she bustled through the room picking up, her long red ponytail swinging side to side.

Caitlin walked to the back of the gallery and up the

iron staircase to the loft door. She knocked and heard Melissa shout for her to come in. Melissa now sat at her computer desk, dressed in flannel pajama pants and T-shirt. Her notepad was in her lap, and stacks of books surrounded her computer. She typed furiously. Caitlin waited for her to reach a stopping place. Finally, Melissa leaned back in her chair, took off her glasses, and glanced up.

"Hey, Caitlin. What's up?"

"Not much. Why aren't you ready?"

"I had to wash my hair, then pick up the apartment so you wouldn't think I was a complete slob, then I thought of a scene for a story I'm working on."

Caitlin smiled. "I'm sorry. I broke your concentration, didn't I?"

"Someone or something always breaks a writer's concentration. But we get used to it. Where are we going tonight?"

"You are so spacey. You've already forgotten. The Back Door Lounge," Caitlin said.

"Christ, I haven't been there in ages. Didn't like it then. I haven't heard if it's any better."

"If we don't like the feel of it, we'll leave. I just want to see Hunter."

Melissa stepped to the bathroom, drying her hair with a towel. "Shit, I still don't understand what you're thinking, Caitlin. After what he did? Maybe we should go somewhere else." She looked at Caitlin's face. "Oh, all right. We'll go. And I'll even be nice to Hunter."

Caitlin sat on the sofa and flipped through a *Time Magazine* on the coffee table. "I don't know why I have such trouble with men. I always seem to attract the wrong type. What am I going to say to Von if Hunter

Rickey Pittman

and I do start seeing each other again?"

"Tell him it was fun, but that it's time for both of you to move on. Caitlin, your only problem is that you are too nice. That niceness works like a psycho-magnet. If a guy isn't mature enough to understand you aren't interested, then tough. In Monroe, if a girl is nice to a guy, suddenly she is the center of his life and becomes his possession. I'm speaking from experience. There was a weirdo I dated for a week or so right after I moved into this place. It was like I couldn't get rid of the bum. He spent one night here once and next thing I know, he's trying to move in. I had to call an Ouachita deputy I know who came over and straightened the jerk out.

"I also think you could be on the rebound," Melissa said. "That second bounce is harder than the first. One should always give themselves a year of playtime after a relationship ends."

Caitlin winced. "Would you please stop preaching? Let's go play. What are you going to wear tonight?"

Melissa cut off her computer. "As little as possible. I want to dress sexy, even though no one wants to look at my flat chest."

"You are such an exhibitionist. And nothing's wrong with your boobs."

"That's easy for you to say Miss naturally-born-with-36-C's. Those puppies of yours are probably ten pounds of your total weight—which isn't much."

"Melissa, there's nothing wrong in being a carpenter's dream girl," Caitlin said.

Melissa raised one eyebrow. "Excuse me? What is a carpenter's dream girl?"

"One as flat as a board and that needs a screw."

Melissa stuck out her tongue.

"But really, you're fine."

"You are such a bullshitter, but thank you anyway," Melissa said. She walked to her turn – of - the-century chifforobe and reached inside one of its drawers and pulled out a shirt. "Here, how about this? I've always liked this one. I know the men love it."

Caitlin took the shirt from Melissa and held up the tiny piece of knitted fabric against her chest. "It looks like a little girl's shirt. I don't see how this tiny thing stretches around your skinny body."

Melissa put the shirt on and stood and posed dramatically in front of the mirror she had hung on a door. "Maybe I too can meet a musician, and like Caitlin, I mean, Ophelia, be swept away in the river of his music."

"Yeah, but Ophelia died, didn't she? I prefer happier endings, Miss Drama Queen," Caitlin said. "Speaking of happy endings, how's your romance novel coming along?" Caitlin asked. "Lots of sex in this one?"

"Not yet, but I'm getting close to a love scene. I think it's going to be really hot."

Caitlin picked up Melissa's manuscript and scanned the first page. "Hmmm. *Lovers' Bayou*. Am I in this one?"

Melissa reached over and took the manuscript. "You know better than to ask that. I don't like to talk about my stories before they're finished. But yes, there is a character in it who resembles you. My heroine falls madly in love with the governor's son who is extremely handsome and charismatic."

"A governor's son?" Caitlin said. "That could only

happen in my dreams and in your books, but I love the thought."

Melissa continued. "But he has a dark side that the heroine can't detect. Her first true love from her past comes and saves her."

The phone rang.

"I'll get it," Melissa said. She picked up the phone. "Hello?"

"This is Von Vermeer, calling for Caitlin Johnson from New York. Could I speak with her?"

"Uh, hold on a minute." She covered the phone with her hand and whispered, "Caitlin, I think it's your African boyfriend. He's calling from New York." She held the phone out. "You must have given him the number for the gallery."

"I might have. I can't remember." Caitlin took the phone. "Von, it's good to hear your voice. I've missed you too. No, I don't know how the store's doing. Well, I resigned from the store. I know I should have talked to you first, but really, Earl can handle things without me. That new girl he hired is doing fine. I'm very busy. Really focused on my show right now. No, I'm not putting you off. I'm just going to be busy, that's all. I miss you too. Well, we'll talk about it at the show, okay? I've got to go, Von. My friend and I are going out. No, I don't have a date, just a girls' night out. Yes, I swear. Goodbye, Von." Caitlin hung up.

"Like I said, Caitlin," Melissa said. "You can't tell guys what they need to hear."

"Weren't you listening? I sort of told him no, I just didn't…"

"I know. You just didn't want to hurt his feelings over the phone. Believe me, it's harder to do in person.

Christ, would you grow up? Your Southern sweetness is going to bite you in the ass someday. I hope you don't feel obligated to say anything about Von to Hunter."

"Hunter doesn't have to know all my business," Caitlin said. "You're talking like we're already back together. I'm not even sure Hunter will talk to me."

"Who are you trying to fool, Caitlin?" Melissa said. "You made up your mind to get back with him the moment you saw his name in the paper."

Chapter Twenty

A true friend is never truly gone. Their spirit lives on in the memories of those who loved them.—Amy Hoover

The next afternoon, Hunter checked into the Fairfield Inn, a motel not too far from the Backdoor Lounge. After he settled in, he called his parents in Caldwell Parish, and told them he had made it to West Monroe and had checked into the motel. He sat outside his room and watched the sky gray as the charcoal and black symmetry of storm clouds boiled into a gnarled pattern of turbulence above him. When rain fell, he dragged the chair back into the apartment and holed up in his room, sitting next to the window. He cut off the light and air conditioner and opened the window.

He sat there, staring through the open venetian blinds at the storm. The thunder was long and growling, and he listened as it rolled spatially across the sky. He willed the thunder to say something, to mean something, but all he heard or felt on the inside were his own song lyrics, all of them saying things about Caitlin. And the words echoed hollowly in some nether region and depth where he had never been able to go before. He was quiet and the room was quiet, and he listened to the rumbles of turbulence and the raindrops as they splashed in a staccato rhythm into standing water and pecked at the pile of beer cans he had thrown outside the door. The chords of a new song rolled like the thunder through his mind, the notes and words coming from somewhere from an unknown sullen muse.

At the Backdoor Lounge, Hunter began his show at eight. He spotted Caitlin and Melissa as they entered the bar. He had just begun John Mellencamp's song, "I Saw You First," when he and Caitlin locked eyes. He tried to ignore her, but she looked good, and he felt her eyes. He tried to focus on the song, wanting to burn his intensity into the crowd, but his eyes kept straying back to hers, and soon he realized he was singing to her again. She smiled and pulled her blonde hair back over her ear.

Shit. I should have known I'd run into her. What was I not thinking when I booked this gig?

Caitlin and Melissa walked to the bar and ordered drinks. He saw the bartender pour Caitlin a glass of red wine. He moved on to Johnny O'Neal's song, "It's True." He noticed how her body swayed to the music, and her lips mouthed many of the words as if she knew the song well, even though he suspected she had never heard it before. The song took over his heart somehow, and he gave up his attempt to focus on the crowd and only looked at her. Caitlin blew him a kiss and pointed to the bar, then moved across the room and sat on a corner stool.

When the song ended, he said, "Be right back, folks. Gonna take me a short break." He signaled the bartender to turn on the jukebox. After setting his Taylor guitar on its stand, he drained the last of his Scotch and walked over to her.

"Hey, Caitlin," he said.

"Hello, Hunter. How have you been?"

"Trying to get myself back together." He caught the eye of the bartender and nodded at their empty glasses.

"Coming right up, Hunter," the barmaid said.

"You really look good, Caitlin." He scanned her red legs and arms. "Did you get some sun today?"

"Yeah, a good bit."

"So how was Africa?" he asked.

"Sad," she said. "So sad, but I'm glad I went."

"I had a little vacation myself, courtesy of Ouachita Parish. Are you seeing anyone?"

"No," she said. "Not really. Are you?"

Not really means she is, but she's undecided. "No. You're still painting, I suppose."

"More than ever. Was that last song yours?"

"No, Johnny O'Neal wrote it. But I wish I had, and the song fits me. I identify with it. Never mind. You don't want to hear me talk about music."

Melissa cleared her throat.

"Oh," Caitlin said. "This is my friend, Melissa."

"So, you must be Hunter," Melissa said. "Caitlin's eternal love." She extended her hand, and Hunter shook it. "He is *fine*, Caitlin."

"Melissa is a writer, Hunter," Caitlin said. "She has a gift for melodrama. Don't listen to her. She's just had too much wine. You can quit batting those eyes now, Melissa."

"I wish some male here would get flirty," Melissa said. "I could use some attention. Hey, Led Zeppelin's on the jukebox. Let's dance, Caitlin. I bet we'll have men dancing with us in no time. "

"Sure." Caitlin said. "Want to join us, Hunter?"

"No," Hunter said. "I'll watch."

"I love for people to watch," Melissa said. "Caitlin does too if she'd admit it." She took Caitlin by the hand and they moved to the center of the dance floor and they danced freestyle. Melissa motioned for an ogling man to join them, and when he did, Caitlin exited and returned to Hunter.

"That girl is so naughty," Caitlin said. "I guess that's one of the reasons I love her so much. Speaking of naughty, how's that Mississippi poet I heard you were so crazy about?" Caitlin dropped her eyes. "Have you seen her?"

"Naw. Not lately anyway. I called her once or twice, but we were never able to get things off the ground. Too many logistical problems." *Like, she had a kid, she was too attached to Mississippi, she was working on a degree. And then there were all those other issues we were never able to get to.*

"I'm sorry," Caitlin said.

"Ending it wasn't my choice, it was hers. I'm not real sure anything with her even got started. How did you hear about her?"

"Monroe's a small town. If one person knows, everyone knows before long. And I know what you're trying to say, Hunter. You're making a point in your usual not subtle way that ending things between us was my choice, my fault."

"No, I'm not saying that. I know I'm not the easiest man to get along with. And just think, Caitlin, you could have stayed with me and had all this." He swept his arm regally in the air. "I think there's an old song that says you could share my smoky kingdom and have a barstool for your throne."

"Some kingdom. Going to hear you play in a smoky bar, as intoxicating as it was at first, isn't my idea of a great date. Fighting off flirting drunks, watching the groupies and floozies hit on you—that part of the scene got old after a while."

"So why are you here tonight? A wild girls' night out?"

"No. Since I came back from Africa, I'm not really into Monroe's bar scene. I don't want to get back in that loop. I saw your name in the paper, and I guess I had a moment of weakness. I just really wanted to see you again. Hope that's okay."

"Yeah, that's fine." Hunter's gut churned. *Goddamn it to hell. Why does she have to be so honest? Moment of weakness, my ass. It's been months, and nothing's changed between us. She's only been around me five minutes and my head is already spinning. And the worst thing about it is that she knows it.*

"I'm sorry about that last letter I sent you." Caitlin said. "Now I wish I hadn't sent it."

"Me too. Last letter? It was your only letter."

"You could have written me."

"And said what? That I screwed up that night? That I didn't want you to go to Africa? Actually, I did write you, a bunch of letters, but I never mailed them. Didn't even know where to send them. I'll even give them to you if you want to read them. You could sell them some day when I'm famous as my jail diary or something."

Caitlin slipped Hunter a piece of paper. "Here's my new phone number. I'm still living on my houseboat on the river. Come and see me when you get up in the morning. I'm going to listen to one more song, then I'm going home to get ready for my show tomorrow and check on my son."

"You have a son?"

"Yes, but you can get that worried look off your face. Tejan is not yours or anyone else's I've slept with. I adopted him when I was in Sierra Leone. He just turned sixteen. He was a boy-soldier of the Revolutionary United Front. His parents were killed along with everyone else in his village. My uncle, the priest I told you about, he helped me adopt him."

"Is he black? Who is the RUF?"

"Yes, he's black. Who are the RUF? We've had this talk before. God, I forget how people here don't keep up with world news at all. You need to at least listen to NPR on KEDM now that you're… back. The RUF stands for the Revolutionary United Front. They are about diamonds, death, slavery, amputations—among other things."

"What other things? Those sound bad enough."

"Don't make me talk about it, Hunter. I promised myself to only think happy thoughts tonight. Come see my art show tomorrow night and you'll understand. It has an African theme."

"I'm not surprised it has that theme." Hunter glanced at his wristwatch. "It's time for me to start my next set." He moved closer and placed his hand on her arm. "It's really good to see you again, Caitlin."

"Still evasive on commitment, I see," she said.

"What are you talking about?" Hunter asked.

Caitlin kissed him on the cheek, and the kiss was soft, and warm, and it reminded Hunter of too many things.

"Look, I *really* want you to come to my houseboat tomorrow, and then to my show that night," she said.

"Promise me."

"I'll try to make it, Caitlin," Hunter said. *I will not be a pushover,* he told himself. *I will not be a pushover.*

"That's not much of a promise. You better not stand me up. It's not like I'm going to ask you to marry me or anything like that. Well, like I said, one more song, and then I've got to leave. What are you going to play?"

"I don't know, but I'll decide by the time I pick up my guitar." Hunter returned to his guitar and stool, turned on his sound system and began, "Ashes by Now."

Caitlin watched him, the way she used to watch him when they had dated. But as he got into the song her face flushed and she looked away. He sang on.

Melissa grabbed a guy she knew at a pool table and dragged him to the dance floor. Melissa signaled for Caitlin to join them, but she shook her head and remained at the bar. She did not look at Hunter.

After the song, Melissa went to Hunter and said, "I enjoy your music. You have the gift, Hunter. But that was a tacky song-choice. I know what you're doing, and I think you hurt Caitlin by doing it. And what really burns my ass is that I think you wanted to hurt her."

"I'm glad you know what I'm doing, because whenever I'm around her, I don't."

"Don't pull that incurable romantic or suffering artist act on me. You knew exactly what you were doing. Look, she's my best friend, so promise me you won't lead her on and hurt her this time? I swear, Hunter, sometimes I don't know how two people who are so incompatible could ever have gotten together."

"I've changed. Well, at least I don't have a temper

anymore."

Someone in the audience shouted out, "Why don't you quit talking and play something good like 'Margaritaville!' "

"Why don't you kiss my ass!" Hunter said into the microphone, then cut it off, and looked at Melissa and shrugged his shoulder.

"What?" he said. "The guy would have pissed me off even if I hadn't seen Caitlin. Cover tunes. They always want the damn cover tunes."

Melissa bristled. "You're ignoring the subject. Caitlin said one reason she broke up with you was because you always felt you had to defend her."

"Sometimes all of us need defending."

"God knows she stood up for your sorry ass enough. I think you should apologize to her. She didn't have to come here tonight."

"Look, just get out of here, Melissa, if you're going to rag my ass all night."

Melissa looked at Caitlin, then back to Hunter. "I mean it, Hunter. Apologize. I don't know what your intentions are, but if you treat her like you did last time, you'll lose her. She's different now. Stronger. She won't put up with all the crap you used to give her. And just for your information, she really wanted to see you tonight. Don't blow this chance with her."

Hunter lit a cigarette and sighed. "Okay, okay, I'll apologize." He flipped on the microphone switch. "Give me a minute, folks. I've got something I've got to attend to." He set his guitar on its stand and walked over to Caitlin. He stood there a minute, then took her hand. "I'm sorry, Caitlin. It seems I can't help getting the dumbass sometimes. I was just hurt by seeing you again and something caused me to lash out."

Hunter felt it was another scene from the past. Another apology to the girl he's always adored and couldn't get out of his head. Another apology just like many others he had offered her. But this time he told himself he meant what he was saying.

****

The phone rang when Caitlin returned to her houseboat. Expecting it to be Von, she picked up the phone. "This is Caitlin. Yes, operator I'll hold." *God, I wish he would give me some space.*

"Caitlin, this is your uncle. I'm calling from London."

"Uncle Ambrose! How are you?"

"Doing well for an old man, child. I'm taking a sabbatical. My health is not what it used to be. Seems I picked up a bug or two during my stay in Sierra Leone. Reaming my insides out they are."

"I'm glad you're taking some time off. You need the rest. You'll be up to speed in no time. I heard on the news that things were not good in Freetown."

"Horrible situation it is. The city is in chaos."

"Have you talked to Mandy?"

"Oh, child…"

"What is it? What's wrong? Mandy's okay, isn't she?"

"Caitlin, Mandy was murdered in her room the night you left. I know I should have called sooner. I'm so sorry. I know she was a good friend, and a fine Christian too."

"The night I left? Who did it?"

"We don't know, child. It is tragic. Her family was devastated. How's my Tejan?"

"Uncle Ambrose, he's doing so well. Healthy, happy. He loves living here with me on the houseboat, and he's such a helper at the art gallery."

"Good, good. Are you still working for Vermeer?"

"No. When I returned from Africa, I wanted to rebuild my business at the gallery, so I quit."

"I'm glad you did. The legitimate Sierra Leone government has declared Von Vermeer *persona non grata*. Assuming the government can regain control, if he ever returns, he will be arrested for smuggling and war crimes."

"Why? Why would they want to arrest Von? He isn't a criminal, and he did so much good for the mission."

"The British ambassador told me that Vermeer has smuggled diamonds and guns for the RUF for over two years, Caitlin. Have you seen him?"

"Von? No, not since I left Freetown, but he's coming to Monroe soon. I've got his artifacts on display in my show at the museum. What should I do?"

"You have to return them, of course. Caitlin, as your uncle I'm asking you to break off all relations with him. As your priest, I could command it, but I won't— at least not yet. I hope I will not have to. Vermeer is an enemy of our faith and to all you're trying to do with Tejan. Are you listening to me, child?"

"Yes. It's just… I just can't believe what I'm hearing. And if it had come from anyone but you, I wouldn't believe it. He assured me his business was legitimate."

"Hopefully, your heart is not tangled up with him, but even if it is, you need to do what's right. When you see Father Robert at mass, tell him I'll contact him soon. Bless Father Robert's soul—he and his congregation were such generous supporters of the mission. Well, I must go, Caitlin. I'll try to call again soon. Take care of yourself and Tejan. May the saints protect you. Remember me in your prayers."

Caitlin managed to choke out, "I will. Goodbye, Uncle Ambrose."

Caitlin set the phone on the hook, went to the houseboat's deck and sat down, reeling from the ramifications of her uncle's call. Images of Mandy swarmed in her head like angry bees—Mandy smiling, fussing, telling bawdy jokes, tending to the boys. A best friend—murdered. She whispered, "She only wanted to help them."

And Von. Was her uncle exaggerating? Was Von really a diamond smuggler, a wanted man and in bed with the RUF—the very ones who had hurt Tejan and thousands of others? The thought of his charade infuriated her, and the thought that she had freely given herself to him sickened her.

Chapter Twenty-One

I grew up among wise men and found that there is nothing better for men than silence
—*Krio Proverb*

The next morning, Hunter drove to Caitlin's houseboat. He paused in the gravel parking lot of the Cottonport Lounge, which had closed after the last flood. The bar's whitewashed concrete block walls were now a dingy gray with a high-water mark about two feet up, smeared with a line of trash and dirt stuck to its surface. The same rusty chairs and rickety tables were stacked on the back patio, and the patio's wall was lined by two church pews, bought or borrowed or taken and brought to this new congregation. This confrontation with the forces of the unseen startled him, and images of Wednesday nights augured themselves into his brain like an old video documentary. He communed with ghosts of parties past, with people he knew no longer, his mind filling with the strains of paean and scolion never to be sung here again.

For over two years he had played here at the Cottonport, and for one of those years he had also used a bass and violin player. They had a good sound, and their relationship had been a good one, but the two other musicians had gone their separate ways with their own ghosts and stories and Hunter returned to playing solo.

He followed the stunted crape myrtle trees and azalea bushes that bordered the patio, his hand brushing brittle summer leaves. He had first met Caitlin here. She had walked down to the bar from her boat and sat alone in front of him as he played. He looked at the spot of ground where he had knelt like a thrall next to her chair, thinking of that moment when he had gained the image for the first poem he wrote her, a poem he still needed to set to music. Maybe someday. After the bar closed that night, they had necked in his truck, whispering shameless things like lovers sometimes do. Hunter believed that Caitlin must think of these things as well, every time she saw this bar. Every time.

The memories brought a smile and twinges of pain.

A hanging basket near the door held a fern—neglected, forgotten, but surviving. A ceiling fan drooped from the Sheetrock ceiling and the blades spun listless and slow, as if tapped by indiscernible fingers of a breeze. A life preserver and broken paddle hung on the wall, untouched and unused, but worn from weather and years. A stack of tiki lights stacked in the corner, the cane poles discolored and splitting. One table sat close to the river and scattered on the ground about it were fish scales and rotting fish heads.

Hunter faced the river, and his eyes darted to a deserted pink condominium, the highest point in Monroe. It sat on top of a decaying brown building that had once been a fine hotel, but was now the haven of bums, bats, and birds. The elevator had long quit working, but the adventurous could still venture up the stairs. He himself had trespassed once and remembered the stairwell marked by the DANGER: CONDEMNED

BUILDING sign.

From the pink, mysterious landmark, his eyes drifted down to the I-20 bridge, then to the railroad trestle, rusted, but solid. Hunter remembered the strange cry of the freight train as it approached the Cottonport Lounge and how the sound of rattling iron filled the air. As soon as he heard the train's horn, he would launch into Johnny Cash's "Folsom Prison Blues" until the train drowned his music, and then he would lay his guitar aside until the graffiti-covered cars passed. Sometimes the train was long, and they all listened for several minutes while the rhythmic cacophony of the train's passing transported each to secret memories.

The trestle rested on huge concrete columns, and the trestle had suffered the ravages of time and the elements. Vines as thick as barge cables draped their leafy beards down the sides of the pillars. Like many people Hunter knew, the vines clung stubbornly to the thin soil of their existence in a place where one shouldn't be able to exist at all. The trestle's decorative veneer of bricks was now colorless, and many bricks were absent, lost to the river's voracious chewing. Occasionally, a pigeon emerged from its roost under the bridge and flew toward deserted buildings lining the Monroe side of the levee.

Growing on the edge of the river and rising above the Cottonport stood a willow, whose trunk split into five sections, each beam a foot thick. Its branches twisted high into the air. Killdeers and curlews, chimney sweeps and gulls, dived into the water and rested on the bank, and Hunter listened to their plaintive cries that questioned, called, and conversed with the ears of unknown recipients. The tin roof of a party barge just downstream creaked as it rocked, and he could hear the wake paddle the bottom boat's barrels like they were drums. The river's waves lapped the shore like a lover's kiss before the river stilled again, and then the sound of the waves was replaced by the sound of locusts.

A bass fisherman chugged upstream, his small outboard humming steadily. Then a jet-ski, then a speedboat, then another party barge. A girl on its deck waved. Another passenger shouted something unintelligible.

Hunter stood here and faced all the ghosts of the river, then walked through the gravel parking lot to the wooden dock with steps winding their way down to Caitlin's houseboat. There was a jon boat tied to its side. As he came on board, he found Caitlin sitting cross-legged on the deck, in shorts and tank top, a sketchpad in her lap. She glanced up and saw him.

"Hello, Hunter," she called out. "Take a seat."

He sat down next to her and lit a cigarette and watched her draw.

"When are you going to lay those cigarettes down?" she asked. "You know I hate smoking."

"Some habits are hard to shake. Like you for instance."

"Habits. They eat up so much of our life that we don't even enjoy them, maybe not even notice them till we try to give them up or are taken away."

Tejan, clad only in a pair of Nike shorts, laid down his fishing rod and moved next to Caitlin, his eyes fixed on Hunter.

"It's okay, Tejan," Caitlin said. "Hunter's a friend of mama's. Tejan, would you get each of us a glass of iced tea?"

"*Oui,*" Tejan said.

After Tejan stepped inside the cabin, Hunter said, "That's your son, I guess. He doesn't seem to have much to say."

"Yes, Tejan's my son. He's on the quiet side, but he's so much better now."

"What do you mean? Was he sick? He looks healthy enough to me."

"Yes, he was very sick. He carried two tropical diseases. He had been shot at least three times at one time or another. But on the inside he was much worse. He was an orphan. One of the mission's priests agreed to help me adopt Tejan because he had known Tejan for many years. When we learned the mission would be shut down, he was afraid that if Tejan were taken to one of the government rehabilitation camps, he would regress and return to being a soldier—only this time, in the government's army."

"Wouldn't the legitimate government be the good guys? Nothing's wrong with a military career."

"Armies there are not like ours. There, armies are the tools of politics, and in Sierra Leone, atrocities were committed by rebels and government soldiers alike. Sometimes it was difficult to identify who was right, who was worse.

"Anyway, for some reason, I fell in love with Tejan. I had to get him away from Sierra Leone. After seeing what I saw in Africa, I feel there's so much evil that I don't know how the universe can hold together."

"What holds you together?" Hunter asked.

"Love. My art. Memories. Tejan. What's holding you together?"

Hunter paused, then shook his head. "I don't know. I'm not even sure if anything in me is sticking to anything."

"I know prison must have been hard on you. I'm sorry you had to go through that. What was it like?"

"Well, it wasn't like being in a Mexican prison, but it was bad enough. The work kept me busy and kept my mind off things mostly. Picked up a lot of trash along the highways for Ouachita Parish. I took every work detail I could get that was outside. That kept me away from the lazy-butt trash inside who got into most of the trouble. No prison time is easy time. But in other ways, it made me more of a musician. I wrote a lot. You'd never guess who I wrote about."

Caitlin blushed. "And Africa made me more of a painter." She touched his chin, turned his face as if she studied his profile. "Still the same Hunter. Strong face. Sadder eyes. This art show tonight is important to me. I want you to come and see it."

"It's Sunday, so I think I can make it. I won't be working."

"Oh, yeah, I've got something for you." She went inside and returned with the *bolon*. "This is for you. It's called a *bolon*."

"It's beautiful. Thank you. I wish I had brought you something."

"Don't worry about it. Seeing you again is gift enough."

Hunter plucked on the *bolon* for a while, then they sat in a wordless silence, drinking tea, hearing and watching the killdeers as they soared and swirled over the river. When Caitlin took his hand, Hunter noticed how different her touch felt to him.

Chapter Twenty-Two

You can recognize a person's tribe by the way he cries.
—Krio Proverb

Hunter left the houseboat about noon. He had only been gone a few minutes when Caitlin remembered that she needed some things from the convenience store.

"Tejan, will you walk with mama to the store?"

"Mama knows Tejan will go. I like to walk."

"Good." Caitlin was amazed at Tejan's energy, but then, a one-mile walk would be nothing to a boy accustomed to the twenty-mile forced marches he had often taken in the tropical bush when he was a soldier.

When they reached the convenience store, Tejan paused in front of the dumpster. His fingertips traced the red spray paint graffiti.

BLOODS RULE MONROE.

"Mama, I fear they are here too. They have come from Africa for Tejan?"

Even thousands of miles away, the RUF still terrorizes my son. "No, Tejan. That is the writing of someone else. It's just graffiti."

When they stepped inside the store, Caitlin said to the manager, "Hi, Barry. How are you?"

"I'm fine, Miss Caitlin. Mighty fine. What can I do for you today?"

"I just need some milk and bread and a few other things." As she gathered up the items on her list, Tejan walked over to the video machine and watched a young boy play a game called *Jungle War*. Camouflaged soldiers jumped out of their hiding places attacking the player's persona with guns and machetes. The boy glanced at Tejan, then turned his attention back to the game. One by one his persona eliminated the soldiers on his screen.

"Do you want to play?" the boy asked Tejan as he dropped coins into the machine.

"No. I've played such games before—in Salone."

"Where's that?"

"Africa."

"You're the first real African I ever met. What were the games called?"

"I do not remember," Tejan said. "But the games were not fun for Tejan or the others."

The boy shrugged his shoulders and kept playing. "You talk funny," he said. "People from New Orleans talk funny too."

"No. Tejan is from Salone. I am come to go to school."

"You're not really from Africa. That's bullshit. I think you're from South Louisiana."

Tejan watched the young boy play at war.

The more Caitlin thought about the graffiti on the dumpster, the angrier she became. "Barry, I want a can of that spray paint behind the counter there."

After Caitlin paid Barry for the groceries and paint, she handed Tejan the sack of groceries, walked to the dumpster and sprayed the white paint over the graffiti. Three boys gathered at the street corner moved toward her. Two wore dew-rags and the other wore a bandana as a headband. They had on sleeveless T-shirts and their knee-length jean shorts sagged halfway down their butt.

"Lady, what do you think you're doing?" one asked.

"Cleaning up the environment. I don't want my son seeing this." Caitlin sprayed over another symbol. When Caitlin finished covering the gang words, she turned to walk away, but the three boys lined up in front of her to block her way.

"You best move those starched britches of yours and let me by," she said.

The three laughed.

"We got us a tough bitch here," the one with the headband said. "Likes our starched britches."

"I'd sure like to get into her britches," one said.

"*Qu'est-ce Qu'il ya, Maman?*" Tejan asked. He had followed her outside carrying their sack of groceries.

"Nothing's wrong, Tejan," she said, searching the dull, burned-out eyes of the three teens. "Let's go home," she said, trying again to step around them.

One stepped over and blocked her path "Tejan?" He adjusted the red scarf on his head, then said, "I thought some of my friends had dumb-ass names. Bitch, is this little black boy your man?"

"Why don't you shut your ignorant mouth. He's my son, asshole, and it's none of your business what we're doing."

"She sure is a sassy bitch," another said. "If he's her son, she must have a thing for black men. Maybe we can help her out."

"*Est-ce-qu'ils song soldats?*" Tejan asked.

Caitlin felt something clawing at her stomach. "*No, ils sont bandits.*"

"What, you from a foreign country or something? Why don't you speak American?"

"It's French, you moron," she said.

The other two laughed. "She nailed your ass, Jamal, didn't she," one said holding out his fist and then banging it on the fists of the others.

Tejan said, "*Qu'est-ce que tu veus me faire?*"

"*Ne fais pas quelque chose jusqu'à je te dit, Tejan.*

"*Je ne le permettrai pas à te faire mal.*" Tejan set the sack of groceries on the ground and motioned for them to take it.

One of the boys said, "Lady, we don't want your goddamn sack of groceries. Why don't you hand me your purse instead."

"Why don't you go screw yourself," Caitlin said. "I'm not going to give you my purse. You can get your crack money from someone else." Her purse hung across her body, and she pushed it behind her back.

"Jamal, sure looks like she's got your number," one said. "How'd she know you wanted some crack?"

"Shut up, man," Jamal said. "Now lady, let me have that purse." He pushed Caitlin against the dumpster, reaching behind her.

As soon as Caitlin heard Tejan groan, she regretted pushing the confrontation. Tejan uttered sounds she didn't recognize. Not an expression of fear, but something digging its way out from Tejan's insides, something primeval and frightening, much more terrifying than the three thugs before her.

When the boy continued to reach for her purse, Tejan stepped forward and pushed him back. "No. You do not touch her."

"Oh, big man. Going to save his white bitch?" He flashed a knife and waved it in cutting motions in the air.

It all seemed like one movement. Tejan fell to the ground and spun, a leg whipping the legs out from under the attacker and then he locked his legs around his chest. He grabbed the knife hand and bent the boy's wrist back so that it snapped. Tejan took the knife from the boy's hand, released him and sprang to his feet. One of the other boys lunged, but Tejan slapped his face with the flat of his foot. When that one threw a punch, Tejan parried, locked the boy's arm and thrust his palm into his face. Blood spurted from the man's nose. Tejan raked his eyes, slipped a leg behind him and straight-armed him to the ground. Caitlin heard the thud of the man's head as it struck the asphalt. His arm was twisted strangely. Caitlin was sure that Tejan must have torn the arm from its socket.

"I don't want none of this kung-fu shit," one boy said. "Let's get the hell out of here." He helped the one on the ground to his feet and together they ran away. The pair vanished around a corner, the two good arms between them wildly flailing the air.

The last one hadn't moved. He pulled a .22 automatic pistol from his back pocket. "I'm not in the mood for getting too active, so I think I'm gonna just pop your ass." He held the pistol sideways, pointing it at Caitlin, then pointing it at Tejan. "I got a T-shirt with your name on it. Who you want to get it first, you or your bitch here?" He swung the gun toward Caitlin again.

The thug never saw it coming—Tejan locked his

arm, snatched the gun from his hand, and tossed it to the ground. As the boy struggled to free himself, Tejan repeatedly slapped his face. For the first time in her life, Caitlin heard the sound of a snapped elbow. Tejan held his lock on the broken arm and ground the boy's face into the pavement.

Caitlin knelt down and hissed in the attacker's ear. "His name's Tejan. He's only sixteen, but he's been a soldier since he was eleven. You punks are sissies compared to him. He's killed over a hundred people in battle. He's used a machete to cut off ears, fingers, hands, feet. And if I tell him to, he'll use your friend's knife and do it to you. Now, will you leave us alone?"

"I'm going to kill this African."

"Tejan, *plus ferme!*"

Tejan thrust the man's face into the asphalt and wrapped one hand around his neck.

Caitlin heard gurgling noises coming from his throat. "I would think twice about your plans of being a career gangbanger. You don't have it in you. Will you leave us alone if he lets you up?"

He managed to squeak out a garbled *yes* sound.

"Let him go, Tejan. *Permettez le d'aller.*"

But Tejan, talking to himself in Temne, didn't let go. Instead, his muscles hardened and he tightened his grip until his nails dug into the boy's skin and streaks of blood dripped from his fingertips. Caitlin again thought she made a mistake. Maybe she should have given up the purse. She had to calm Tejan before he killed this attacker.

Caitlin placed her hand on Tejan's shoulder. "*S'il vous plait, pour mamá.* Tejan, please, for mama."

Tejan finally released his grip and hooked such a

vicious kick into the boy's ribs that Caitlin winced. Tejan picked up the pistol and the knife and dropped them into the grocery sack. He was breathing hard. He pointed down the street and shouted, "Get up! Leave us alone! We have no diamonds!" He kicked the man in the ribs again.

The man struggled to his feet and half-running, half-limping, followed his friends' trail around the corner. Caitlin looked at Tejan's face. She didn't like what she saw in Tejan's eyes—the battle between the boy and the monster, the instinct for self-preservation, the struggle between the human and the soulless, the struggle of the sweet Tejan with the boy soldier who had played the machete games, all so black and white hands could end up full of diamonds—bloody diamonds, blood diamonds.

A baseball bat in his hands, Barry ran out of his store. "Are you okay, Caitlin? I heard the ruckus and came out as quick as I could. I've just called the police. They should be here any moment."

Caitlin was dizzy from hyperventilating. "Good. I hope they catch them. They shouldn't be hard to find. Tell the police that three boys with broken arms tried to snatch my purse and hurt us, but Tejan stopped them. We're going home. If they need to talk to me, send them to the boat."

"Broke arms? Who broke their arms?"

"Tejan did, but he was protecting me. They threatened us, Barry."

"You probably should wait until the police get here."

"No, we're going home. I really don't want to talk to the police. Tell them whatever you want."

Caitlin and Tejan said nothing on the walk home. By the time they reached the boat, Tejan was crying. He moved to the far side of the boat, retrieved the pistol from the sack and sighted down the barrel. Turning it over in his palm, he studied it. He turned as if facing an imaginary person. "Boy, do not bring your rebel ways here," he said, quoting someone Caitlin did not know. Tejan tossed the pistol into the river, then he did the same with the knife, then turned to Caitlin. "Tejan is sorry, *Mamá*. He promised to not be soldier again. You will send Tejan away now?"

Caitlin clutched him to her. "No, Tejan, never. Today, you were a good soldier, and you protected your *mamá*."

Caitlin sat next to Tejan for two hours while he cried all the tears he had inside of him. Only once before had she had seen him cry like this. In Sierra Leone, after Tejan had agreed to talk of his experiences, she and Father Ambrose took him to the banks of the Mabole River. They had spent the afternoon on the river's banks talking. There, the priest told Tejan about all the things Tejan had done to the people of his own district, and how he had seen Tejan kill his own grandfather.

Chapter Twenty-Three

The role of the artist is to not look away.
—Akiro Kurosawa

Hunter returned to his room and slept until late in the afternoon. When he woke, he sat on the edge of the bed and reached for a cigarette. "I'm getting too old for this late-night shit," he said out loud to the nothing he greeted each time he woke. His body felt like it had taken another beating. He wondered why he put himself through this grueling routine, then just as quickly, he thought of the answer. He was driven to see what was there, to see what life and music really had to show him, and there was no other way to know life's arcane secrets other than by showing up and having the guts to not turn one's head when she spoke.

During his nap, Hunter had dreamed of being with Caitlin again, and the dream was sweet, without sex, just him and her together. The same dream had often haunted him while in prison, and in the morning the dream's memory drove him crazy because it was only a dream and would likely never be a reality.

Hunter dressed and walked down to the Waffle House. After he ate, he walked along Highway 80, until his head cleared and his energy level rose, then he walked back to his room to clean up and get ready for Caitlin's show.

Hunter went to the hotel desk and asked for an iron. In his room, he showered, then dug into his duffel bag and pulled out the only pair of dress khaki pants he had and a white Oxford shirt. He ironed his pants and shirt carefully on the dresser top. After he dressed, he studied himself in the mirror, trying to remember what he looked like a year ago when he and Caitlin had dated. She looked the same—the long, curly blonde hair, the blushing skin of her fair face, the blue eyes. Yet, somehow, she looked more beautiful than ever.

Hunter saw himself differently, and he felt that if Caitlin couldn't see the difference, she must be blind. His body was much more scarred than the body she had known before, and he knew his insides were as well. Scars—injuries, wounds, badges of shame, of stupidity, of failure. Many things can happen to a man in prison. And the jabs of pain he felt occasionally were more than the bruised and broken ribs from prison fights, or from the scar left by the prison shank that had nicked his kidney—or the sore spot in his heart.

The Lost Bazaar was crowded with people and Hunter could feel and hear the buzz of the energy her work generated. Inside, Hunter spotted Caitlin. She was dressed in black—a short skirt, and a top sheer enough that he could see her bra underneath. She was talking to a couple and she gave him a small finger wave. While she was occupied with them, he picked up a glass of red wine from Melissa's tray when she walked by, then strolled through the exhibit. A collection of African artifacts hung on the wall. All of Caitlin's paintings were of Africa —mostly oil and watercolor—and they were unsettling. He noticed several boys in the paintings had Tejan's face

He found a stack of Caitlin's artist statements on a table and picked one up.

BLOOD DIAMONDS: A STORY OF AFRICA
BY CAITLIN JOHNSON

My time in Africa was the richest, yet most painful journey of my life. The worst was the suffering I saw, and the best was the fact that I gained a son, Tejan. It is his face you see in many of the paintings. The images in this collection are our story of Sierra Leone, once a beautiful land with beautiful people, now a land ruined by greed—greed for power, and especially for diamonds.

It is hard for Americans to grasp the horror this land suffers as a result of diamonds—these pretty little stones, which Marilyn Monroe described as "a girl's best friend." Today, the diamonds of Sierra Leone are mined by slave labor and exchanged for guns in a vicious cycle of suffering. Children are taken into forced slavery as laborers, prostitutes, or soldiers. They are beaten and drugged and used until they are soulless. Citizens are often the victims of pillage, rape, torture, and amputations. Salone is a place where a diamond can literally cost an arm or a leg. These images have haunted my mind for over a year, and in the creation of these paintings, I have experienced a strange catharsis.

I have inexpressible joy when I remember my time at the Xaverian Mission in Freetown, Sierra Leone. But I also have moments of terror and anger and deep sadness as a result of having watched this beautiful land disembowel itself. View these paintings with your heart. None of them are for sale at this time. Perhaps at a later time I can bear to part with them. This exhibition is scheduled to be presented at several diamond conventions this summer, and for the Louisiana Senate in September when I am scheduled to speak on behalf of State legislation requiring proof of origin for all diamonds sold in the United States. I am asking our state government to allow Louisiana to be the first to implement this legislation.

"Good luck on getting Louisiana to be the first at doing anything," Hunter said out loud. "We tend to study the failures of others states and then imitate them."

"Excuse me?" a man next to him said.

"Nothing. Just thinking out loud."

Hunter folded and stuffed Caitlin's artist statement into his pocket, then strolled around and studied the paintings. There was a painting of her Uncle Ambrose, one of a worker whose name was Mandy, and another of a group of boys in a class at the mission. The centerpiece of the show was called *Blood Diamonds*, and in it a boy held out two arms. One arm was missing a hand, but the good hand held diamonds which sparkled and flashed. The boy stared at the diamonds as if mesmerized.

He moved on to *Operation No Living Thing*, which portrayed soldiers moving through a burning village. The ground was covered with dead bodies. Next, he saw *Operation Pay Yourself* in which villagers were stopped at a roadblock and piling their belongings at the feet of some very young soldiers. He moved on to the next, *So You Won't Vote*, an image of a line of people behind a block of wood where a youth had raised a machete to cut off a villager's hand. Another, titled *Boy Soldiers*, pictured a marching regiment of very young boys carrying AK 47's and machetes. Next to it was

Sierra C-section. In this painting, a grinning, wild-eyed soldier held a machete in one hand and in the other what seemed to be a very small baby. On the ground at his feet lay the naked body of a young woman.

Soon, Caitlin did something Hunter didn't know she could do. She moved to a podium and made a speech.

"I want to thank all of you for attending this reception at the Lost Bazaar. Every day, a constant stream of men make their way to the bazaars of diamond merchants in Sierra Leone, Liberia, Guinea, and Angola. The men—miners, thieves, and soldiers—arrive alone, or in small groups. Some would have walked a month or more with one or more stones wrapped in cloth or newspapers and hidden in jean pockets or body orifices. They would arrive, having successfully evaded roadblocks, soldiers, gangs, and armies. After they are paid, the travelers slip back into the bush and return to their families or the place they were sent from. And once there, each man resumes his thieving, soldiering, or the backbreaking work of mining. They will break their backs, ruin their health, and risk prison seeking the little stones they hope will deliver them from their poverty-ridden existence.

"Now, the citizens of Sierra Leone sigh when they remember how organized and beautiful the mining districts of Sierra Leone were before the civil war. The earth itself had paid a high price for man's voracious quest for diamonds. In Sierra Leone, the diamonds are close to the surface, nearer to man's hands than anywhere else in the world. Without tight government controls, riverbeds and dry land had been dug, panned, sifted, and searched until the earth was pocked as if stricken by an eruptive disease. Parts of the once beautiful country are now so full of craters and holes that it resembles an artillery-blasted World War I battlefield.

"These small milky-colored diamonds are the smuggler's perfect commodity. They are virtually undetectable in transport. The stones' exodus from West Africa might be by plane, by boat, by pigeon, in letters, in sandwiches, in watchbands, or packed inside tourist souvenirs. The stones' destination would be Israel, Antwerp, Amsterdam, or India to be cut and polished before being sold again. The journey of the blood diamonds ends when they are set in gold, silver, or platinum, and then as multi-faceted tokens of love and beauty, placed on the hands and wrists and necks of American and European women. Yet, as Cupid's trophies, the stones would say nothing of the sad and gory stories of their genesis or the terrors and travail from whence the stones came, or the life of crime the stone had lived, or the bloody or corrupt hands that have handled them."

Caitlin's speech and paintings jarred something loose on his insides, and Hunter felt queasy. He decided he had seen and heard enough. He moved to the refreshment table and quickly drained two glasses of wine. As he was about to pour another glass, he felt Caitlin's hand on his shoulder.

"Hey, Hunter, slow down on that stuff—as you used to say to me."

Hunter spoke without looking at her. "How can you produce work like this, Caitlin? This is nothing like the art you used to do."

"No, it's not. I've given up painting swamp and

Cajun scenes for a while. I admit, the show is intense, but it's a story that must be told."

"But Caitlin, I liked the Louisiana paintings. And these… they're so graphic. I wasn't ready for what I saw in your paintings. Looking at your paintings is like going to a horror show. You're telling me you came up with this because of your stay in Sierra Leone? Jesus Christ!"

"Jesus wasn't there, Hunter. He really wasn't. Most probably don't believe the conditions were as bad as I've tried to portray them. And really, they weren't— they were worse." Caitlin decided to not mention what happened to the statue she had made for Hunter since he didn't even seem to notice its absence. Let the river hold its secrets.

"Who's the white dude in a couple of the paintings?" Hunter asked.

"A diamond merchant I met. I used to work for him, and we dated a few times. He's very rich and very talented. He's supposed to be here tonight."

"You also use Tejan's face in your paintings," Hunter said.

"Yes, I use his face. I love him, I hurt for him, and he is Africa to me. I wonder what songs you'd write if you went to Africa."

"Going to Africa is not at the top my list, but I do wonder what songs I could have written if we hadn't split up."

She leaned over and kissed him on the cheek. "You're not done writing about me yet. I've missed you, Hunter. I mean, I have really missed you. You'll come to my reception party on the boat tomorrow night?"

"Yeah, but I can't get there till after midnight. Jed's hired me for the Back Door Lounge."

"Well, come anyway. The party will go way beyond midnight. And bring your guitar. I want Tejan to hear you play."

Three men entered the Lost Bazaar. One waved and called out, "Caitlin!"

"Excuse me, Hunter. He's the owner of Vermeer Diamonds and the benefactor for the African artifacts. I need to introduce him to the guests. The *News Star* reporter is here somewhere, and I need to find her so she can interview him."

"All right. I'm tired, so I need to get back to my room anyway."

"Oh, don't leave yet. Hang with Melissa and drink some wine."

Hunter did take another glass of wine, and he studied the three men. In her painting, Caitlin had portrayed Von Vermeer well in her painting. Tonight, he exuded arrogance in his high-dollar suit. Hunter didn't like him.

The large black man and the other white man also wore suits, but they lacked Von's refinement. Their faces were harder and their bodies more muscular. Hunter eased up behind Caitlin as she talked with them.

Von put his arm around Caitlin's waist, pulled her to him, and kissed her. "Caitlin, I'm so sorry we're late for the reception. We missed our connection in Atlanta, and that threw us off schedule a couple of hours."

"I'm glad you made it here safely. Well, Biko and Rilke. I wasn't expecting to see you in Monroe. Does Von need security that badly?"

"Hello, girl," Biko said. "Yes, Von, he be bad boy.

He cause trouble everywhere. He needs us with him."

"Caitlin," Rilke said, "I'd still like to steal you away from Von."

"Rilke, you are still the patronizing flirt I met in Sierra Leone."

"Biko and Rilke are multi-talented men, Caitlin," Von said. "Not only do they provide excellent security, they have good business sense. How were the artifacts received?"

"People are in awe, Von." She hooked her arm into his. "Biko, you and Mr. Rilke can help yourself to the cheese and wine. There's a reporter here that needs to interview Von."

Caitlin passed by Hunter without a word or introduction to Von. Hunter saw Melissa and picked his way through the crowd back to her.

"So, that's Caitlin's old boss," Hunter said. Caitlin and Von now were talking to the reporter. As the reporter took their picture, Von put his arm around Caitlin's waist and kissed her on the cheek. "Seems like a friendly sort of fellow, a real kissy sort too."

"He certainly has the gift of gab," Melissa said.

"Gab. That's another word for bullshit, isn't it?"

"Hunter, I do think you're a little jealous."

"So, are the three of us going to do something after the show?"

"I can hang out with you, but Caitlin can't. She has to meet with Von."

"Why?"

"She kept books for him in Africa, so she has to turn those over to him. She's also going to explain why she quit the diamond store." Melissa took Hunter's arm. "Let's get some more wine. I'm sorry I was such a bitch at the Back Door Lounge, Hunter. I didn't mean anything by what I said. Really. Caitlin will be happy you came to our little soiree tonight."

"Don't worry. I deserve a good thrashing most days." Von's hands seemed to touch Caitlin constantly. "This guy is acting like she's more than an employee."

"She dated him in Africa." Melissa leaned over and whispered, "But just so you'll feel better about things, she's also going to make it clear tonight she's not interested in dating him anymore."

"Oh," Hunter said. "Maybe I will hang around. How long can it take to break up with someone?"

****

Von dropped Rilke and Biko at the hotel, and he and Caitlin drove to a diner. After they placed their orders, Von said, "At last, we are alone, even though I'd rather we be alone in a room somewhere."

Caitlin set a small bookbag on their table "Here's the records I kept for you in Freetown."

Von nodded, then placed the bag on the seat beside him. He scanned the diner and shook his head. "Why would you want to come here? I could have taken you to a much nicer place."

"Because we need to talk, Von, and I want you to listen to me. This is hard for me to say, but I don't think we should date anymore. I've decided to get back with Hunter."

"Your old boyfriend? You're kidding me. You want to jeopardize what we have for some country bumpkin?"

"Von, stop it. We've had a great time, but it's time for both of us to move on. I'm not suited for your world. I don't belong there. I don't even want to be in it."

"You are talking crazy. Haven't I been good to you? Give me one reason why you don't want to be in my world."

"Because you worked with the RUF for one thing. I don't know exactly what you did with them, but if you did anything, it's too much."

"Where would you get such a ridiculous notion?"

"My uncle told me. He said you'd be arrested if you ever returned to Sierra Leone."

Von sipped his coffee and signaled the waitress for a refill. "Business is complicated in Africa, Caitlin. It's like working in a madhouse—one day something's legal, the next day it is not. One day the government official you see has complete authority, the next day he's in prison. You saw firsthand the extent of graft and bribery there. If you fail to pay the right person, or fail to pay enough, they will use whatever influence they have to coerce you to do so. In this case, I think my competitors poisoned the well so to speak by attaching me to the RUF. It's like calling someone a child molester here. How can you prove you're not?"

"Is that really what happened? You weren't running guns and getting diamonds from the RUF?"

"Caitlin, I am a simple businessman. I assure you that whatever transactions I entered into, I did so with a clear conscience and the tacit approval of the government. And every diamond I've ever purchased or exported had a certificate of authenticity. My diamonds are legitimate. They are not conflict diamonds."

"Oh," she said. After her stay in Africa, Caitlin could see how a businessman could easily find himself in awkward situations that would require ethical compromises. Bribery seemed to be ingrained into the West African psyche. The mission staff itself had been forced to bribe some officials from time to time to insure they had electricity and security. Nearly every passenger on her flight out of Freetown had slipped the customs officials money to avoid a time-consuming search of their luggage.

"But the RUF? Do you really do business with them?"

Von drummed his fingers on the table, and his lips tightened the way a man does when he wants to think as he talks. "Everyone in Sierra Leone does business with the RUF. Even those who succeeded in blacklisting me. I'm not worried though. My approved status will be restored, once I find the official I neglected to bribe. So, does that explanation satisfy you?"

Caitlin set down her Reuben and wiped her mouth with her napkin. "Yes, Von. I'm sorry. God, I must have sounded so accusing. I had forgotten how complicated doing business in Africa can be."

"And I understand your wanting to see this Hunter. I probably have been rushing you a little. Just don't dismiss me entirely, okay?"

"I don't know, Von. If you can handle the fact that I'm also seeing someone else, I guess we could still go out once in a while—at least until things become more serious. Can you accept that?"

Von snapped his finger to get the waitress's attention, signaling her to bring the check. "I'm not worried. You'll change your mind about this hick. You belong in my world, and you know it. What are you doing tomorrow night? Let's go to a movie and a decent dinner."

"I would love to, Von, but Hunter and I already have plans. Can I have a rain check?"

After Von drove Caitlin home, he called one of his contacts in Sierra Leone.

"Why do you have to ask?" Von said. "You know what I want you to do. Find out who it was that put my name on that list and either get him on our payroll or kill him. I expect to hear from you tomorrow."

He hung up the phone. This situation was more of an annoyance than a problem. Africa had no shortage of annoyances.

Chapter Twenty-Four

Music doesn't lie. If there is something to be changed in this world, then it can only happen through music.

–Jimi Hendrix

Outside the Backdoor Lounge, Hunter took a slow deep breath. The air was balmy and warm, with a dense humidity that felt like a kiss to his skin. After he packed his truck, he drove to Caitlin's boat. He parked in the Cottonport Lounge parking lot, opened the truck's topper, and retrieved his guitar. He walked toward Caitlin's houseboat, following the waning light of a trail of candle lanterns.

As he came onboard, he saw Melissa sitting on the gunwale, her dress hiked up to her thighs and pressed down between her legs. She said, "Hey, Hunter."

"Good crowd for the party?"

"The boat was packed, but everyone's gone now except for me. I think Caitlin is in the cabin doing dishes." She looked over her shoulder and called out, "Hey, Caitlin! Hunter's here."

"Good. Tell him to take a seat and I'll be right out."

As soon as he set down his guitar, Tejan thrust a steaming ceramic plate into his hands, heaped full of fish and shrimp and red gravy over rice. "Mr. Hunter has worked hard tonight. *Mamá* says he must eat."

"Thank you, Tejan," Hunter said. "This smells great."

Caitlin came out of the cabin, wiping her hands on a dishcloth. "Tejan's a wonderful cook. And I think cooking is therapeutic for him. He insisted on cooking with palm oil. I had the devil of time finding it."

"Men in Louisiana have always cooked the special meals. He'll fit right in with our tradition." Hunter stuffed a forkful into his mouth. "It's good. He could start his own restaurant or catering business."

"That's a good idea," Caitlin said. "Monroe needs some food variety. I don't think we've ever had an African restaurant."

"What's he going to do about school?" Hunter asked.

"I'm home schooling him now. I'm hesitant to send him to a public school until he has some time to adjust. We're going to enroll him in West Monroe High School in January, though our priest wants me to send him to St. Fred's."

"Don't try to shelter him too much. I don't think it's healthy. Don't you want him to be around other boys his age?"

Caitlin poured Hunter a glass of Merlot and handed it to him. "No. He's not ready. I learned that today."

"Good God, and you say I'm overprotective. What do you mean you learned that today? What happened?"

"Tejan had a little run-in with some boys hanging out at Barry's store. But he's okay. I'm glad you brought your guitar. Would you play us some songs?"

"I can't believe my ears. You are asking me to play some music?"

Caitlin slapped at his arm. "Stop that teasing. You know I like your music. It's just better when it's not at a bar."

"I admit I've thought that myself a couple of times." Hunter set down his plate and lifted his Taylor from its case. He lightly strummed a few chords to check it for tuning, then began playing. Even though he was buzzed from the wine, his fingers deftly moved along the guitar's neck, his right hand plucking notes to a melody swelling in his heart, fingering chords in a minor key. He sang softly, the lyrics describing a lonely sailor looking at the stars and thinking of his true love.

Tejan sat near him, his bare legs pulled up to his chest. "The song is sad, Mr. Hunter. I understand such songs."

As Hunter made a transition to the second verse, Tejan kept time with the African rattle, and hummed the song's melody as if he had heard it all his life.

Amazing, Hunter thought. *Maybe I didn't write this song. How can he know it?* Tejan picked up enough words of the chorus that soon they were singing together in harmony. Hunter then did a faster song, one about the Southern Cross. Tejan accompanied him on a *djembe*, striking the leather drumhead with his hand. Hunter noticed three distinct tones Tejan drew from the instrument, and some rhythms he had never heard. When he ended the song, he said, "Where did you learn to play?"

"My father, he teach me to play *djembe*. *Mamá*, she buy the drum for me."

"Now, you play, Tejan. Just you and the drum."

"This is a song of our village, written long ago. It honors the strong and brave men that came from our village in Guinea."

Using the three basic strokes of the *djembe* drummers, Tejan slapped out a rhythm that was fluid, complex, polyrhythmic, throbbing, at times rolling. Tejan closed his eyes and lost himself in its cadence that ebbed and flowed as strong as an ocean tide. He accelerated the beat into a blistering tempo, then slowed and softened his strikes so that the song faded into the night. A ten-minute song the night of Monroe had never heard.

Hunter's head reeled from the impact of the song and the images it evoked. "I've heard conga players in New Orleans, but I've never experienced anything like this. I feel like I've been in Africa. I think people would pay good money to hear you play like that. You could be a star. Do you have more songs?"

"I have many, but I will not give them for money. A star?" Tejan looked up at the black scrim of the sky with the stars splattered brightly across it. "My people say the stars are fireflies that flew too high. A man must know when to stay on de ground."

Hunter played another song, and Tejan listened with rapt interest. When Hunter finished, Tejan said something in French to Caitlin. She leaned toward Hunter. "He asked me if you will teach him to play guitar."

"Sure. Tell him I'd be glad to. We'll start whenever he wants."

Tejan smiled. "Thank you, Mister Hunter."

"I think he speaks English better than he lets on," Hunter said.

Caitlin reached for Hunter's hand and squeezed it. "Yes, but sometimes he chooses not to, because he wants what we say to just be between us."

Melissa drained her wine and refilled their glasses. "I'm going to get drunk tonight."

"We're all going to get drunk tonight." Caitlin raised her glass. "To art. To borrow Auden's phrase, 'art for our sake.' "

"The savior of our souls," Melissa said.

"The mistress of our hearts," Hunter said. He fixed his eyes on Caitlin. "And to the muse who gives us our songs."

Caitlin handed Hunter another bottle of wine and a corkscrew. He opened the bottle and they filled their glasses again. "Now I have a toast," he said. "To the Lost Bazaar and my friends."

"To the Lost Bazaar, where anything goes," Melissa said. "The gallery of our erotic dreams," Melissa said.

"Naughty girl. To the Lost Bazaar," Caitlin said, shifting her eyes to Hunter. "Where one can find one's self, friends, or the love of her life."

"Oh, brother," Melissa said. "Let's not get mushy here. You two are so obvious. Why can't you be raunchy like me?"

"You're a writer, that's why." Caitlin turned on her CD player. The words of the songs she had chosen rattled Hunter's insides, songs that brought back memories and that seemed to tell their story. Caitlin pulled Hunter to his feet. "You're going to dance with me tonight." As they danced, she occasionally repeated lines of the song in his ear.

"It's been a long time since we danced together," she said.

"Too long," he replied.

"I wish we could stay like this forever."

The next song jumped to a faster tempo and Caitlin pushed Hunter away and danced freestyle, wiggling and shaking her hips, and once in a while giving Hunter a shimmy. Hunter wildly jumped about, slinging around his arms. Caitlin covered her mouth with her hand for a moment, then said, "You're a damn good musician, but you sure can't dance!"

Tejan set down his tray of dirty dishes and danced with them, mimicking Hunter's spastic movements. Hunter laughed until his face and chest hurt.

Melissa sat on the edge of the boat's ladder and dangled her feet in the water. "The water's warm. We should all go for a swim."

"I assume you're skinny dipping again?" Caitlin said.

"I didn't bring a suit. Besides, it dark," Melissa answered. "So, do you want to join me?"

"No, thanks. We'll just sit here till you're done."

Melissa moved to the other side of the boat. Hunter heard a small splash and rose to see.

"Hey," Caitlin said. She grabbed Hunter's shirt and pulled him down. "You're supposed to be looking at me tonight. That's something else, Hunter. I don't know if I can trust you around other women."

"Just checking out the scenery."

"Uh huh."

"I thought anything goes at the Lost Bazaar."

"It does, but not on our first night together in nearly a year."

When Hunter lit a cigarette, he saw three men standing under the streetlight on top of the levee. They seemed to be looking at the houseboat.

Caitlin noticed his gaze. "What's wrong?"

"I thought I saw some men looking this way. Over by the levee."

"Maybe they just heard the music."

Melissa finished her swim, dressed, and joined them.

Hunter set his guitar in its case and watched Tejan as he tied up the last sack of trash from the night's party.

"Will Mr. Hunter play his sad guitar more tonight?" Tejan asked.

"No. The world's heard me enough tonight. Like Tejan, I want to listen to the quiet. I want to hear a heartbeat." He looked at Caitlin.

Caitlin placed her hand on Hunter's shoulder.

"I like Mr. Hunter, *Mamá*," Tejan said. "He is a good man. *Il est amoureux de ma mère?*"

"*Oui, et je suis amoureux de lui.*"

"*Mamá*, Tejan will sleep outside tonight. He will watch stars move across the sky and guard the boat so Mama can sleep well." He looked at Hunter and smiled bashfully.

"Yes, thank you, Tejan," Caitlin said.

"You are good man, Mr. Hunter. Tejan not see many good man in his short life."

"I'm not a good man, Tejan. I've made many mistakes."

Tejan patted Hunter's chest. "No, you are good man. The eyes do not lie to Tejan. Tejan too has done many wrong things, but *Mamá's* eyes tells Tejan that he is good. And now Tejan feels like he is good man. Mama says you are good man too. And my *mamá* could never be wrong about a man. The heart is what makes the man."

Tejan went inside and fetched a pillow and quilt and climbed up on the top deck.

"I *was* wrong about you before, Hunter," Caitlin said. She moved to the cabin door and held out her hand to Hunter. "But I'm not wrong about you now. Am I?"

Hunter leaned over and kissed her. "No, you're not wrong."

Caitlin stood gently pulled him toward the cabin. "Goodnight, Tejan. Goodnight, Melissa."

"Oh, I guess I should be going," Melissa said.

"You're welcome to sleep here tonight, if you want, Melissa. Tejan will get you pillows and blankets."

"Why don't you take this good-looking man inside your boat and worry about yourself for once?" Melissa said. "The gallery's only a block away. I'm going to walk home."

Hunter fell asleep in Caitlin's arms, listening to the water lap at the boat's bottom and the wind whistle through the small window, rustling the curtain window above them, tossing, and playing delicately with the thin fabric. Hunter thought he had grown used to being alone, but the feeling of having Caitlin next to him proved he had not.

****

For the first time in many months, Caitlin didn't wrestle with insomnia. The soft shuffle of Tejan's bare feet on the deck above them and the sounds of the river were familiar, but tonight they were like a lullaby. She wondered if this night really meant she and Hunter were a couple again. And if it did, how long would it be before Hunter's old restlessness kicked in, before Lady

Music called him to some new place, before he screwed up with one of the easy groupies who followed musicians like Hunter around? Maybe he wouldn't find a way to screw things up. Perhaps things would go well this time. Maybe Hunter was *the one* for her and Tejan. The only certainty Caitlin felt was that even though she and Hunter had hurt each other deeply in the past, they loved each other, and because of that their destinies had to be connected in some way.

****

Hunter woke later that night and made his way to the bathroom. He stepped out on the deck and lit a cigarette. He saw a man in the Cottonport parking lot, digging in the dumpster. Odd. He rubbed his eyes and looked again. There was the ripped open trash bag from the party down on the ground, but no man in sight. On his way back to bed, he opened Caitlin's refrigerator and took out a bottle of water. As he chugged the water down, he saw a letter on the cabinet. It was addressed to Caitlin and had African stamps. He picked it up and in the dim light of the open refrigerator read it. He pitched the letter down and returned to Caitlin.

He slipped in the bed, stroked her cheek and shoulder, and whispered, "Caitlin, are you awake?"

"Hmmm? You hand feels so nice on my shoulder. Kiss me."

Hunter kissed her cheek. "Caitlin, This Von, how important is he to you?"

The question slapped Caitlin awake. She sat up in the bed and pulled her knees to her chest. "I meant to tell you about him, Hunter. Really, I did. Von was only my boss. I did date him in Africa."

"I know. Melissa told me. Are you in love with

him?"

"Was I attracted? Yes. In love? No."

"There was a letter by your icebox. I shouldn't have, but I read it. He seems to be nuts about you."

"Oh, yes, the letter. He writes and calls constantly. He says he's in love with me, but I think it's more of an infatuation."

"He's the diamond merchant in the painting? That came to your reception?"

"Yes."

"He seemed more than a little interested in you, don't you think?"

"Hunter, it's awkward. I agreed to date him, but that was before—before you and I got back together. In Africa, I wasn't counting on getting you back. I told him about us, told him I didn't want to date him seriously anymore."

"You don't have to do that. See him if you want. Maybe we are moving a little too fast here. I've no right to demand anything from you."

"You don't want us to be together?" she asked.

"I want it more than anything. I've wished for it every day since that night. But I want you to want it too."

"Oh, I do, Hunter. I do. I realize how much I've missed you and how incomplete I am without you. Besides, you've always said I was your muse. How can you create great music without a beautiful muse?"

"I can't." Hunter hugged her tightly. "Come to me, muse. Let's make some more music tonight."

****

Caitlin, with a mother's ear, heard Tejan groan. When she sprang from the bed, Hunter sat up.

"What is it, Caitlin?" Hunter mumbled.

"Something's wrong with Tejan. Go back to sleep, Hunter." She slipped on a pair of shorts. "I've got to go see about him. Sometimes he has nightmares. Please, go to sleep. It will be all right."

Caitlin touched Tejan's forehead. He burned with fever. "Oh, Tejan." She hurried to the sink, wet a washrag, and wiped his face. He opened his eyes and she knew he was lost in some alien dream. And the thought of where the dreams might take him—to the diamond pits, to the battlefield, to the villages—those thoughts oppressed and hurt her. But she knew that if she held him, if he heard her voice, he would be better in the morning, and he would wake up and realize he was on the Ouachita River with his new mother. At least the dreams recurred less often. *Time can heal us all. Time can heal anything.*

Chapter Twenty-Five

As you sell yourself, so the world will buy you.
—Krio Proverb

Von flew from Monroe to New York and delivered to his contacts a hundred diamonds he had hidden in sandwiches and suitcase linings. He negotiated another delivery in three weeks. Diamond Salone, Incorporated had rented an office in Manhattan and hired a full-time secretary to help him with the paperwork. From New York, he flew on to New Orleans.

Once in New Orleans, he rented a car and met with a jeweler who was interested in acquiring stones from Sierra Leone. Afterwards, he met Biko and Rilke at his hotel in the French Quarter.

"What about the firearms, Von?" Rilke asked.

"Well, first of all, we chose the right city to do business. I didn't realize these cowboys had so much money. Purchasing firearms will be no problem. Our friends in Sierra Leone have arranged for us to load a ship that will arrive at the port here soon."

"Are there any potential loading or export problems?" Rilke asked.

"No, none at all. The government is focused on looking for drugs, not for guns leaving the country. We'll have some losses eventually, but not as much as the drug dealers. We'll factor that projected loss into

Rickey Pittman

our expenses and the RUF will bear the expense. The Feds are understaffed here, so we'll feed them enough leads on some big drug deals to draw their attention from anything we would want to do."

"Playing head games with the government?" Rilke asked.

"Yes," Von said. "Government here is more efficient than in West Africa, but it still has obvious weaknesses."

"Biko wishes to go to Dallas, J.R.'s city. I see him on the telly many times," Biko said. "He is hero to me. He is rich man like Biko hope to be."

"I have no doubts you will succeed in your endeavor, Biko," Von said. "And getting you to Dallas will be no problem. Now, drink up so we can go and purchase some personal hardware. I'll show you how easy it is. Where are the diamonds?"

"In the lining of my suitcase," Rilke said.

"Good," Von said. "I've a buyer here in New Orleans."

"Well, let's go handle our business, then we'll take a road trip to North Louisiana." Rilke snorted. "You're going to see that flaky Yank girl again, aren't you?"

"Caitlin is expecting me, Rilke. I cannot disappoint her."

Biko said, "Perhaps when we finish our work in Monroe, we go to Dallas, J.R.'s city?"

"Sure," Von replied. "I'll take Biko to Dallas, and at my expense. Now, let's go to this gun show and see if we can place some orders."

At the gun show, Von used a fake ID to purchase three Glock .9mm's, three boxes of hollow point shells, a machete, and a large sheath knife. He also networked

250

and probed until he found one man with a Federal Firearms license willing to ship him a large quantity of semi-automatic rifles and pump shotguns—no questions asked.

Rilke was amazed. "Living here must be like living in a toy store, eh, Biko? I thought Africa was backward." He picked up an AK 47 from a table, slid back the bolt, then snapped it shut. "It's easier than I thought to buy a gun here, and they're in better condition than what we could buy in Freetown."

"Amazing, isn't it?" Von said. "There's a gun show here almost every month of the year. No wonder criminals here are so well armed."

As they drove from the gun show Von saw a smiling Biko in his rearview mirror, thumbing the edge of the knife he had bought, and studying his reflection on the blade.

"Do you like the knife, Biko?" Von asked.

"Yeah, mon, I like the knife."

Rilke chuckled. "Biko likes any blade. And you ought to see what he can do with them."

Von took Biko and Rilke on a tour of New Orleans. Outside of St. Louis Cemetery, they passed a gang of boys gathered on a corner.

Von said, "American youth at its finest. They stay high all the time. They steal, they fornicate, and they are violent. They like to do everything we had to force our boys to do when we first got them. Building an army here would be much easier than even in Africa if a man could recruit and train them quickly. They look like they'd make good soldiers."

"No," Biko said. "They're too soft, and too old. Biko likes young boys to make soldiers, so he can teach them everything they need to know." He opened an aspirin bottle and popped down a white pill.

Von, still glancing at Biko in the mirror, said, "How long have you been using speed, Biko?"

"Since I can't find Kola nuts here."

From the gun show, Von drove them to Monroe and checked them into a suite at a hotel. Von called Caitlin several times, each time leaving a message. He glanced at his watch.

"Von, it's late," Rilke said. "Be patient. You'll reach her. She's probably the type of woman who goes to bed early."

"Yes, she go to bed," Biko said. "But not to bed alone. One man can't fill de box!"

Chapter Twenty-Six

I can resist everything except temptation
—Oscar Wilde

Hunter booked himself gigs with several other clubs in Monroe and Ruston to get back into the Monroe loop. His income was enough to live on, but not enough to provide what normal people liked to have—things like insurance, a house, nice clothes, but he knew that sometimes one must choose between one's passion and material comfort and security and stability. Music was Hunter's passion, and sometimes the music provided these other things. As his routine set, so did the grinding physical weariness and mental fatigue. His days became a blur—work till midnight or beyond, unwind until two or three in the morning, sleep and rise late the next afternoon.

After a gig at the Backdoor Lounge, Hunter returned to his apartment and turned on the old television, which only picked up Channel 8, a local station. A late-night movie was on—*The Beast with Five Fingers*. Hunter studied the detached hand of the composer as it crawled about terrorizing and searching for its victims as if guided by a vindictive memory. He held up his left hand, then closed and opened his fingers twice. He reached for the remote and turned off the TV. There are some things one shouldn't think about.

Still wired and knowing that sleep would not come easily that night, he took his notebook and walked down to the Waffle House. A waitress brought his menu and water. He ordered coffee and eggs and bacon. The black cook listlessly scraped at the grill, lost in the inner world late night workers travel to. At the jukebox, Hunter selected some songs by Lyle Lovett and Pat Green and returned to his seat.

In a booth sat a mother and two daughters. The girls were very young and wore tiaras. Their tired faces were caked with makeup. One was asleep, face down on the table. The mother lectured the other who wore a filigreed sash across her chest that read, *Watermelon Queen.*

Stern of voice, the obese mother said, "You got to eat honey. We got a long drive to Atlanta tomorrow." The little girl with a woman's face nodded and rubbed her blank red eyes. She nibbled at the grilled cheese sandwich in front of her, then took a drink of her chocolate milk. She smiled at Hunter. A pageant smile—chin up and scarred by some forced facial contortion. She had an enormous puffed-up hairdo and long false eyelashes. Her hair and eyebrows were dyed. Raccoon eyes peered out from her mask of pancake foundation and rouge. Beneath her beaded lace jacket, she wore a blue rhinestone and sequin-covered dress split up the side almost to her hip. Somehow her outfit reminded him of the drag queens he had seen in New Orleans. All baubles and spangles. A painted doll with porcelain grin. Young child-bride of Frankenstein all dressed up.

The mother unbuckled her wristwatch and shook it. Her eyes met Hunter's. "You got the right time?"

Hunter glanced at the clock on the wall above the grill, then at his wristwatch. "It's three. I don't know that I've ever had the right time though. You folks traveling?"

"Yeah. Gotta get my pretty babies here to Atlanta. I been entering them in beauty contests. That's how we're going to pay for their college education. They already won over a dozen pageants each. Gonna take them all the way to the top." She gazed out the window like a desert monk who had just seen a vision.

"Yeah, I'm trying to get somewhere myself," Hunter said. He wanted to tell her that he's been at it long enough to know that it's a long way to the top of that mountain. And when you get there, it's never what you thought it would be. And after you've reached the summit, your strength is spent, clouds shroud the view, and what you wanted to see, you can't. And it's always a long, precarious way down. But at least the way down is always quicker. He wanted to tell her all these things, some of which he felt better than he knew, but he did not. *Elusive horizons*, Hunter thought. He remembered an English teacher and a poem of Stephen Crane. You lie, we tell each other, then we keep running for the horizon. One mirage replaces another, and soon you've gone so far you've lost your bearings and you don't know where it is you came from. And the horizon behind you fills with other mirages, but if you turn around and return that too will not be what you expected, and you wish you had kept going. And he and other musicians and the beauty queens and the hobos and the salesmen, traveling together toward that horizon, eking out a living, eating fast food or worse, spending weekends cooped up in cheap hotels, were all just moving along a crazy-quilt pattern of existence.

"I competed in beauty contests myself," the woman said, "until a few years ago. Ever since I was six years old, just like my little Skittles here. Won a whole bunch of beauty contests."

Hunter tried to envision the obese woman in another life, slim and bikini clad, sashaying coquettishly across a stage to the cheers of the audience and the delight of the panel of judges. Somehow the thought depressed him. "What does their daddy think about them entering these contests?"

"He's real proud of them," she said. "Real proud. Wish I could get him to come with us more. But he drives a truck and usually he's too tired out from working all week. He drives all over the nation. He's in New Mexico tonight.

"What do you do?" she asked.

"I'm a musician." He leaned over and pointed at the Backdoor's neon sign. "Name's Hunter. I'm playing at that bar yonder."

"For how long?"

Hunter shrugged. He didn't know. He never knew. His was the constant movement of the displaced. Even when the crowds loved him, they never asked him to stay. Didn't expect him to. Didn't care if he did or didn't. Only Caitlin had cared, and after things had gone bad, even she didn't care. Hunter shuddered at the thought of permanently trying to make a living with his music in Northeast Louisiana. On the other hand, he had tried living in Mississippi, in Texas, but it seemed like some dark hand of fate kept dragging his ass back.

"What did you say you did?" the lady asked. "Did you say you were a hunter? I'm tired and I done forgot what you said."

"Don't worry about it none. My name's Hunter. I'm a musician. I'm kinda tired myself but you'll be slap wore out by morning. Atlanta's eight or ten hours from here. Depends on if you have a heavy foot."

"I've gotten a few speeding tickets in my day." The mother left her beauty queens and went to her car. Returning with two plastic hangers and a suit bag, she sat down, lit a cigarette, then poked the sleeping daughter. "Skittles, you wake up now." She reached into her giant purse and shoved a jar of cold cream and a clothes hanger toward the girl. "You got to change out of your dress and put on your tanning cream. It'll be cool in the car, so you won't sweat none and you'll look real purty when we get to Atlanta. Take your flippers out first."

The little girl opened her mouth and unclipped a pair of false teeth that replaced lost baby teeth. She dropped the teeth into the mother's hand, stuffed the jar of cold cream into her own handbag, took the hangar, and vanished into the restroom. She returned in cutoffs and a T-shirt that said, BEAM ME UP SCOTTY; THERE'S NO INTELLIGENT LIFE HERE, and Hunter could see a patina of the cream on her face. She winked salaciously at Hunter as she passed him.

"Okay, Doodlebug, you're next," the mother said as she stuffed Skittles' dress into the suit bag.

"Oh, Mama," Doodlebug said. "I'm tired. I don't want to change."

"Your daddy worked long hours to pay for that dress and we want to take care of it. You'll get it all wrinkled if you wear it in the car all the way to Atlanta. Now, go on and show the nice Hunter man how a beauty queen walks."

The girl stood in the classic beauty queen pose, rear foot parallel to shoulder, front foot extended and pointing forward, her eyes scanning the Waffle House and flitting from customer to customer as if they were the judges she would see tomorrow. As she sashayed toward the restroom, she gave Hunter the same forced grimace of a smile she would give the judges in Atlanta. Hunter watched the mother pay for their meal and parade the girls out to their station wagon. Hunter wondered if a normal kid had a chance in winning beauty pageants.

This thought made his mind jump and wonder if he could make it in the music business. He knew a few locals had made it. They had gone to Nashville, gone on the road, and somehow obtained recording contracts. Some were not what Hunter considered great musicians or singers or song writers, but they had some kind of look, some kind of voice that was labeled as *commercial*. Most had used agents, but Hunter, who had known several of these musicians well, noticed that many things changed when they took on an agent. Every detail of their musical and social life was regimented and determined by the agent. They were told what to wear, where to play, what songs they could play, what to say in interviews, what songs they were to record, and what they were to say in interviews. Hunter knew of performers who hadn't raised their level of skill since he had known them. Some famous singers and performers sometimes didn't even sing or play an instrument in their concerts—it was a taped, carefully orchestrated performance full of special effects. To Hunter, the artist's soul seemed like a lot to give away.

Signing the agent's dotted line was like signing a devil's book. Too much fine print.

Hunter glanced at a man who sat alone in a booth under a sign that said booths were reserved for two or more. The man muttered to himself. Both of his hands were wrapped around his coffee cup. He thought he looked like the man he had seen at the Sundown Tavern. There were lost and lonely people everywhere.

"You want a refill?" the waitress asked Hunter.

"Yeah. Can I take a booth?"

"No," she said. "It's going to be busy before long. The after-hours bar crowd will come in."

He pointed to the man. "He has a booth and there ain't nobody else with him."

"He sure is having a talk with someone. Besides, I want to keep you close to me." She smiled.

Hunter looked at the tired, but pretty green eyes and sensed some sadness.

"Long night?" he asked.

"Yeah."

Hunter laid two dollars on the table and slid them toward her. "Do I have to leave now? I've got insomnia bad tonight."

"Like I said, I'd like the company. I don't get off till five. I heard you say your name was Hunter and that you were a musician?"

"Yeah, that's what I hope to be when I grow up."

"I'm Veronica. I like that name, Hunter. What do you hunt?"

"Old joke. But I do like to chase down good-looking girls now and then."

"You are so funny, and so cute!" She reached behind her and grabbed a Polaroid camera, sighted it at

Hunter, and snapped his photograph. The flash blinded Hunter's eyes. It had been over a year since anyone had taken his picture. He heard an echo in his memory telling him to turn right.

"Why'd you do that?" Hunter asked.

"For my scrapbook," she said. "I can tell my friends I knew a handsome musician who used to play at the Backdoor Lounge before he became famous." She wrote *Hunter* on the back of the picture and then set it on top of one of the coolers.

"Ain't it illegal to try and scare your customers by sticking ugly pictures like that on the wall?"

"Pshaw. Listen to you. Ugly, my foot."

Hunter and she talked till her shift ended, and then he left without saying goodbye, knowing if he had asked, he could have taken her to his room. She was truly pretty, and like him, on the low end of thirty. But as he walked back to his room thinking these things, something in him felt bad, like he was being unfaithful to Caitlin in some way.

Caitlin doesn't own me. Nothing's been said by either of us about committing fully to a monogamous relationship, he said to himself. *If Caitlin wants to go out with someone, let her. It won't bother me.* But he knew it would. And he knew she would cry if she knew how easily he was tempted by this Waffle House girl. *Hunter, don't do this to yourself. Some things are better not thought about. Yes, you could have taken this sweet girl to your room and enjoyed the night, but you can't do that to Caitlin. Not now. Don't think about it.*

Not thinking had often been his answer to difficult choices. Sometimes it worked.

Chapter Twenty-Seven

The jealous are possessed by a mad devil
—Johann Kaspar Lavater

The next morning Von called room service for coffee and the local newspaper. In the "Accents" section, Von found a featured interview of Caitlin. The article focused on the reopening of her art gallery, reviewed the recent show, and told of her experiences in Africa. As he read, he sipped slowly at the coffee, his tongue savoring the slight bitterness of the added chicory. Caitlin was brilliant in the interview, of course, and Von marveled at the creative and well-turned phrases she used to promote her gallery and comment on her recent show, *Blood Diamonds: My Year in Africa*. The writer also praised Von's collection of paintings and artifacts.

In the article, Caitlin ranted about the usual political issues surrounding Sierra Leone, issues he considered to be exaggerated by a few sensationalist politicians and their media cronies—conflict diamonds, child-soldiers, child-slavery, and amputees. He was amused to read of her intent to promote legislation banning the importation of any diamonds from Sierra Leone until conditions had changed and the land had stabilized.

Von chuckled. What an idealist his Caitlin was. As

if laws could change these problems. He studied her black and white photograph.

After breakfast, Von drove to the Lost Bazaar in West Monroe. He couldn't wait to surprise Caitlin with his appearance. They would go to lunch, then back to his hotel to catch up on things. Entering, he was greeted by the slim, redheaded woman who lived above the gallery.

"Can I help you, sir?" she said.

"Perhaps. Can I see Caitlin?"

"She's having coffee with her boyfriend at the moment. They should be back any moment. They're just across the street at the café."

"Boyfriend?" Von asked.

"Yeah. I remember you. You're Caitlin's boss, right? The one that donated the African artifacts."

"Yes. Who are you?"

"I'm Melissa, Caitlin's friend. I work here at the gallery with her. Is there any way I can help you?"

"Not at the present time. Please tell Caitlin that Von dropped by to see her." Von turned away tight-lipped, feeling confusion, and something else that bordered on rage. He crossed Trenton Street and stood at the restaurant window, scanning the tables of customers until his eyes found his Caitlin. The longhaired man he had seen at the gallery sat with her. They were holding hands and talking and looking into each other's eyes. Von imagined himself marching into the café, wrapping his hands around the man's throat and throttling him.

Von returned to his car and drove blindly around until he came to a Waffle House. He entered and sat down at the counter. "Coffee please."

"Sure thing," the waitress said. She poured and set down a cup. "Cream?"

"Yes. Black coffee or tea is quite an American thing."

"Where are you from?"

"I'm African."

"African?"

Von saw the surprise in her eyes. It was an old confusion that he was used to and enjoyed. "Yes, believe it or not, some Africans are white."

"I knew by the way you talked you weren't American. Where in Africa are you from?"

"West Africa, Sierra Leone exactly, though I did live for a while in South Africa."

As Von sipped his coffee, he spotted Hunter's photograph on the wall behind the counter. He was sure that it was the same man he had just seen with Caitlin.

He nodded his head at the photo. "Who is that?"

"That's Hunter, my boyfriend."

"Tell me about your boyfriend." Von could barely contain his laughter. *Her boyfriend? He doubted Caitlin knew about that bit of news! Caitlin had chosen a player.*

"Well, I don't know a lot about him because we just started seeing each other, but he's a stud. He's a musician and plays at the Backdoor Lounge. He's there tomorrow night, in fact."

"You seem quite taken with this Hunter."

"Oh, I am."

He looked at her nametag. "When will you see him again, Veronica?" Von asked.

She bent over and pulled a stack of plates from the dishwasher. "I didn't tell him, but I'm going to take off tomorrow and meet him at the Backdoor Lounge."

"I think I may go and hear this new boyfriend of yours play Friday night. If I see you there, I'll buy you a drink."

"Great," she said. "That would be nice."

No, Von thought. *It won't be nice at all.*

****

Von returned to the Lost Bazaar and stood at the door. Caitlin, Melissa, and her black boy were hanging paintings on the gallery's wall. Caitlin finally noticed him, but he was not pleased with the expression on her face. He walked over to her and held out his arms. "Caitlin!"

She avoided his offered embrace. "Von, what a surprise. How was your trip?"

"Tedious." He glanced over at Melissa as he lowered his arms.

"Melissa," Caitlin said. "You remember Von."

"Oh," Melissa said. "Actually, I forgot to tell you that he came by earlier. Sorry."

"Could you excuse us a minute, Melissa?" Caitlin asked. "Why don't you and Tejan go out to the patio and frame the new painting. Von and I have to talk a moment. It won't take long."

"Sure. Come on, Tejan."

After Melissa and Tejan left, Caitlin said, "Look, Von, I meant to call you, but things were so busy here, I had a million details to attend to, I've got Tejan to worry about, and…"

"Then there's Hunter," Von said. "Your new boyfriend."

"How the hell did you know about Hunter?" She looked over at Melissa.

"Don't worry," Von said. "Your friend did not betray you."

"Von, I'm sorry. I'm not very good at things like this."

"You mean, like leading someone on? I adore you, Caitlin. Come and have dinner with me tonight."

"I can't, Von. I have too much to do. I'm in the middle of putting together another show."

"Tomorrow then. There's plenty of time. I made arrangements to handle all my business from Monroe so we could have some quality time together."

"I'm sorry you had to waste your time and money. You should have talked to me first, and not assumed…"

"You don't mean what you're saying. You need me, Caitlin."

"No, Von, I don't need you. I'm doing fine. Please, don't pressure me. We had some good times in Africa. Let's not spoil those memories."

"You don't have time for me? You found time to drink coffee for half an hour with your new boyfriend. I understand that a woman has needs for a man now and then. But really, to fall for a second-rate musician? I could make things so much easier for you. You can come back to work for me, then you wouldn't have to hustle your paintings or give art lessons, just give yourself to your painting."

"Von, keep your voice down. I like teaching art. And I certainly don't want to be a kept woman of yours. Make my life easier? I'm beginning to wish I had never met you."

"I see you haven't lost your sense of humor or your sense of the melodramatic," Von said. He looked away in anger, only to have his eyes land on a painting entitled *Making a Killing*, showing a man with a face much like his own. He looked closer. The man was dressed in a business suit and sat at a rough wood table, counting out diamonds. The table was in the middle of a field of dead people. His smile vanished and his face flushed. "A man's got to make a living."

"Actually, in your case, it's making a killing."

A lady entered the gallery and stood near the door obviously waiting to speak to Caitlin. Von noticed how Caitlin's eyes kept shifting impatiently toward her. "You didn't seem to mind the way I made a living when we had sex," he said.

Caitlin's customer turned abruptly and walked out of the gallery.

"Great, Von. Just tell the whole world everything you know. That lady wanted to talk about commissioning a portrait. I think it's time for you to leave."

"Caitlin, I'm sorry. What I said was inappropriate. I didn't mean it."

"Goodbye, Von." Caitlin turned to walk away.

"That Hunter is not who you think he is. He has other women on his string besides you."

She spun around. "Von, jealousy doesn't become you. You don't know the first thing about Hunter, or really about me. I screwed up things between Hunter and me once before. I won't do it again."

Von heard Tejan laughing outside. "We belong together, Caitlin. Don't make things difficult for me. I have friends who have influence with the INS whom I could persuade to send your black African son back to Sierra Leone. And I have other friends who could do far worse."

"Now you're threatening me? How can you expect me to take your profession of love seriously when you talk to me like that? And you dare to demean Tejan to me? Do you really think bribery and pressure are going to make me love you?"

"I get what I want, Caitlin."

"Not this time."

"You prefer that peckerwood guitar player over me?"

"I see you're picking up the use of Southern idioms. I'm not impressed and I think you need to leave Hunter out of this conversation."

Von smiled. "It's hard to have a relationship with a dead man."

When Caitlin gasped, Von knew he had made the point. He could, and would, do anything to possess her. Genuine terror was etched on Caitlin's face, and he felt a rush of adrenaline. Von was amazed as to how easily he could read Americans, even his Caitlin. They wore their feelings and thoughts on their faces, without duplicity. Such facial honesty would easily kill a man in Africa.

"I really think it's time for you to leave," Caitlin said. She glanced at the gallery door just as Hunter entered.

"Hunter is my boyfriend now," Caitlin said. "He's standing at the door waiting. I hope you understand why I don't want to introduce him to you. Please, just go. If you cause a scene, I *will* call the police."

"So, this is your boyfriend. He's dressed like a slob, so I knew he wouldn't be a customer. I'll leave you two alone." Von passed Hunter as he came in and turned his head in time to see Hunter kiss and embrace

Caitlin. *A player*, he said to himself. *A polite one, but a player. This situation won't be difficult to repair. He is definitely the same man I saw in the Waffle House picture*. He was not impressed and wondered what Caitlin saw in this loser. The thought of Hunter touching his Caitlin nauseated him.

****

"Looks like word is getting around about your show," Hunter said. "Lots of traffic?"

"Yeah," she said. "Word is getting around. Did you forget something?"

"I wanted to see if you wanted to come hear me play and get together after work tonight. Are you okay? Your face is red."

"I'm fine. I just have a lot on my mind. Where are you playing tonight?" she asked.

"The Backdoor Lounge. Do you want to go?"

"No, sweetie. That's really not my type of crowd. Besides, I think I need to spend some time alone again with Tejan, okay?" Caitlin felt a twinge of guilt at the half-lie, but she also needed some extra time to think of how to handle Von. Maybe she should go to his hotel for one last talk to break off things completely. She didn't want any repeats of today's confusion. And his artifacts. Another issue to resolve.

"No problem," Hunter said. "I'm a little on the tired side myself. I've been working hard."

"I know you have." She gave him a quick kiss. "Now, you better let me get back to work."

"Okay, but take off tomorrow so we can visit my parents. I really could use the moral support."

"Sure. I'd love to meet them. Do you realize that the whole time we dated, you never took me home to

268

meet them?"

"I decided that a lot of things in my life are going to be different. I'm really trying, Caitlin."

After Hunter left, Tejan asked Caitlin, "Who was the tall man here before Mr. Hunter? He no talk like people in Louisiana. He talk like white men in Africa. Tejan think he see this man before."

Caitlin nodded. "You have seen him before—at the mission." Tejan had actually seen Von many times, but his mind was so clouded during his rehabilitation that she wasn't surprised that he couldn't recall him.

What bothered Caitlin the most was that Tejan's eyes were wide and he was sweating profusely. His face bore the expression of a fearful little boy who has just learned the RUF had entered his village to play.

Chapter Twenty-Eight

Without hearts there is no home.
—Byron.

The next day, Hunter drove Caitlin and Tejan to visit his parents in Caldwell Parish. Hunter felt it was time to go home. There was some kind of ache inside that he thought going home might cure. *Home is supposed to do that.* His parents still lived in the house where Hunter had been raised.

There were amends to be made, too. It would be easier to face his father if Caitlin were to be with him. His arrest for the pot possession had hurt his parents, but his father especially. Hunter knew his father would never be able to understand why a man would want to use any kind of recreational drug. His father was a farmer, and son of farmers, a solid man, good of heart but definitely one to whom the wildness and infatuation of the fast-living music world Hunter moved in would have had little appeal. Drugs could never be a part of his father's world. Hunter remembered his father warning him about the alcoholics and dope fiends and adulterers in the music industry. Now Hunter wondered if his father thought of him as having joined those casualties. Some days, Hunter wondered if he truly had. Was he doomed to join the ranks of the countless worn-out, burned-out musicians who never reach their dreams and often never even find themselves?

In spite of his apprehensions, Hunter smiled as they approached the house. It was a gray, one-story cypress board plantation-age home, resting on a gravel road along the banks of the Ouachita River. Its porch extended along the whole front of the house and had been screened in for protection from mosquitoes so the family could sit outside on hot summer evenings. The windows were large, and long, reaching from the ceiling almost to the hardwood floor, a floor that creaked at night in response to the lightest of footsteps.

Hunter parked underneath one of the pre-Civil War live oak trees next to a shotgun house. As they stepped out of his truck, a yellow hound ran up to them barking. Tejan froze.

"Stonewall! Behave yourself!" Hunter said. "Don't worry, Tejan. Come here, boy." Hunter patted his leg and Stonewall trotted amiably over to him, his tail wagging. "He doesn't bite. He just likes to call attention to himself. All that barking and noise makes him feel important."

"So, he's just like any other redneck male, eh, Hunter." Caitlin knelt down and rubbed Stonewall's head. "Come pet him, Tejan. See? He's a good dog."

Tejan squatted and cautiously rubbed Stonewall's back, then pulled his hand back quickly. He touched him again, and when Stonewall licked his face, he laughed.

"He's not used to dogs?" Hunter asked.

"Not as pets. Sierra Leone had a lot of dogs, feral ones mostly. Pye-dogs, they called them. There were packs of them everywhere in Freetown. They were bad to bite and often carried rabies. The government said they were planning on a pye-dog extermination program, but first they needed to figure out what to do about the packs of wild boys in Freetown. What kind of dog is he?"

"Stonewall is what they call a Blackmouth cur, and a very good hog dog. But he's of questionable origin. Daddy likes to say that his mama was a feist, and the father was just a real good friend she met somewhere. By his build and his blue eyes, I'd say one of his parents was a Catahoula Cur."

Hunter heard the screen door slam. He saw his mother step outside. She wiped her hands with her apron.

"Land's sake alive, Hunter, it's about time you found your way home." She wrapped her arms around Hunter and he gasped as she squeezed the breath out of him.

"This is Caitlin, Mother. The love of my life."

Then she held out her arms for Caitlin and embraced her. "Hello, Caitlin. Hunter used to talk about you all the time. It is so good to finally meet you."

"Hello, Miss Belle," Caitlin said. "Hunter talked about me?"

"All the time. Caitlin, you are as purty as can be. You look a lot like I did when I was your age. I'm happy that you and Hunter are seeing each other again. I hope you can keep this boy of mine out of trouble this time around."

Hunter thought that maybe mothers have some kind of radar that automatically kicks in when it's needed.

"Your daddy's out in the garden," his mother said. "Why don't you go say hello, Hunter."

"Sure," he said, but hesitated.

"Don't worry, son. He won't give you a hard time. We done talked about it. Go on now. I'll fix us all some iced tea. Tell your daddy to come to the porch."

****

After Hunter was out of earshot, Miss Belle looked at Tejan. "And who might this young man be?"

"That's my son, Tejan," Caitlin said. "I adopted him when I was in Africa."

"Is that right? Hunter told me you went to Africa, but he didn't say anything about you having a kid now." She held out her hand and smiled. "Good to meet you, Tejan. You can call me Miss Belle."

Tejan took her hand and pumped it once. "Hello, Miss Belle."

"Go take a look around our place if you want while your mama and I talk. Stonewall will go with you. Call him."

"Come, Stonewall!" Tejan said. Stonewall barked and followed, his tail thumping their legs like a metronome as he passed by them. Tejan ran laughing to the tire swing, stuck himself inside and hurled himself into the air while Stonewall barked and jumped, dashing in and out of Tejan's path as he swung.

Caitlin and his mother walked to the house and Caitlin sat in the porch swing while Hunter's mother went inside to pour glasses of iced tea.

"You have a beautiful place, Miss Belle," Caitlin said when Hunter's mother returned. "I may ask Hunter to walk me out to that high ground over there so I can see the river."

Hunter's mother set the tray of glasses down on an end table next to the swing. "That high ground yonder

273

is what folks call Jayhawk Hill. Near the end of the Civil War, Jayhawkers hid out there. They were a criminal sort mostly—deserters from both sides, thieves, rapists, murderers, vagabonds, smugglers. Seems like every unsavory man who came into Louisiana found his way to that hill. My daddy said that the White Camellias finally ran them out—at least all the ones they didn't shoot or hang. Tejan," she called out. "Would you like a glass of tea?"

"*Oui!*" he said. He and Stonewall galloped toward the porch. He gulped down the tea, smacked his lips and he and Stonewall ran back to the swing.

Belle said, "I'm going to tell Hunter what I think today."

"Ma'am?"

"I think it's time he gave up whatever dream notions or idle fancies he has in his head and settled down. He needs to give up that gypsy life. I don't want no old-maid son. You'd make him a fine wife, Caitlin. I can see it in your eyes. I know Hunter thinks he wouldn't make a good husband, but the fact is there ain't no man that's a good husband right away, and he can learn how to be one just like every other man has to do. I think that spell on the pea farm broke that bad temper of his. If he had any sense at all, and since he's my son I'm inclined to think he does, he'd ask you marry him before next week. That shotgun house on our property would make a fine starter home for you. Now, I know with this new boy you got, and that means if he takes you, he's got a black son to raise too. That might slow Hunter down a bit, but Tejan seems like a good boy. Louisiana ain't as bad or prejudiced about such things like it used to be, so I don't think his being black will cause you much trouble as long as you don't go on a crusade or something. Where do you live now?"

From Miss Belle's words Caitlin realized how Tejan was a difficulty factor to consider if she wanted to add any man permanently to her life. But Tejan was non-negotiable, and any man that couldn't accept Tejan, could just kiss her ass and move on. "Tejan is very important to me. He and I live in a houseboat on the river in West Monroe. But I'm not that attached to it. I heard Hunter say he wanted to settle down in the country. If Hunter and I end up together, I guess I could sell the houseboat."

"Pshaw. There ain't no doubt in my mind you and him will be together, but there ain't no need to talk of selling anything to do it. You could hook that houseboat on the river here just as easy as you could there if you're attached to it."

Then Hunter's mother looked at Tejan sailing through the air in the swing. "But then, sometimes you got to do what feels right, even if it don't seem quite natural. Don't you think so?"

Caitlin wasn't sure exactly what she meant by *natural or doing what feels right*. Her sentence seemed to be a cryptic Southern aphorism, containing wisdom that Hunter's mother thought Caitlin needed to hear. "Yes, ma'am, I think so."

After meeting and talking with his parents, Caitlin understood Hunter a little better. She also got a glimpse of what Hunter could be like in his later years. *Worth thinking about because all of us grow old.*

When Caitlin returned home, she found a brightly wrapped package propped against the door, and an envelope taped to the door. She opened the letter and recognized the handwriting.

Caitlin:

My dearest. I am so sorry we quarreled. I behaved like such an ass. I miss you. I need to see you so much. I don't want you to feel pressured. I can't bear the thought of living without you. Please call me at the hotel and let me know what you think of the gift. Maybe this will make amends for my horrendous behavior this afternoon. I hope to see you wearing them soon.

Yours always,

Von.

Inside the package were a diamond necklace and a pair of diamond earrings. The attached tag said that the stone for the necklace was one carat and the earrings were one-half carat each.

Caitlin called Von's hotel and asked for his room, wanting to tell him that there was no way she could accept the gift, that he would have to come and pick up the diamonds up tomorrow. Von needed to know that she could not be bought. There was no answer when the operator connected to his room, so she left a message on the voice mail.

Later that night, after she was sure Tejan was asleep, Caitlin stood naked in front of the bathroom mirror, wearing only the diamond necklace and diamond earrings. The stones sparkled and glittered in the light. She hated herself for wanting to keep the diamonds.

Chapter Twenty-Nine

On the streets, unrequited love and death go together almost as often as in Shakespeare
—*Scott Turow*

The next morning after coffee, Caitlin called Von.

"Caitlin, I thought about you all night. Did you like the diamonds?"

"Yes, Von. You knew I would, but we have to talk. Can I come by for a moment?"

"Certainly. I'd love to see you."

She wrote down his room number and told him she'd be right over. She returned the diamonds to their velvet case and stuck them in her purse. She coveted the diamonds, but she knew the strings attached were strong and reached all the way back to Africa. Accepting the diamonds would indicate Von saw her as a commodity, as someone for sale, and if she kept them, he would be right.

When she arrived at his hotel, she asked the clerk to ring Von's room and tell him she had arrived.

The clerk said, "You must be Caitlin Johnson?"

"Yes."

"Mr. Vermeer is expecting you. He called the desk a moment ago, and asked that you come to his room, number 268."

"Thank you very much."

There was a *Do Not Disturb* sign on the doorknob of Von's room. She rapped on the door noticing her knuckles were specked with red paint. Von opened the door almost with a bow, and Caitlin stepped inside. The room was a large suite, and an elaborately table set for two stood next to another table which was loaded with Sterno-warmed pans of pastries, eggs, bacon, potatoes, and gravy.

"Oh, Von," she said. "You shouldn't have gone to the trouble. We could have met in the hotel restaurant."

"This is more intimate, don't you think? Would you like coffee first?"

"Please, but no breakfast. I really have to be on my way."

"Surely you aren't in that much of a hurry." Von poured their coffee and placed them at the table with place settings, and ignoring her refusal of breakfast, prepared each of them a plate. She sat down and sipped the coffee, trying to dredge up the right words to tell him what was on her mind. In spite of herself, she picked up a fork and began eating.

"How do you like my room?"

"First class, but then, I can't picture you settling for anything else."

"The bed is wonderful, but it's too large and comfortable for only one to enjoy."

Caitlin dropped her fork. Hunter had told her that when a person dropped a fork at the table, it predicted something, but she couldn't remember what it was.

She bent over to pick up the fork, but Von said, "I'll get it." He walked slowly around the table and knelt down next to her. "So, you liked the diamonds?" He set the dropped fork on an empty saucer, unwrapped another set of silverware, and carefully wiped the fork with a cloth napkin before setting it next to her plate.

"I did Von, and that was one of the things I wanted to talk to you about. I can't accept them." She dug in her purse for the jewelry cases, and then slid them toward him.

"Why?" Von placed his hands on her shoulders and kneaded them with his strong fingers.

"Because it would give you the wrong message about me."

"Caitlin, I can't give you up. I love you. In Africa—"

"In Africa I was lonely and vulnerable. You're a good man, Von, handsome and very attractive, but I don't love you. Hunter and I are going to repair things. I think the year apart helped both of us. I want you to stop calling me, Von. Don't write, and please don't surprise me with expensive gifts. Listen to me. I won't meet you anymore for lunch or drinks or for any reason. We had a good time together in Africa, so let's just end things on a pleasant note."

"You will change your mind," Von said. He stepped back to his chair and sat down.

"No, I won't. Please make arrangements to remove your artifacts from my gallery. I thank you for your generosity, but it would be best for you to take them. As soon as possible. Goodbye, Von."

Caitlin stood and walked out the door. She made sure she didn't look back.

****

Von, Biko, and Rilke waited in the BMW outside the Backdoor Lounge and watched the crowd entering the bar.

Von stepped out of the car and spoke into the open window. "After I talk to the girl, I'll be back."

Once inside, Von made his way through the crowd. Veronica, the Waffle House waitress who claimed Hunter as her boyfriend, sat at the bar with the other barflies. She wore shorts and a red tube-top, flirting with a man next to her who didn't appear interested. As far as Von could tell, Hunter avoided even looking at her.

The cowboy sitting with her joined friends at another table, and Von moved behind Veronica just as the bartender brought her a drink. As Veronica dug into her purse, Von pitched a twenty onto the bar. "I'm buying the lady's drinks tonight. And you can bring me a double whiskey—no water."

The girl at the bar turned around and said, "Why, you did make it! And thanks for the drink. This is my friend, Von," she said to the bartender.

The girl tending the bar slung a rag on her shoulder and said, "Okay." She yelled out, "Bobby! Wake that man at the back table and get him outside. His cab should be here by now."

"Can I sit here?" Von motioned to the empty stool next to her.

Veronica leaned her face on one hand as if depressed. "Sure. I could use some company. Hunter isn't paying me much attention."

"It's his loss." Von sat down. "So, you really do like the musician?"

"Yeah, I like him, but I understand. I mean, he *is* working. But I'm really crazy about him. He's so cute and he sings so goddamn good. But then, you're cute too."

"Tell me again. Tell me honestly this time. How well do you know this Hunter?"

"Well, we just met this past week after he came to the Waffle House. I had seen him before, but it was about two years ago, and I don't think he even noticed me then. He was with some girl that runs an art gallery on Trenton Street. I love this accent of yours." She leaned on her elbow. "I think I could listen to it all night long."

"All night sounds interesting. And I do like to talk."

"I've always wanted to see Africa, ever since I saw that movie with Meryl Streep in it. I bet it's beautiful there."

No, bitch, I won't offer to take you to Africa. There is no way a tramp like you could compare to my Caitlin. "Yes, sometimes, Africa's very nice. Sometimes the movies portray the continent very realistically. Sometimes, they do not." He lit a cigarette and laid the package on the counter.

"I've never seen cigarettes like those," she said. "Can I have one?"

"Of course. Excellent tobacco blend." When she picked one out, he flipped open his lighter and lit it. "I would like your help tonight."

"I bet you would."

Von couldn't believe she actually batted her eyes. He laid down a hundred-dollar bill. "I think you could drink a while on this. Are you interested?"

"Depends on what you have in mind." She covered the bill with her hand and slipped it off the bar and into her purse. "But sure, I'm interested. What do you want me to do?"

"As it turns out, your Hunter and I have a mutual friend, and my friend wanted me to find Hunter and discuss some business. I want you to persuade him to go outside on his next break and occupy him till I get there so we can talk privately, then you can come back inside. That's all. But it's imperative you get him alone. I'll come around from the back and meet you."

"Why don't you just walk up there, introduce yourself, and talk to him?"

"You see, he doesn't know me. He arranged our meeting through a friend who wanted me to get him some, you know…" Von imitated smoking a joint. "You know how these musicians like their pot. So, this is not the kind of business I can prudently discuss in front of others. How about it? If you don't want to, I'll understand."

"I don't get it. A hundred bucks just so you can meet Hunter? I can call him over next break and introduce you. No one would hear what you were talking about."

"No, I want him outside. Besides, this deal is bigger than most I do."

She laughed and nodded. "Oh, I see. Sure. I'll be glad to help him kill a few brain cells. You have some for me too?"

"Oh yes, I've got something for you. But you can't tell him I gave it to you, or tell him my name, or say anything else about me. It is important that I remain anonymous."

"Okay. But what do I do until you get there?"

Von cringed inwardly. He found the stupidity of this girl annoying. He stretched the top of her tube top out a little, peeked down it, and allowed the elastic to pop back. "I think a good-looking woman like you can think of something to get his attention. Just make him feel good enough so he won't go back inside for a few minutes. Think you can handle that?"

"Oh yeah. And enjoy it, too. Maybe I'll get lucky. I think he'd enjoy a quickie."

"Now you're talking." Von signaled the waitress. "We'd like to buy the musician a drink. What does he prefer?"

"Scotch and water," Veronica said. "I've never seen him drink anything else."

"I've never understood why someone would want to ruin the taste of a good Scotch by adding water." He signaled the barmaid to come over. "Take a Scotch and water to the musician for us please and tell him that is from this beautiful woman here." As the waitress prepared Hunter's drink, Von put his arm around Veronica. "A man likes a woman who buys him drinks. The act suggests certain things. It also makes it harder to deny a simple request, especially one that is in the interest of his pleasure. As I mentioned, he also has a weakness for this." He slipped a joint into her hand. "Ask him to take a break and tell him you have something outside to give him. He won't say no."

"You seem to know a lot about people."

"I'll be waiting."

****

The waitress carried a Scotch and Veronica's note to Hunter. "It's from that girl at the bar."

Hunter scanned the bar and saw the waitress from the Waffle House smiling at him. One of her hands suggestively fingered the rim of her tube top. With the other, she imitated someone smoking a joint. Hunter

283

toasted her and drained the glass. He sang "Steam Roller" and then said, "Folks, it's time for a short break." The jukebox came on and he made his way toward Veronica, stopping along the way at a couple of tables to thank them for their tips and coming to hear him.

He sat down next to her. "Thanks for the drink, Veronica," he said. "I'm sorry I haven't talked to you sooner, but I've got a lot on my mind and I wasn't sure if you were with anyone else or not."

"You're welcome. God, your music is so good! And as far as meeting someone, I came here hoping I could see you. Hey, I was just about to go outside and uh…" She showed him the joint cupped in her hand. "Want to share?"

"Sure."

Jed, the Backdoor's owner walked over to them. "Hunter, you ready to go outside?"

"Yeah. Veronica's coming too."

Veronica leaned over and nibbled on Hunter's ear. "Actually, I'd rather he not come. After we blow this joint, I wanted to blow you."

"Jed, let's catch each other next break. I've got to have a private talk with Veronica here."

"Sure, no problem." Jed grinned. "You two have a nice talk."

Hunter followed the girl out the bar's side door. After they smoked, she set her beer on the ground, put her arms around his neck and kissed him. "I knew you would be a good kisser." She slipped down her tube top. "As promised."

Hunter removed her arms from his neck and gently pushed her away. "Sorry, but I can't do that. I'm seeing someone. But let's light that joint. We better hurry up. Jed will come out here looking for me in a minute."

She looked toward the parking lot.

"What are you looking at?"

"Nothing. I thought we had an audience for a moment."

Hunter heard footsteps in the gravel. Hunter glanced over his shoulder at three men silhouettes. A camera clicked and there was a bright flash.

A voice he didn't recognize said, "Okay, Veronica, you've earned your money, you can leave now."

"Who the hell are you?" Hunter said. "Paid you for what, Veronica?"

She pulled up her top. "He said he knew a friend of yours. I'll see you later, Hunter."

After she went inside, one of the men shut the side door, and the three circled him. Hunter knew the men had not come to book a gig.

"Hunter," Von said, "we have business to discuss. You're causing me some very real distress."

"How's that?" Hunter said. "I don't recollect holding up a mirror."

"Funny man. My name is Von. I believe you are interested in Caitlin. Well, as it turns out, I am too. And that means that you're going to quit seeing her."

"Oh, so you are Von. Mr. Lovenote himself. Caitlin told me all about you. You're as ugly as she said, and twice as ugly as I thought you would be. And your friends are just as bad. I tell you what—you can go straight to hell."

The black man hooked a punch into his belly. "Watch your mouth, mon."

Hunter doubled over as the pancake size fist dug

into his gut. A black vice clamped onto his throat and squeaking sounds came from Hunter's mouth.

"I wouldn't irritate Biko," Von said. "Once, he cut off a man's head, and then ate his heart and liver. I could kill you now, and the most the paper would say is that a second-rate musician died after a fight at a local dive with unknown assailants. Tomorrow, you *will* say goodbye to Caitlin, pack your bags and leave town, or by God I'll find you again, and I promise the pain will be much worse. And not only for you, but for Caitlin's black boy and her friends. Caitlin is no longer going to be a part of your life."

Hunter felt like his insides were paralyzed. He had never been hit that hard before. He couldn't breathe and the huge hand was cutting off circulation and he knew he was seconds away from passing out.

"Now just to emphasize the importance of your decision…"

Hunter felt jolts of pain at first, but then he felt nothing, but he knew the fists and boots and the blackjack were battering his face and body, and he felt a rib snap, then another, then he lost consciousness.

****

When Hunter was twenty minutes late for his next set, Jed went out the backdoor to look for him. Hunter's truck was still there, but the musician was nowhere in sight. He circled around the building and found the bloodied, beaten Hunter on the ground.

"Shit, goddamn it to hell!" he said, and then went inside to call the sheriff's department and an ambulance. He told one of his bouncers to go outside and watch over Hunter until help could arrive. Jed entertained the crowd inside with a few karaoke songs.

He cursed Hunter for messing up another gig. He wondered what Hunter had done this time.

Chapter Thirty

Stalking is a cruel and incessant crime with often terrifying consequences.
—Amber Rudd

The next morning, Caitlin met Melissa at the gallery and sat down to schedule shows for the next year.

"So," Melissa said, "how is the woman no mortal man can resist?"

"Just call me dud-magnet."

"After all this drama of yours, you're fast becoming story material."

"You wouldn't dare. Besides, I've settled things with Von, and Hunter and I are doing fine. He hasn't called has he? I can't believe he hasn't phoned me yet."

"Musicians are notorious for sleeping late. He works nights, remember?" When the phone rang, Melissa said. "I bet that's him. Caitlin, there's a phone call for you." She rolled her eyes. "It's a man with an accent."

Caitlin took the receiver and covered it with her hand. "You better get that smirk off you face, Melissa before I slap it off." She turned so Melissa couldn't see her face. "Hello, Von."

"Caitlin, please, we need to talk."

"About what?"

"About us."

"There is no *us*, Von. Now please, I need to get back to work. Stop this. You're acting childish." She hung up.

The phone rang again.

Caitlin blew out her breath in exasperation. "What is it, Von?"

"Don't hang up on me this time. I saw your cheating boyfriend with another girl last night. I saw her mouth on his—"

"You are a lying son of a bitch."

"Well, you ask him if you want. I think he got in some kind of scrap involving the girl and they had to take him to the doctor. I'm not exactly sure where they took him. I put an envelope in your mailbox. Something's inside it you may find of interest."

"Please. No more gifts."

"Just go to your mailbox at the boat. I'm doing you favor. You won't try to give this one back."

The phone went dead.

"That's a first, Melissa. Von hung up on me." She called Jed at the Backdoor Lounge.

"Jed, this is Caitlin. Did something happen to Hunter last night?"

"Somebody whupped up on him pretty bad last night, Caitlin. The ambulance took him to emergency at Glenwood and they patched him up. He's all right, but pretty banged up."

"What happened? Did he make some girl's boyfriend mad?"

"You better talk to Hunter. I learned a long time ago to not get involved in shit like this."

Caitlin called Hunter's hotel, but there was no

answer. She told Melissa she needed to go out for a while and left the gallery.

His truck was outside the motel. She knocked, quietly at first, then pounded on the door with her fist, the envelope from Von in her purse. She heard the chain rattle, then the door opened. Hunter's face was swollen and badly bruised. Hunter wore only boxers, and he had Ace bandages wrapped around his torso. His eyes were bloodshot, and his hair matted and wild.

"Oh, Hunter… I thought you had changed."

"Thanks for asking. I'll be all right. Just a mashed-up face, a couple of broken ribs, and some wounded pride. Come in." He turned, limped to the small fridge and pulled out a beer. "Want one?" He opened a pill bottle, swallowed two Tylenol 3's, and sat on the bed.

"It's a little early to start drinking, don't you think?"

"I'm in no mood for a lecture if that's what you came for. It wasn't a fight. I didn't get to throw the first punch. Three men jumped me. One of them was your psychotic African boyfriend."

"Von?"

"Yeah. He said this would just be taste of what I'd get if I didn't stay away from you and get out of town. He also said bad things would happen to Tejan and your friends if I didn't."

"He called me with this story about you getting beat up because you were with a girl. Is that true?"

"You were the only girl whose name was mentioned."

She took the picture of him and Veronica and flipped it at him. "You are such a liar. Same old song, isn't it, Hunter? Same old song. I wonder how many blowjobs you got when we were dating?"

"It's not what you think, Caitlin. Nothing happened with that girl. She came on to me and they took that picture before I pushed her away. Can we talk about it later?"

"No. Tell me what you feel, Hunter. Tell me what you honestly feel."

"I feel like I should go to Daddy's and get a gun. I feel like shooting the son of a bitch."

****

After Caitlin left, Hunter drove to Jed's bar, told him he wanted to take off work a few days. Jed nodded, paid him, and wished him the best. Hunter loaded up his equipment and drove to his parent's house. Stonewall ran up to him, and as if he understood Hunter's hurt, licked his hand and walked alongside him to the house.

His mother was on the porch shelling peas. When she saw him, she said, "Lord have mercy, Hunter. What has happened to you?"

"I got jumped last night at the club. I'm all right. Where's Daddy?"

"He's at the table drinking coffee. He'll be glad to see you, even in your present condition."

Hunter walked to the dining room.

His father set his coffee cup down and shook his head. "Lord, what kind of trouble are you into now? I thought you'd give up scrappin'."

"It wasn't a fight, Daddy. I was jumped by three men."

"You owe somebody money?"

"No, sir. There's some guy who thinks he owns Caitlin. He and his two friends did this to persuade me to stay away from her."

"Did it work?"

"Not hardly."

"Is this man likely to do it again?"

"Yes, sir."

"What are you going to do about it?"

"I don't know. You got any ideas? I'm taking off work a few days and do some thinking."

Hunter spent the night with his parents. The next morning he woke at sunrise and joined his father for coffee on the porch. His father rocked slowly, and Hunter remembered the sound of that steady rhythm that sometimes had rocked him to sleep as a baby. A soft creaking sound that even now soothed him. The chair itself was ritually symbolic of his father and would be as long as chair or father lasted.

They watched the sunrise together. The neighbor's cotton field was blanketed with fog, and the sunbeams brushed the clouds with pastel strokes as they crept south.

His father said, "So, were you able to sleep, or were you too churned up?"

"Didn't sleep much or well. I'll be damned if this woman ain't messin' with my redneck head. And I'm not going to let this son of a bitch Von scare me away or bother Caitlin anymore. I'll kill him if he does." He shouted it again at the stream of eighteen-wheelers passing him. "I'll kill him!"

His father filled his pipe and tamped it down. "I know you're just talking how you feel, not how you think. But you need to get those violent thoughts out of your head. When a man starts deciding who he's going to kill, the devil puts that man's own name on the list too."

"I know, Daddy. I'm going to stay here a few days if that's okay. I'm still stove up, and I don't feel like working."

Hunter's father lit his pipe and waved the match out. "You're my boy, Hunter. You stay here as long as you need to."

****

Hunter returned to his hotel. At the desk, he asked if he had any messages.

"No messages," the clerk said, "but you did have a visitor. One of your lady friends came by looking for you. Ain't none of my business, but she was a looker. There was something odd about it though. She seemed a bit on the nervous side, and she had this boy with her, a black boy who called her mama. I know times are changing, but I thought it a mite bit odd, a white woman coming in with a young black boy."

"She adopted him when she was in Africa. What she'd say?"

"She wanted to know if you had changed rooms. I told her you were gone for a few days, but you didn't say where you were going. She asked if you left a number. No, I said. He didn't say much at all."

"What did she say then?"

"Didn't say much. She was crying though when she left."

****

By the time Caitlin reached the houseboat later that afternoon, Von had left a half-dozen messages on her phone, pleading with her to come to see him or call him. He promised to explain everything and to change and do anything, if only she would marry him. He said he couldn't bear the thought of living without her, and he had even thought of killing himself if he didn't hear from her soon. That was the only part of his messages she felt he didn't really mean. Von was too selfish to do something noble like ridding the world of himself. She went outside and saw Tejan sitting sullenly on the deck, his knees drawn up to his chest.

"What's wrong, Tejan?"

He looked past her. "Nothing is wrong with Tejan's world, but he feels something is wrong with his *mamá's*. Maybe *mamá* works too hard. Call Mr. Hunter and ask him to come. He will make your heart feel better."

Caitlin sat down next to him. "I'm not sure Hunter will come over again, Tejan."

"Why, *Mamá*? You love Mr. Hunter. Did Tejan make him angry?"

She put her arm around him and pulled him to her. "No, silly boy. Hunter angered me. I think he was with another woman."

"Mr. Hunter does not love *mamá*?"

"That's not the point, Tejan. I don't know that I can be with a man I can't trust to only love and want me."

Tejan stood and placed his hands on the gunwale, looking into the river. "I do not understand, *Mamá*. In Sierra Leone, a man can have many wives. I think he love them all, though he always have one he loves most. I think Mr. Hunter love you most of all the women in the world."

"It's just not the Christian thing to do, Tejan. You're Catholic. You know that."

"I once heard Father Ambrose speak to us of David

and Solomon. They were great men in the Bible, and Jesus came to us through them. They had many wives. Why should a man only have one woman? It does not mean Mr. Hunter does not love you."

Oh, great, Caitlin thought. *I'm being lectured by my son. He's only been here a short time and he argues like a left-wing philosopher.* "Why would he be with another woman?"

"Why were you not with him? If you had been there, Mr. Hunter would behave himself. A man can be strong in battle and his work, but tremble before a woman who owns his heart. When Mr. Hunter is your husband, he will change his ways."

"I just can't stand the thought of him being with another woman."

Tejan shrugged his shoulders. "Then tell him." Tejan stretched, his eyes touching the cloud-laced sunset. "But *mamá* should forgive him first."

****

The next morning, Caitlin woke to Tejan shaking her arm.

"*Mamá*, someone is outside."

"Who is it?"

"It is the white Africa man. I tell him *mamá* is asleep, but he say for me to wake you. So, I come and wake you."

"Tejan, would you make *mamá* some coffee?"

"*Oui.*"

Caitlin stepped out on the boat's deck, pulling her robe together at the front. She squinted in the daylight and sat down on one of the deck chairs.

"Good morning," Von said.

"What do you want, Von? Do you always wake up

people who don't want to see you?"

"Why are you treating me this way? You don't return my calls, you don't write me, you won't come and see me…"

"Yes, that's the idea of not seeing someone anymore. I'll call you if I ever change my mind, but if I were you, I wouldn't hold my breath." She stood up. "I'm going back inside. You can find your own way off my boat."

"You're a whore, Caitlin. A dirty whore."

Caitlin wanted to spit in his face. "Get out of here! I don't want to see you again—ever. You're a moron if you think you can pressure me. After what you did to Hunter? He's so hurt he can hardly stand up. After threatening me? Leave! Go!"

"He said I hurt him? What about how he hurt you? What about that slut I saw him with?"

"Leave!"

Von turned over a small ceramic tile table, scattering dishes and books. "You will change your mind."

After Von left, Caitlin called Melissa. "Hey, I need your advice. Von is becoming more of a problem. Did you know he broke a table? He's starting to act a little crazy."

"A little? This guy followed you all the way from Sierra Leone. And to be honest, Caitlin, it sounds like you led him on a little."

"Well led on or not, he needs to be grownup enough to understand I've changed my mind and I don't want to see him anymore. And he and two other men hurt Hunter."

"I don't know what to say, Caitlin. But don't worry

about it. His fight with Hunter was just the typical male fight for dominance over the female. He'll probably give up after a while."

"I hope so. Hey, I've got to shower and have some coffee, but then I'll come down to the gallery."

"Okay, see you in a few."

After cleaning up and spending some time with Tejan, Caitlin walked to her car. The gas cap lay on the ground. "Damn!" she said. She screwed the cap back on, thinking someone had siphoned the tank. The Civic's gas gauge indicated the tank was still full, so she thought that maybe the thief had been interrupted before they could siphon the gas. Before she had pulled out of the Cottonport's parking lot, the engine began to shake and sputter, and then the car died. She got out of the car, called her mechanic, and walked on to the gallery.

Her mechanic called the gallery a couple of hours later.

"What's wrong with my car, Paul?" Caitlin asked. "It won't be expensive I hope."

"It's not too bad. About fifty bucks, counting the tow. Now, about what was wrong with it. Well, if you hadn't told me you found the cap on the ground, I would have thought it was bad gas, but the best I can tell is that someone put some sugar or something like that in your gas tank. I drained it, flushed it as best I could, and put some clean gas in it and now it's running fine. I'd suggest you get a locking cap. This was probably just someone pulling a prank. Do you want me to drop it off for you?"

"That would be great. Thanks Paul."

Someone sabotaged her car. Why? Who? Was it

Von? If so, what did he think to gain by doing it?

Caitlin didn't see Von the next week, but she was reminded of him daily. One day flowers and a note were sent to the gallery, the next day a letter, the next day a gift certificate, the next day more flowers, another letter, and every day he left phone messages, both at the gallery with Melissa, and on her machine on the houseboat.

She called Melissa's friend at the Ouachita Parish Sheriff's Department.

"Is this Deputy Stewart?"

"Yes, it is. What can I do for you?"

"I'm Caitlin Johnson, a friend of Melissa's. She said I should call you. I need your help. There's a man who bothering me, bothering me a lot, and I want to know what I can do to make him leave me alone."

"Come and see me."

Caitlin met Deputy Stewart and told him everything that had happened—how Von and she had met, the things he had said, the things he had given her, his phone calls, his letters, the gas tank, his jealousy over Hunter, his obsession to marry her.

"He's not just bothering you, Caitlin," he said. "He may have been a boyfriend in the past, but now he's stalking you."

"Am I in danger? How can I make him stop?"

"I don't know if he's dangerous. Let's hope he's not. This type of situation is not easy to fix, Caitlin, and you may have to make some radical changes."

"I'm not going to change my life because I'm being stalked."

"I'm sorry, Caitlin, but once someone stalks you like this, your life has changed, and changed forever."

"I hardly know this guy."

"Exactly how long have you known him?"

"Not very long. We dated a few weeks when I lived in Africa. Certainly, I don't think it was long enough for him to expect marriage."

"Hmmm. That short a time is not a good sign. It could mean he is a hopeless romantic that you just affected at a vulnerable time in his life, or he could be really disturbed individual, perhaps borderline erotomaniac."

"Which is…"

"Erotomania is a condition where a person believes without justification that someone else is in love with him and pursues the notion that the object of his affection reciprocates his romantic feelings and fantasies. That's the dictionary definition, but I'm sure you get the idea."

"So how bad can this erotic condition be?"

The deputy shrugged his shoulders. "Depends. When rejected this type of individual can spiral out of control and demonstrate expressions of anger, rage, frustration and violence."

"But I've told him I'm not interested."

"I know it's strange, but the erotomaniac typically does not see the victim's lack of interest. He is delusional, maybe psychotic and definitely no longer in touch with reality. Often, such men are so flipped out that they construe any negative reaction to pressure as a signal of approval."

"This is crazy. He says I'm his life."

"Believe him."

"It's not fair!"

"No, it's not."

"I feel sorry for him," Caitlin said. I don't want to crush anyone. Maybe I should try one more time and let him down easy."

"Don't feel sorry for him. Odds are that he has a criminal history not related to stalking."

He paused, studying Caitlin's silent face.

"He does, doesn't he?"

"I don't know for sure. I have a friend who warned me about him. He said Von was a diamond and gun smuggler."

"You're kidding me."

"No, I'm dead serious."

"I've many files on stalkers, but no diamond merchants and gun smugglers."

She pounded her leg. "What should I do?"

"Telling him *no* or that you're not interested is not enough. Start by never speaking to him again. He just won't get it any other way. Don't offer explanations, certainly do not allow time limits, and don't let him plea bargain. Any act of kindness you show him will be blown out of proportion into a deeper delusion of intimacy."

"Am I in danger?"

"Usually not."

"Usually? So that means I could be. He did hurt my boyfriend and tried to get the government to take my son away."

"To be on the safe side, I'd get a dog and a good alarm system. Block your address at the DMV. Move if you have to."

"I can't leave Monroe! Stalking me? But I'm not famous. I've got no money. I'm no Rebecca Shaeffer or Jodie Foster."

"The vast majority of stalking victims are not celebrities at all. If you thought someone like yourself could never be stalked by a crazy stranger just because you aren't a model or famous or rich, you are so wrong."

Caitlin sighed. "I'm getting sick of his messages. I guess I could change my phone number."

"No. He will only find the other number and that will make him angry and things will get worse. Leave him this outlet. Let your voice mail or recorder handle all the incoming calls on the other line. Leave a long, pleasant message on it. Perhaps the sound of your voice will soothe him. Then, get another phone, perhaps a cell, with an unlisted number and only give it to the people you know. You can even block it from receiving any calls at all."

"Would a restraining order keep him away?"

He took a pencil and tapped the eraser end on his desk. "Yes, certainly you could try that. However, from what I've seen, they are seldom effective, and violation is only a misdemeanor unless he packs a gun. A restraining order can also anger him and make things worse. On the other hand, if he does try something really weird, at least he might go to jail for it. You might get some justice, but you won't get safety. In the meantime, document everything that he does, and be extremely cautious. Write down anything you see that you think is suspicious."

She thought of Hunter. Maybe he could move in with her for a while and would bring Stonewall. Tejan would like that. "I think I'll take a chance on angering him. How can I get a restraining order?"

Chapter Thirty-One

Salomé, Salomé, dance for me. I pray thee dance for me. I am sad to-night. Yes, I am passing sad to-night. When I came hither I slipped in blood, which is an evil omen; and I heard, I am sure I heard in the air a beating of wings, a beating of giant wings. I cannot tell what they mean.
—*Oscar Wilde*

After the deputy sheriff left, Von laid the restraining order upon the coffee table, poured himself a double whiskey, drained it, then read the document again. He threw the empty glass and it shattered against the wall. He couldn't believe she would do something like this on her own. Someone must have pressured her to do it. But who could have this much influence? Her redneck lover? Her girlfriend? Did they really think that a piece of paper would stop him from being with his Caitlin? Maybe Caitlin just needed some space and time to see the error of her thinking. Fine. He would give her that. But he was not one to turn the other cheek to those who damage his relationship with her. No, his cheek did not know how to turn.

He drove to downtown West Monroe. Inside the coffee shop across from the gallery, Von watched the gallery. He drank coffee, then ordered lunch, then after he had eaten the spicy Cajun Po Boy, he ordered more coffee and waited. When he saw Caitlin and Melissa leave the gallery, he threw his money to the table and stepped to the door. As their car pulled out of sight, Von studied the gallery. A dark-haired, fair complexioned girl was the only worker in the gallery. He crossed the street and walked into the gallery.

"Hello," she said.

"I haven't seen you in the gallery before," Von said.

"I'm not here often. My name's Bronwynn."

Von, amazed at how personal and open Southerners tended to be with strangers, popped a cigarette in his mouth. "Can I smoke?"

"Oh, not in the gallery. Let's step outside and I'll join you. I could use one myself." Bronwynn picked up her purse.

"At last, I meet a woman who understands the joys of tobacco. Do you have a light?"

"Sure."

She handed him a book of paper matches. On the cover was a black silhouette of a naked girl, and underneath the girl, the name of a club: The Mer Rouge Lounge. Von lit his cigarette and handed the matches back to her. "Thanks," he said.

"You keep them. I've got plenty."

"I was hoping to talk to Caitlin. Do you know when she'll return?"

"I'm sure she'll be gone the rest of the afternoon. She's helping her boyfriend move in with her."

"On her boat?"

"Yeah. You know Caitlin?"

"Yes, I do. Well, I must be about my business. I'm sure we will speak again."

****

Bronwynn's tips were good that night at the Mer Rouge, but the fast pace of the evening had worn her out. When she came down from the dance floor after a set, the floor manager met her.

"You got three table dances lined up with those men over there," he said. He pointed to three men sitting at the end of the bar to three men—two white and one black. They were dressed in suits and had a bottle of champagne on the table. They had the look of moneyed men. One was the man who had stopped by the gallery earlier. She cursed under her breath. Monroe was certainly too small a town.

"They asked for you specifically by name. Your real name, not your stage name."

"I'm tired. I want to shower and get ready for the closing dance."

"The dances are already paid for." He slipped three twenty-dollar bills into her hand. "They said there's a lot more for you if you're interested. You can take them to the VIP room and give them a little extra if you want. I'll even cut off the security camera if you'd like."

Bronwynn wondered how much money the three men had given the manager to set this up. The manager didn't care what his dancers did away from work, but in the club he had a "no extra's given" philosophy.

"How the hell do they know my real name?" Bronwynn asked, but then she remembered telling the man earlier her name, and that she had given him the matchbook. "A table dance is all anyone will get from me tonight. I'm tired."

"Suit yourself. But whoever they are, they've got a pocketful of money. So just get your skinny ass over there."

In the dressing room, she slipped on a halter-top and a pair of shorts over her G-string, then walked to their table. "Hey guys, I heard you might want a table dance."

"We might. First, sit down and let's talk a minute. My name is Von. Biko, Rilke, this is Bronwynn. She's a friend of Caitlin's." He pulled out a chair and slapped a hundred-dollar bill on the table. "That's just to talk to us and let us buy you a drink."

"Sure. I'll take a large gin and tonic." *Von? The man Caitlin was trying to shake?*

Von signaled a server to come over. "I guess you've figured out who I am by now. I can tell by your face that Caitlin's been talking about me."

"I really don't have a lot of time," Bronwynn said as she sat down in the vacant chair between Von and Rilke, "We're going to close soon. If you want a dance, we've got to get on with it. So do I dance for you one at a time or all at once?"

Von chuckled. "I don't want a lap dance."

She slid the hundred back to him. "Well, you just keep your money because you won't get anything else from me tonight."

Von took his wallet from his jacket and replaced the bill. "Suit yourself. Though, if I really wanted sex, I'd get it elsewhere." He looked at Rilke. "You know what they say about strip clubs—the place where you can get screwed but never laid."

"So if you don't want a lap dance, why the hell did you ask for me? I don't sell drugs. I'm really not a good counselor. I don't play the talk-dirty-to-me game. If mama's not good to you gentlemen at home, I really

305

can't help that. I'm tired, so I probably won't be the kind of company you want."

He leaned forward, then slowly and deliberately said, "I want you to take Caitlin a message. She needs to reconsider my offer. I want her to come with me to New York, then back to Africa. I'll be in Monroe until next Saturday. I expect her decision by then."

"Von, you must not know Caitlin as well as you think. I *know* she doesn't want to go anywhere with you. You're wasting your time."

"She *will* see me, and she will go to New York with me."

Von's face grew hard and stern, and his words were spoken with a fierceness that frightened her.

Now, Bronwynn remembered where she had seen his face—he was the white man in Caitlin's paintings. *The Merchant of Blood Diamonds*. The same one who had wanted to marry Caitlin even though they hardly knew each other. The one who had inundated Caitlin with phone calls, letters, gifts, and demands. The stalker who had forced Caitlin to file a restraining order.

"Caitlin is afraid of you now. You've come on too strong."

"You are mistaken. She's not afraid of me. She's just confused and pressured by others to avoid me."

"If I were her, I'd be afraid of you. From what she told me, you're suffocating her. I'm claustrophobic, so I understand the feeling."

"If you were her, your fear might be warranted. But you're not her; you're nothing like my Caitlin."

"Screw you."

Biko hissed like a snake, then said, "Maybe we should take her and lock her in small, dark room. She be nice to us then."

"You men are creepy, but you don't frighten me," Bronwynn said.

"Biko's joke was inappropriate." Von leaned closer to her. "Actually, I sense you are afraid, and you should be. But don't be ashamed of your fear, Bronwynn. We all have our private terrors, little neurotic phobias that sting us like scorpions. Some have more than others."

Bronwynn stood up. "You are so full of yourself, so full of shit."

"I know what you're thinking, Bronwynn. You regret sharing with me anything personal. You don't understand why you did it. You're used to controlling the conversation with the drunken losers who come to this club, men who can't even get an erection, who drop money on this stage or slip it in your garter because it makes them think they're still men. But they're not men, Bronwynn. Not anymore. They're losers who have wasted their life. You know it every time they whisper how beautiful you are and what they'd like to do to you. Do you think a man who could get a decent date would be here on a Saturday night? I doubt it. And you yourself—it's probably difficult for you to get a decent date, isn't it?"

"So why are you here, Von? Does that mean you can't get a date? You sure won't get one with Caitlin."

"I'm not here to find a woman like you. I knew you were a friend of my fiancée, and that you worked here and I wanted you to tell Caitlin that I'm running out of patience." He thumbed through several hundred dollars bills. "I could be very grateful for your help. Just persuade Caitlin to be more open to reason and to meet me again."

"Fiancée? You're kidding me. You must be insane."

"Perhaps, I am insane. Perhaps you don't know Caitlin as well as you think you do. Carry my message to Caitlin. After you dance, you can leave, Bronwynn."

He and the others turned their attention to the stage. It was suddenly like she was a non-person, someone who wasn't there at all.

The three men were still at the table when she danced, downing Tequila shots and draining beers as fast as the waitress could bring them a new tray. She felt uncomfortable stripping before Von's leering eyes, and she tried to dance in areas away from their line of vision.

The three grew louder and more obnoxious with every round of drinks. When their waitress taking orders refused to return to their table, the manager walked over and told Von they would have to leave if they didn't settle down.

"I apologize," Von said. "We just got a little carried away." He handed the manager a twenty. "Send the waitress or a dancer with one more round, then we'll be on our way."

As Bronwynn finished her last set before the grand finale, Von dumped a handful of change on the dancefloor. "This tip is especially for you, Bronwynn," he called out as they walked toward the door. "I've known gutter whores who could dance better."

She knelt, scooped up the change, and pelted their backs with the coins. "Sorry sons of bitches! Caitlin said you were a psycho!"

"Bronwynn!" the manager shouted. "Settle down."

"Losers!" she shouted. "And you better not bother

Caitlin anymore!"

****

After Von, Rilke, and Biko returned to the hotel room, Von once more went over his itinerary. Biko watched the television, engrossed in *Rambo: First Blood* on HBO, and Rilke was brooding, nursing his drink.

"What's on your mind, Rilke?" Von asked.

"Von, America is not like Africa. I'm worried that you've gone completely daft over this American girl. Forget her. Forget her boyfriend. Let this matter slide. We've wasted too much time here, and if you get any crazier about her, you'll screw up our business deals. Let's get out of Hickville and get back to work. I know you're picking up the tab for this, but watching you chase this girl is boring."

"He is right, mon," Biko said. "Biko is watching too much TV. Makes him crazy and stupid." He took a puff of a cigar. "And Von become soft, like boy who cries when little girl calls him names."

Von felt his face redden. "All right. Give me one more week."

Rilke set his glass on the table and stood up. "Naw. I'm going to New York for a few days, then back to Freetown. I'll see you there when you get this girl out of your head."

"Wait a minute, Rilke." Von looked at Biko. "You remember what you told me about the Lebanese girl? That if I wanted her, I should kill the man and take her?"

Biko smiled. "Ah, but this Caitlin is not Lebanese. She will not be wife who obeys. I do not think she will come with you, even if you kill her man."

309

Von looked out the curtained window. It was late and the traffic on Louisville had slowed. "She will come. I just need to be more persuasive."

"How, Von?" Rilke said. "She's a horse that hasn't been meeked."

"Rilke, tomorrow I'll rent a car. I want you to take it and go to New Orleans tomorrow and deliver one of these diamond parcels. I also have a contact there whose specialty is creating identification. I want new identities for each of us—in our business, one never knows when he might need one. And just in case she proves to be difficult, I also want one for Caitlin. I'll drug her and drag her ungrateful pretty little ass all the way back to Africa if I have to."

He opened his briefcase and handed Rilke passport photographs of himself and Caitlin. "My contact can use these for the passports. Biko will stay with me and help me tidy up things here. By the time you finish your business, we'll be ready to go."

Chapter Thirty-Two

*If they carry you on their back, you won't know
that the road is long.*
—*Krio Proverb*

"Now, if you gentlemen will excuse me, I have a
wife to claim," Von said. Leaving the hotel, he parked
his sedan in the lot near her houseboat and boldly
walked onboard.

Caitlin was on the deck, working on a half-finished
painting of the Xaverian mission compound. She
glanced up at Von. "I guess you don't understand what
a restraining order is, Von," she said. "But after the
sheriff finds you tomorrow, you'll know."

"I have some business to attend to in New Orleans
and New York. After that's done, I want you to come
with me to New York. I have a wonderful apartment
overlooking Central Park. You will love the life I plan
on giving you. You can even bring the… boy," he said.

"Aw, you would do that for me, Von? You would
accept the same boy you threatened to take away from
me? That is so sweet."

"I'm serious, Caitlin. Please."

"You are so full of shit. I regret ever meeting you.
Now get off my boat before I call the law and they
carry your white African ass to jail."

Von grasped her arms. "Caitlin, that's enough of

this foolishness. Why are you playing so hard to get? I know what you are on the inside—lonely, an opportunist like myself, and I know you truly care for me."

Caitlin struggled to free herself, but his hands gripped her arms like a toothed spring trap. "Von, you're hurting me. Let me go."

"Not till you tell me what I want to hear." He pulled her toward him as though he would kiss her.

Caitlin turned her face away from him and closed her eyes. "No. No, I won't. You won't hear it from me. Go to hell. Leave me alone!"

Von shook her like she was a rag doll. "Caitlin, listen to me. I love you. I need you."

"Let her go, Von," a voice said.

Von glanced over his shoulder at Hunter and Tejan who had just come on board. He shoved Caitlin away and moved toward Hunter. "You. Everything would have been fine between Caitlin and me if you hadn't been around and turned her against me."

Von didn't see the short iron pipe that Hunter held behind him until it was shoved into his gut. The blow took the wind out of him.

"Surprised to see me?" Hunter said. "You don't seem so tough without your two friends to hold me."

Hunter then truly did surprise Von by pounding his body and face with the pipe and then his fists.

"Hunter, that's enough," he heard his Caitlin say.

When the blows stopped, Von rose from his knees, then staggered into the parking lot. He wondered why Hunter had not killed him. It was another sign of weakness.

"You'll like our sheriff, Von," Caitlin shouted.

"You can explain everything to him."

Von looked through his bloodied and bruised eyes and saw Caitlin and Hunter embracing. He didn't like what he saw at all.

****

Hunter called the sheriff after Von left and told him about the altercation. The sheriff issued an all-points bulletin for Von Vermeer's arrest and promised Caitlin he would deal with Von as soon as possible. He promised to send a patrol car by the houseboat and art gallery periodically through the night in case Von returned. Hunter spent the night with Caitlin, but their sleep was fitful. Early that morning, the sheriff called and said that Von had checked out of his hotel.

Feeling that Von had at last gone and would be out of her life, Caitlin felt much better. She prepared a huge breakfast for Hunter and Tejan of coffee, eggs, bacon, and pancakes.

As Hunter finished another cup of black coffee, she said, "Thank you for being there, Hunter. For once, I was happy to see those angry fists of yours. I was really frightened. And Hunter, I'm glad you stopped when you did. The old Hunter wouldn't have."

Hunter looked down at his hands, at the bloodied knuckles and scars. He flexed the fingers. *Fighting is not what a man's hands are designed for. In a man's hands reside the secrets of his art, the memories of the women he has touched, the earth he has held, the people he has helped, the songs he has played. Von, you did me a favor by forcing me to defend Caitlin. I am not proud of hurting you. I don't like fighting anymore.*

"A penny for your thoughts," Caitlin said.

Hunter laid down his fork and looked at Caitlin. "I

want you and Tejan in my life—permanently this time. I'll give you space. I'll work my ass off to make sure you both have everything you want. I'm afraid though. Afraid I'll screw up. There's still too much wrong with me."

"Mr. Hunter," Tejan piped. "You are still a good man. You and my *mamá* belong together. If I know my *mamá* will be happy, Tejan would be willing to die."

"Well, we have much to talk about then, don't we?" Caitlin said. "However, today I want to focus on getting the gallery for next week's show. The walls need to be painted, and I don't know when I can get to it since I've got to finish these paintings I plan to show."

"Since tomorrow's Monday, the museum is closed, right? Why not let me paint them today?"

"Right," Caitlin said. "That will give the walls time to dry and time for me to hang the new show."

Hunter said. "I can have it done before tomorrow."

"That's so sweet. Do you want Tejan to help?"

"Naw. Just send him to get me when supper's ready."

****

Von drove mindlessly for several minutes, fighting the rage and shame that blistered his mind worse than Hunter's fists had his face. He rolled down his window and lit a cigarette. At a stoplight, a young black boy sat on a bicycle, leaning against a street sign pole. The boy's eyes widened when he saw Von's face. Then he grinned.

"Mister, shore looks like someone tore your face up. You better get yourself to a clinic and get fixed up."

Von flipped his cigarette at him and rolled up the

window.

As he entered his hotel room, Biko laughed when he saw Von's face. "Mon, I hope that girl did not hurt you this way." He chuckled. "You are sure you want her?"

"That's enough of that, Biko. Her boyfriend jumped me when I wasn't ready for him."

"Biko is happy that it was not the girl. Where is this boyfriend? Take me to him."

****

Hunter rolled the beige paint onto the Sheetrock walls quickly, and after he had washed out the rollers, attacked the wooden trim with a brush. He was concentrating—not on the painting, but on the future, on how good life would be, how much life and energy a happy relationship with Caitlin would bring to his music. He was so lost in his thoughts that he didn't hear the footsteps of the two men who had entered the gallery through the open back door. The thump of the blackjack was no louder in his head than the thumps of his conscience.

When Hunter woke, he was in the back portion of the gallery and his legs and one arm were tied to a chair by Caitlin's desk.

"We're going to play a little game," Von said, "the way we played it in Sierra Leone. Biko, are you ready to play the game with Hunter?"

Biko grabbed a handful of Hunter's hair and jerked his head back. "Yeah, Mon, he play with me tonight." He lifted a lock of Hunter's hair and slowly cut it loose with his knife. "The white man's hair, it feel light, wispy, like the hair of a woman."

Von laid a machete upon the desk. Hunter watched

315

as Von folded and tore a sheet of paper into several pieces. He wrote a word on each slip.

"*Hand, ear, arm, toes, foot, leg, nose, head,* and just to make it interesting—here's one I never used before—*go free.* Here's how it works." He lifted a paper sack from the trash and dropped the small anatomic squares into the bag. "You reach into the sack and whatever body part you draw, Biko will cut off."

Hunter grinned when he saw Von's two blackened eyes. "You look like a raccoon with those black eyes." Hunter looked at Biko. "Did he tell you who blackened his eyes?"

Biko slapped Hunter so hard he heard his own teeth rattle.

"Play the game, mon," Biko said.

"You are a couple of sick bastards."

"You came between me and my Caitlin. You should not have interfered."

"And you think killing me is going to make her want you? What an idiot. What will you do after you kill me? Caitlin still won't go with you."

"Then I'll kill her and her boy too. Now, reach into the sack."

"I won't play your sick game."

"Okay." Von took a slip and wrote *Tejan* and dropped it into the sack. "You will play. If you don't, then I'll draw for you *and* for him. Now you only have to draw once, and who knows, you might get lucky and draw the one saying I have to let you go."

"Somehow I don't feel lucky tonight," Hunter said. Images of Caitlin's paintings flashed through his mind like a slide show. This man and this moment is the Africa Caitlin had given months of her life for.

Von patted him on the shoulder. "Understandable. If I were you, I wouldn't feel lucky either."

Biko took Hunter's hand and stuffed it into the sack. "Choose, Mon."

"Go ahead, Hunter," Von said. "I'll even draw and play the game with you."

"You don't have the guts."

"Biko, I want to play the game."

Biko held out the sack. Von reached in and took a piece of paper. "I'll even play first." Von unfolded the paper. "Go free." He showed it to Biko. "Isn't that right, Biko?"

"Yeah, Mon, that is right. Go free."

"Now, Hunter, you draw."

Hunter felt his fingers clasp one of the small pieces of paper and withdrew his hand. Biko snatched it, read it, and smiled. "Hand," he said. "Today is your lucky day."

"Well, Hunter, I must leave you in the care of my friend. I'm going to finish my business with Caitlin and inform her that you are no longer available as a boyfriend. Biko will draw the next papers for you. And since I've already drawn the one that had *go free* written on it, you can't leave here alive. You don't have to be gentle, Biko, but don't drag it out too long." Von sighed. "I do owe Caitlin that much." He wadded up his paper and threw it to the floor. "On second thought, have as much fun as you like."

"Biko will kill this mosquito carefully. He want to see his guts."

Hunter rocked the chair as he struggled with his bonds. Biko laughed. "The turtle wants to box, but his arms are too short." He untied Hunter's left arm and stretched it across the table. There was a lightning-fast flash of a machete, then Hunter saw his detached hand twitching on the tabletop as if the fingertips were stretching for the notes of a sad minor song.

****

"Tejan!" Caitlin said.

"Yes, *Mamá*?"

"I'm going to go to Pecanland Mall and buy a gift for Hunter. I don't feel like cooking, so I'll pick up something for us to eat on the way home. Would you go help Hunter finish painting? I ought to be back by the time you've returned and cleaned up."

"*Oui,*" Tejan said.

As Tejan neared the gallery, he stopped. He felt the violence inside even before he heard Hunter's groans. He moved to the window and peered in. A black man with a raised machete stood over Hunter. Tejan pounded on the glass and screamed, "No!" The man merely smiled and brought down the blade. Tejan heard the sound of the blade as it bit into the wooden desk and saw the blood spurting from Hunter's arm. He tried the door, but it was locked, so he ran around the building to the back patio and he picked up a shovel, which he used to break out the back door's glass window. He reached in and unlocked it, opened it and stepped inside. The man inside now faced him with the raised machete, but Tejan smashed his face with the shovel. The force of the blow didn't knock him down, but it did turn the man's head and daze him. A gold tooth tumbled from the grinning bloody mouth and bounced across the floor. Tejan knew that if this man were a soldier, he would be an adept grappler and skillful fighter, and he dare not give him a chance to grasp him. Tejan's strength would be no match for this big man. He plunged the shovel's blade into the man's exposed neck. This time the man fell to his knees, his hands clutching at the gurgling hole in his neck. Tejan then drove the shovel into the thick chest like it was a bayonet and pushed the man until he fell. He dug in the man's chest until he heard the blade scraping the ground, and he leaned on the handle until his huge frame stiffened and stilled.

Tejan threw down the shovel, pulled off his T-shirt, and tied off Hunter's arm.

"Caitlin…Von's gone after Caitlin," Hunter said.

Tejan slung Hunter across his back in a fireman's carry and marched double-time toward the houseboat. He had carried others like this before, but this time there was no alcohol or drugs to numb the ache of his muscles or the pain inside. There was nothing to fill the hollow of his very live heart and he wept. A car passed him slowly, but the driver did not stop to help or to ask why a weeping teenage black boy carried a longhaired handless white man on his back. Maybe there are some things people just do not see.

As Caitlin's car was not in the parking lot by the houseboat, Tejan knew she had not returned yet. He did not know how to find her, so he kept walking, down Trenton Street, across the Endom Bridge, to Saint Francis Hospital.

Tejan staggered into the emergency room and told a worker, "You must take care of my *mamá's* friend." A drop of Hunter's blood splattered on the floor.

"Good God, what's happened to him?"

"He need your help. Soon."

The door into the emergency treatment area opened

and Tejan saw a gurney. He plopped Hunter down, turned, and rushed out.

The admittance clerk followed after Tejan. "Who is he? There are papers you must fill out."

"He is Mr. Hunter."

"I'll call the police! You can't just leave him here like this!"

"You will help him or he dies," he said. He remembered what Hunter had said about Von and ran back to the houseboat. "I must go help my *mamá.*" He felt he ran faster than he had ever run before.

****

Von studied the houseboat. He could see Caitlin's shadow-form as she moved through the boat. She was naked except for a towel wrapped around her waist. He quietly made his way closer. As he spied on her, he cursed her for making him love her, for causing him to be miserable without her. He opened the cabin door and stepped inside.

"Hunter? Is that you?"

"No, it's not Hunter."

"You better get out of here. Right now. Hunter's already given you one ass whipping. You don't know him, how angry he can get." Caitlin snatched a shirt from a clothing basket and hurriedly slipped it on, fumbling at the buttons. "He'll kill you this time when I tell him you broke in." She reached for the phone.

Von snatched the phone and backhanded her. "Stupid bitch."

Caitlin cringed from the blow and started crying.

Von held out his arms. "Caitlin, I'm sorry. I didn't mean it. Really. Come here."

"Von, please, just go away and leave me alone! Let

me have a life. I love Hunter—not you. You and I could never have a life together now."

"Well, Hunter is no longer a complication to our relationship."

"What do you mean?"

"I mean he's gone. You'll never see him again."

Caitlin wildly flailed at him with her hands. "You killed Hunter, didn't you? Listen to me, you sorry excuse for a man, I would be a gutter whore and give myself to the whole world before I'd let you touch me again!"

"Caitlin, Shhhh. Shhhh." He placed his pistol against Caitlin's temple. "I love you so much. Now, I'm not going to have to use this, am I?"

Caitlin shook her head.

"Where's your black boy?"

"He went after Hunter."

"Biko will take care of him. Okay, then. Let's pack some clothes so you come with me to New York." He stuck the pistol into his belt and watched as she packed.

****

Tejan saw Caitlin's and Von's shapes through the curtained windows and he was again assaulted by the intuition of violence. Tejan picked up a piece of wire in the parking lot and wrapped the ends around each hand. He had learned to garrote in Sierra Leone from a white Ukrainian mercenary.

Von pushed Caitlin out the cabin door. Caitlin held a small suitcase. Von followed toting another. As Caitlin rounded the cabin, she saw Tejan. He held a finger to his lips. She nodded and kept walking.

As soon as Von walked past him, Tejan slipped the wire around his neck and pulled it tight. That was when he saw Von reaching for the pistol in his belt. He yanked Von backward to keep him off balance, hoping that he could strangle him before he could get the pistol out. Von did grasp its handle, but Tejan fiercely jerked him backward again until they both slammed into the gunwale, causing Von to drop the pistol. Tejan kept pulling Von until the momentum pushed both of them over the side into the river. As they descended into the dark water of the Ouachita, Tejan felt Von's hands clawing at his throat. The dark world of the river was all he could see, but he managed to hold his breath and pull the wire tighter. *Don't let Tejan die in the dark*, he prayed to whatever god was listening. Tejan managed to raise his head above water, gulp a breath, then sat on top of Von, pulling the wires until his hands crossed, and he felt the wire cutting into his hands as it bit into Von's neck.

Von stiffened in death throes, and his arms and legs flailed wildly beneath Tejan. He held Von under for a long time, until Tejan felt himself losing strength and breath. Von's weight was now a weight too heavy to hold any longer. Treading water, he unwound the wire from his bleeding hands and released Von's body. Von's corpse bobbed to the surface briefly, and the head rolled to the side in a peculiar manner. The wire garrote had nearly severed Von's neck completely. As Von's body sank below the surface and into the river's current, Tejan took his bearings. He could barely see the houseboat's lights.

Chapter Thirty-Three

When a cunning man dies, it's a cunning man who buries him.
—Krio Proverb

When Tejan slammed into Von, the impact knocked Caitlin to the deck of the boat.

"Tejan!" she cried as Tejan's momentum carried him and Von overboard. She saw Von's pistol on the deck. She picked it up and called 911, then waited at the edge of the boat, calling Tejan's name, the pistol at the ready. For just a moment, she heard them struggle in the water. When those sounds faded, she heard the river lapping at the side of the boat and a faint siren in the distance, but there was no sign of Tejan. She laid the pistol down on the deck and fetched the small bat she used to kill gar and waited, hoping it would not be Von's face she would see next.

The police arrived, and they called the Ouachita Sheriff's Department and the Wildlife and Fisheries requesting boats to search for Tejan and Von. A half-hour later, a Sheriff's boat with spotlights arrived and chugged slowly downriver. Caitlin begged the police to go to the gallery and check on Hunter. A patrol car went at the gallery and found the dead Biko, the machete, a great deal of blood, and a severed hand, but no Hunter. The deputy called the hospital on a hunch, and sure enough an injured Anglo had been dropped off at Emergency by a young black boy. His hand had been amputated and he was still in shock. The man fit Hunter's description. The deputy radioed the other car waiting at Caitlin's boat and the deputy there relayed the news to Caitlin.

"You're sure they said his hand was amputated and that it was Hunter?" Caitlin asked.

"That's what the report said, Caitlin."

"What about Tejan?"

"The emergency nurse said that after he set the man down, he dashed out."

Inside her heart, Caitlin cursed herself for being the cause of Hunter's tragedy. She cursed Von, and she cursed Africa. She saw the rattle Von had given her, and she hated the sight of it. Feeling an indescribable rage at Von and at anything that reminded her of him, she picked it up and smashed it against the cabin door, blow after blow until she heard the gourd crack and the leather tear, and the small rocks inside spilled onto the deck.

The officer with her picked up one of them. "Looks like some kind of quartz."

Caitlin knew they weren't just rocks. "They're diamonds," she said. "Blood diamonds." What a laugh Von must have had using her as a smuggler.

"You're shitting me," the officer said.

"I wish I were. What should I do with them?"

"Hell, I don't know. Are they stolen?"

"No. No more stolen than any other diamonds people wear."

"Then keep them."

She saw flashing blue lights pull into the parking

lot, and then a weary, wringing wet Tejan rushed from the car, up the boat ramp, and into her arms.

****

On the third day in the hospital, Hunter opened his eyes. Caitlin and Tejan sat by his bed. Caitlin had one black eye and a scrape on her face. Caitlin stood, her lip quivered and she leaned over to kiss him. "You lost so much blood. I was afraid we had lost you."

"I've never wanted to do anything but play guitar and sing." Hunter held up a bulbous gauze-wrapped stump. "But I guess I'm out of the music business now."

Hunter cried, and it was the first time Caitlin had seen him cry without a guitar in his hands. His sobbing was the sound of despair and heartache.

"Not hardly." She laid a sack on his chest. "There's three harmonica's there—a D, an A, and a G—and a tape called, 'How to Play Harmonica for the Musically Hopeless.' Tejan said I should get them for you. He remembered seeing a harmonica player once in Sierra Leone. And besides, you can still sing. We'll figure out a way. I'll take care of you till you get back into the groove. You've got a lot of practicing to do."

"How is Tejan?"

"He's fine, thank God. He saved us, Hunter—both of us. And you know what?

He wants to go to a regular school now, and then go to college. He also says he wants to return to Sierra Leone someday and use all he learns to help the people there. I don't know what I think about that."

"It's his homeland. One's sense of home runs deep. I guess that's why I never could get out of Northeast Louisiana," Hunter said.

****

Because of fever and infection, Hunter wasn't released from the hospital as quickly as Caitlin had hoped. As she sat by his bedside, she flipped through the dozen channels on the television, and for a while landed on KNOE News. The reporter related an abbreviated account of the attack on Hunter, the story of how Tejan had rescued him, and how two local benefits had been arranged to help Hunter financially. The hospital darkened and grew still and Caitlin left Hunter to check on Tejan.

****

Hunter woke, rang the nurse, and asked for a sleeping pill.

When the R.N. came into his room and offered him a white paper cup, he inadvertently held out his left arm to take it. The nurse hesitated.

Hunter studied the bandaged stub in the air, turning it over, as if he were searching for the lost hand. He saw the pain in the nurse's face. "Sorry. I forgot my hand's gone. I swear I can still feel my fingers moving."

"Those are phantom pains. Don't think about them," she said softly. "They'll fade eventually. Here, open your mouth." She placed the pill on his tongue, then held a glass of water to his lips. "Nighty, night, Hunter. These pills work well."

Even with the help of the pill, sleep still didn't come quickly, and the phantom pains blurred with the real pains as sleep continued its evasion, but eventually he drifted into sleep, and he slipped inward into his dreams.

Hunter heard Tejan singing and the words told their stories and were such as he and Tejan could have written together, happy songs of family and love that had been found. Soon unknown musicians joined, playing rattles and drums that kept time with Tejan's song. As Tejan sang, he began to see those about him. Two men who looked like brothers drowning in the river. Boys and girls who in sadder times had been soldiers, diamond miners, sex slaves, and porters. Some tapped drums with stumps and prosthetic hands, others shook rattles and danced together in the street outside the Lost Bazaar. A circle of boys raised handless arms and danced around Hunter and Caitlin as Tejan sang. The stars above them were blood red at first, but as his song continued, they became sparkling splashes of white in the sky forming familiar and unknown constellations. The stars shined and sparkled like the cut and polished diamonds on the black cloth of a diamond merchant

An angel, bearing Caitlin's face, floated down from heaven. She kissed the sad children on their foreheads, then made her way to Hunter and kissed his wrist and took away the guitar.

And somehow Hunter felt in his heart that all they had lost, all that had been damaged, all that had been taken from every one of them because of man's greed for wealth and power, all of themselves that they had sold—all would be returned. All of the hands, the dignity, the opportunities that had been lost would blossom in future serendipity and epiphanies. All the lost souls faded with the song, and Hunter walked with Caitlin and Tejan into the Lost Bazaar, a gallery where one can find one's self, one's friends, or the love of one's life. A bazaar, but one where nothing and no one was for sale.